# What Bae Won't Do Saga

# What Bae Won't Do Saga

*Genesis Woods*

URBAN Renaissance

www.urbanbooks.net

Urban Books, LLC
300 Farmingdale Road, NY-Route 109
Farmingdale, NY 11735

What Bae Won't Do Saga

ISBN 13: 978-1-62286-453-9
ISBN 10: 1-62286-453-0

First Trade Paperback Printing May 2017
Printed in the United States of America

10 9 8 7 6 5 4 3 2 1

Distributed by Kensington Publishing Corp.
Submit Orders to:
Customer Service
400 Hahn Road
Westminster, MD 21157-4627
Phone: 1-800-733-3000
Fax: 1-800-659-2436

# What Bae Won't Do Saga

by

*Genesis Woods*

# JaNair

*Beep . . . Beep . . . Beep!*

*Smack!*

I had just hit the snooze button on my alarm clock for the third time in a row. I hated Monday mornings. Hell, I hated mornings—period. I was a night owl, so this waking up at the crack of dawn with the roosters was not for me. Besides, I just got home almost two hours ago, so I didn't get much sleep. I went out with my new boo Jerome last night. It was the first time we had sex, and it *definitely* won't be the last.

While I was in the middle of snoozing again, my door suddenly swung open, and the irritated look on my face could be seen from a mile away.

"Hey, bitch, rise and shine. Wake your ass up. You knew you had class this morning when you went out hoeing last night," my cousin Mya said as she skipped her ass to my dresser and started smelling the different bottles of perfumes I had lined up.

"Ooooh, this is new!" she sang.

"Mya, put my shit down. If you want some smell-good, look in the basket and use the stuff from Victoria's Secret."

I lazily got out of my bed and snatched my new bottle of Dolce & Gabbana Rose out of her hand. This was my favorite perfume, and she was not about to use it. As I stood there and looked at her sort through the different body sprays I had from Victoria's Secret, I just shook my head.

For the life of me, I couldn't understand how someone who has as many sugar daddies as she does is always broke. Her pockets should be lined with cash, and her dresser should be lined with real perfume bottles and not that cheap knockoff shit. Her car note should be up to date, and *our* house bills should all be paid.

"So how was your date with Jerome?" she asked while spraying her wrist and smelling it.

*Jerome.* I couldn't do anything but smile. "It was fine."

She stopped what she was doing and looked at me. "Fine? Fine like what? He tapped that ass fine, or he didn't try anything and just kicked it fine?"

See, this is the other thing I hated about Mya. Just because you tell me all of your business doesn't mean I have to do the same thing. I've never been one of those chicks who tells how my man's dick game was in the bedroom. All that does is make a bitch wonder. And I didn't trust anything that bleeds once a month just like me. Family or not.

"It was just fine. Nothing else. Now can you get your ass out of my room so I can start to get dressed?" I said to her as I shifted through my closet for something to wear.

"Yeah, Okay. I'll go. But I'ma stop telling you my business since you can't do the same with me." And with that, she exited my room. I hoped she didn't think I really gave a fuck about her not sharing her sexcapades with me, because I could surely do without them. The water coming from my deluxe showerhead had me feeling some kind of way this morning. Maybe because the tiny drops of water hitting my skin resembled the way Jerome peppered kisses all over my body last night, or I was just yearning for his touch again. Man, oh man, I got it bad. I hope this nigga has some act right. I do not and will not tolerate any form of bullshit, regardless of how good the dick is.

After getting out of the shower, I air-dried and moisturized my body with some raw shea butter. The loud whispering outside of my door kind of caught my attention. I was so glad I had a bathroom in my master suite and didn't have to share one with Mya and her rotating men.

I knew she had company before I even heard the voices. She never comes in my room to "wake me up" in the morning unless she does have visitors. I could also smell some bacon and eggs being cooked. Breakfast is the only thing she can make without burning the kitchen down. Whoever she had over here must've been good in bed, because she doesn't reward them with breakfast unless they are.

*"Shhhh. Nigga, keep your voice down. I told you my cousin is already up. I don't want her to come out here being nosy,"* she said as they passed my door going back to her room.

I don't know what the hell she said that for, because I could give two fucks about who she has up in here. As long as they respect this house and don't try to move in, we're good.

After I got dressed and grabbed my backpack and keys, I headed out the door. I didn't even stop in the kitchen to see if there were any leftovers for me, because that would be too much like right. I really should've thought about who I let move in with me when I decided to get a roommate to save a little money. This living situation right here is not going to work much longer.

When I stepped outside, the sun was shining bright and feeling good. I was glad that I picked my short denim skirt and pink crop top to wear today. Before I made it to my car, I had the sudden urge to turn around because I could feel someone watching me. As soon as I looked to the left, our eyes connected, so I couldn't be rude and not speak.

"Hey, you!" I called out to dude that lived next door. I couldn't remember his name for shit.

"What's up, Jay. You're looking good this morning. How are you?"

"I'm fine, just on my way to class, and thanks for the compliment."

He just nodded his head and stared at me. I didn't know if I should've asked a follow-up question or complimented him.

The awkward silence though was my cue to leave. I waved good-bye, hopped in my car, and pulled off. I was kind of embarrassed because he's told me his name a few times, and for some reason, I never remember it. *Donte, Kevin, Ronnie, Bobby, Ricky . . . Mike.* Oh well, I'll ask him or his cousin Li'l Ray again one day.

One name I do remember though is Jerome. The way he had me screaming his shit last night, I bet the neighbors know it too.

*Bzzzz, Bzzzz, Bzzzz!*

Speaking of the devil. I had a flirtatious smirk on my face as my phone vibrated and Jerome's picture flashed across the screen. I hurried up and swiped "talk," then said in the sexiest voice,

*"Hey, baby, I was just thinking about you . . ."*

# Mya

"Nigga, you almost got us caught. I told your dumb ass to stay in the room." I couldn't believe this fool. If Jay would've seen who I was fucking last night and cooking breakfast for this morning, it would've been some drama popping off.

"Why would she care anyway? She dumped me a few months ago. And didn't you say she fucking some new nigga now?"

"You mad or nah? Because your face was kinda screwed up with that last statement," I asked, getting a little upset.

"Hell no, I'm not mad. I'm just saying she shouldn't be tripping off me moving on too. Especially since she fucking homeboy."

Damn, that was the fourth time he said something about Jay having sex with someone else. Last night before we even made it to my bedroom, he wanted to know where she was. I told him that she was at her new boo's house. As soon as those words left my mouth, he was firing off questions. At first, they were regular ones like, who, what, where, and when. But then he started asking me shit like, "Does he spend the night over here? Does she spend the night over there? Has she said anything about them fucking? If so, how long has it been?" I had to tell that nigga to snap the fuck out of it. Why the fuck did he care anyway? Especially when he was in *my* bed about to get some of this A-1 pussy.

"You must still be feeling Jay or something, because you're a little too worried about who she letting slide in between her thighs."

"It's not even that. I was just making sure it wasn't while we were together," he said, finishing the last of the bacon, eggs, and toast I made for him.

"And if it was? What the hell could you do about it now? Y'all ain't been together for months," I said, laughing at this dummy. Who gets mad at some shit that happened in a relationship that's been over for almost a year?

"There's nothing I can do about it at all. The only thing that will happen, though, is her image will change for me."

"What the hell does that mean?" I asked, confused as fuck.

He went on to explain to me that JaNair is considered a *"good girl."* Faithful to one man, can count the number of niggas she slept with on one hand, good head on her shoulders, career minded, can take care of herself, respects her body, and doesn't tolerate being disrespected. Of course, I had to correct him on a couple things. I don't understand why everyone thinks JaNair is this sweet little angel.

With her now sleeping with Jerome, she would need both hands to count the number of dudes she slept with, and she has cheated on a boyfriend before. It was to get revenge for the way he did her, but nevertheless, she did.

After I told him that little tidbit of information about his precious Jay, I wanted to know what kind of *"girl"* he considered me. I kind of got offended when this nigga laughed and said that I definitely was *not* considered a "good girl." He told me that I was what they called a *"fa'sho girl."*

"And what the hell is a 'fa'sho girl'?" I asked somewhat with an attitude.

"A fa'sho girl is a chick that you know that will do anything for you, fa'sho."

"Huh? That doesn't make any sense."

He shook his head and slid both his hands down his sexy-ass face. For some reason, he just stared at me for what seemed like twenty minutes. Finally, he answered my question.

"This is what it is. With you, there's no limit to what you'd do for a nigga. Your answer will never be a no. When it comes to getting anything, especially some pussy and head, you will do it, fa'sho."

I sat there smiling, because, to me, being a fa'sho girl was way better than being a good girl. What nigga wouldn't want the world given to him or pussy on demand whenever he wanted? The thought of that being a great thing though immediately left my mind when he started to speak again.

"What you over there smiling for, Mya? A fa'sho girl *isn't* a good thing. Low key, it's a step above being a ho," he said, then started laughing like that shit was funny.

"Nigga, I ain't no ho," I yelled with my hands on my hips and stepping into his personal space. I was mad at the fact that he said some shit like that to me.

"I can't tell! Let me ask you this. Can you count the number of niggas you've slept with on your hands?"

*Yes . . . if I could use my toes too,* I said to myself.

He smirked when I didn't answer. I guess my silence told him what he needed to know, so he asked me another question.

"OK, well, how about this? How many of your cousin's boyfriends have you slept with?"

That was an easy one. "Including you . . . four."

He laughed. "You're saying that like you're proud. You couldn't find your own man, so you sleep with your cousin's." At that time, he was laughing a little too hard for my taste. "That isn't a ho to you?"

I socked him in his chest, because what he just said pissed me off. Yeah, I slept with my cousin's exes, but only because they came after me. Obviously, she wasn't doing them right, or they wouldn't be coming my way. This nigga included.

He did have me thinking, though. I have done some scandalous things behind JaNair's back. I know if it were the other way around, I'd get in her ass about that shit. I guess I could stop—hell, she let me come live with her when I didn't have anywhere else to go. She also helped me out with finding a job and enrolling back into school. If it wasn't for her, I don't know where I'd be today.

I laughed to myself. Who the fuck was I kidding? I'm not about to stop that shit anytime soon. Especially not until I see what this new nigga Jerome is like. The bitch didn't want to tell me how he was in bed either. That just made me want to find out even more. I'll give it a little time, though. She seems like she really likes him. Then again, it's only going to be a matter of time before he comes knocking on my bedroom door in the middle of the night like all the others.

"Yo, earth to Mya!" my guest yelled while snapping his fingers in my face. "I'm about to head out. I have to go take my grandma to the doctor."

"OK, but can I get that before you leave?" I asked with my hand out. He reached in his pocket and pulled out the $300 I asked for so that I could get my hair done.

"See, that's another thing about JaNair that makes her a good girl. She never asked for nothing. She took care of herself."

"That may be true, but I bet she don't have that fiyah-ass head like me," I said while running my hand over his dick. That mini-monster in his pants instantly bulked up.

"Yeah, that's true. How about you hit me off with some of that before I leave?"

I kissed him on his lips, then got down on my knees and unbuckled his pants. Before I took him into my mouth, I looked up at him and said, "I got you, baby. Fa'sho!"

# Semaj

After watching JaNair pull off, I had to adjust myself. Just by looking at her in that short skirt with those thick thighs and that pink top that showed her perky C cup titties made my dick get hard as hell.

To me, JaNair was one of the most beautiful chicks I've ever met. Her light, smooth skin, full, pouty lips, long, black hair, cocoa-brown eyes, then her perfectly shaped and molded body got a nigga every time.

Whenever she was within a few feet of me, I always smelled peaches. I don't know if it was the type of body wash she used or just her natural scent. Whatever it was, I loved it.

I was still standing in the same spot thinking about Jay when the front door of her house swung open.

When her cousin Mya stepped out on the porch, my dick instantly got soft. Although Mya and Jay could pass for twins in the looks department, there was something about her that didn't sit well with me. I turned my head in the other direction and took another pull from my blunt when she looked my way.

"Match one, nigga!" she yelled over to me.

"I'll only match one if your shit is high grade like mine," I countered back.

"Boy, I only fucks with that fiyah."

"Shit, I can't tell. You came over here the last time with a weak-ass bag of stress."

See, this is why I like to smoke my weed in the house, away from begging-ass motherfuckers. I hated when someone wanted to get a higher buzz off of my shit. Normally, I'd be in my room blowing, but my aunt Shelia was home today, and she didn't like the smell of Cali's finest throughout the house.

"I'll be back. Let me drop him off around the corner!" she said as a nigga I haven't seen in months walked out behind her. I laughed at homeboy because he had the nerve to mad dog me. If it was because of Mya's ass, my nigga could miss me with that. I'd never stick my dick inside of her. From the looks of things, she was more scandalous than I thought. Besides, I wanted homie's ex, not his next.

I finished my blunt, flicked the roach in the street, and headed into the house. I was hungry as hell, and the sausage, eggs, and homemade biscuits that auntie was cooking hit a nigga's stomach as soon as I walked in the door.

I grabbed my plate she had already laid out and went to work. Once I downed the last of my OJ, I went to the den, flopped down on the couch, and stretched out for a bit.

I was flipping through channels trying to find something to watch on TV when my cousin came to the back to let me know that I had a guest at the front door.

"Man, who is it?" I already knew, but I really didn't give a fuck. I sat there still flipping through different channels.

"Ol' girl from next door."

"Tell her I went to sleep."

Li'l Ray laughed. "Nigga, I didn't even say *who* it was from next door."

"I already know *who* it is. The person I want to see from next door left about thirty minutes ago."

He couldn't do anything but laugh again. Li'l Ray then tried to convince me on why I should kick it with Mya and get her superhigh.

"She tends to get real loose when that greenery hit her lungs just right," he said wiggling his eyebrows up and down.

I shook my head. *I bet it does get her loose too,* I thought. But I wasn't that hard up for pussy that I had to get a bitch high. I had no problem getting my dick wet, and my cousin knew that. Especially after middle school. Back then, I was the ugly kid that no one liked or wanted to be friends with. But after I got to high school, all of that changed.

By my junior year, I grew to stand six foot three. With me being on the track and football teams, my body got toned, and muscles I didn't even know I had started to appear. The girls who didn't pay any attention to me in middle school now knew who I was in high school. If they weren't gawking at my washboard abs or perfect body, they were drooling over my milk chocolate skin, brandy-colored eyes, and neatly twisted dreads. So, yeah, I didn't have a problem with getting pussy. My dick was just selective on what it dipped into.

"Nigga, you dumb as hell. I would of had Mya's ass bent over this couch digging her back out," Li'l Ray hollered as he came back from shooing Mya away.

"That's because you like hoes and hood rats, my dude."

"You ain't never lied!" he said laughing. "I don't discriminate, and neither does this dick."

I couldn't take too much more of this nigga. Plus, he was messing up my high. I finally found something to watch on TV, and all I wanted to do was laugh at Dave Chappelle's crazy ass before I dozed off.

For some reason, though, this nigga Li'l Ray wouldn't shut the fuck up.

"Aye! Real talk, I know what your problem is, J. You trying to holla at JaNair, and it ain't happening. She don't even remember your name half the time."

I threw the pillow that I was lying on at the nigga and hit him right in the head.

"Semaj Nasir Edwards, I know damn well you ain't throwing my decorative pillows at RayShaun. Get your high ass up and put my shit back where it belongs. You do it again, I'ma put my foot in your ass!" my aunt Shelia yelled from out of nowhere. She must have x-ray vision, because how in the hell could she know what I did when she was most likely in the kitchen? I went and picked the pillow up and sat back down in my same spot.

I looked at my cousin who was balled over on the couch laughing at how his moms just got at me. Aunt Shelia wasn't nothing to play with, so whenever she spoke, I had no problem falling in line. She was my saving grace and the reason why I lived in California now. I will always have respect and love for her even after she cusses me out.

After Li'l Ray stopped laughing, I decided to respond to the little jab he said about JaNair forgetting my name.

"She may not remember my name now, homie, but best believe, she won't forget it once she does!"

# JaNair

I was beyond tired when I got home from school. I couldn't wait until this semester was over. I would be free from the books, studying, and waking up early in the morning. It'll all be worth it in the end, though. I already had a bachelor's degree in business. I was back in school for my MBA now. I had just a few more semesters to go before I graduated.

In typical Mya fashion, the kitchen was left a mess after she cooked. I went to my room and changed into a pair of yoga pants and a white tank top. Once I made it back to the kitchen, I cleaned it, and the entire house, from top to bottom.

I was taking the trash out to the front when I heard a female laugh. I looked over to next door and saw Li'l Ray's cousin outside hugging some girl. She was cute, in a Lauren London kind of way, but I think that he could do better. I was on my way back inside but was stopped when Li'l Ray called me over.

"What's up, Jay? How's everything?" he asked, licking his lips as he looked me up and down.

"Everything is chill. How are you, RayShaun?"

"I'm fine, li'l mama, but I'd be much better when you stop playing around and give a nigga some play."

"Some *what?*" I asked as I folded my hands underneath my breasts and shifted my feet.

"Time, JaNair, some time. That's all a nigga wants."

"RayShaun, you are way too young for me, and you know that. I was changing your diapers a few years ago. Plus, you fuck with my girl, so what would I look like?"

He smacked his lips. "So, you gon' play a nigga like that, baby mama? As far as your girl goes, I haven't talked to her in a minute. And as far as my age, I'm only a few years younger than you and my relli."

His mentioning his cousin made me look over in his direction. He and the girl he was hugging were still outside talking. Our eyes met, and he smiled. I quickly turned my attention away when ol' girl took it upon herself to look in the direction that he was.

I looked back at RayShaun, aka Li'l Ray, and had to admit to myself that he was a handsome young man.

He was a twenty-two-year-old, six foot one brother with a peanut butter complexion. His eyes were a deep mocha color that I noticed would change whenever he laughed. He had a nice, fit body and dressed pretty decent.

When he graduated from high school, he got a full scholarship playing basketball for Texas A&M University. A few semesters in, he got caught up with some drug charges. When the athletic department tested him, they found marijuana and cocaine in his system. He was immediately kicked off the team and ended up losing his scholarship. Now he just attends a city college and smokes weed all day, aspiring to be the next big rapper.

LaLa said he had a mean sex game and all, but I wasn't interested in him like that. So, yeah, he was cool and all. But definitely not for me.

"RayShaun, you are so silly. Besides, I have a man already." With that being said, I turned around and was headed back into my house. Before I got too far, though, I turned around and asked him what his cousin's name was again.

"Damn, girl, this is like the twentieth time I've told you. His name is Semaj. SA-MAH-J. It's actually James spelled backward. His mom didn't want to name him after his dad, but then again, she did," he said shrugging his shoulders. "I don't know, but that's that nigga's name, and don't forget it."

I waved bye to Li'l Ray, then looked back over at Semaj. Just like before, he was looking at me too. I gave a small smile and waved to him as well.

When he sent the gesture back, ol' girl looked over at me, rolled her eyes, then jumped in that nigga's arms and kissed him. I just shook my head and went into my house.

*Bitches are so funny and basic.*

I didn't want her nigga in any way, shape, or form. So that "marking your territory" shit was really uncalled for.

If you had to do all that to show the next person that this was your man, then he really wasn't.

If I'm with a nigga, best believe everybody knows we're together. No PDA need.

# Semaj

"Tasha, what the fuck you do that for? I don't know where your lips been," I angrily said as I pushed my baby mama off of me.

That was one of the reasons why we couldn't make what we had work. She loved staying in the middle of some mess. Although Jay wasn't checking for me like I wanted her to, I still didn't want her to see me and another chick getting down.

"Ahhh, Semaj, did I make your little girlfriend mad?" she teased, trying to get a reaction out of me. "You're so concerned about the feeling of a bitch who doesn't even know your name."

See, this is why some females get the shit knocked out of them. They never know when to shut up. I couldn't even entertain her messy ass anymore, so I kissed my princess good-bye, then headed for Li'l Ray's and my hangout spot . . . the garage.

It wasn't anything special, but it was a place where we could go and get away or work on perfecting our craft. There were a couple of couches in here, along with a sixty-inch flat screen, refrigerator, and a small dining table to eat or roll up on. It sorta reminded you of a bachelor's pad, except we had a small studio in here as well.

Whenever Li'l Ray got high, he wanted to be a rapper. He could spit a little too, but he still needed some help.

Me, on the other hand, I was more into doing things behind the scene. I liked making beats and producing. I'm pretty good at it too, if I do say so myself. I've sold a few tracks to some local MCs. I was just waiting for the chance to get my shit into the hands of someone A-1.

After we smoked a few blunts, I was still feeling some kind of way about JaNair seeing Tasha hug and kiss all on me. I guess that's why I was at her door right now ringing the bell.

For some reason, I felt like I had to explain myself. I don't really know why, though. This Bob Marley had me tripping.

The faint smell of peaches invaded my nostrils, so I knew she was close. I turned around to face the door with my hands in my pocket. I was totally in a trance when she appeared in front of me.

"Hey, Semaj. What can I do for you?" Her voice sang as she cracked the door open a bit.

She must've just gotten out of the shower because she had one of those big white fluffy towels wrapped around her perfect body. Her skin was still kind of damp but had this certain glow to it.

"Hey, Jay. I didn't want anything. I was just stopping by to say what's up. I didn't get a chance to speak when you were talking to Li'l Ray earlier." She stared at me for a minute before she spoke.

"Oh, OK. I started to say something when I was talking to RayShaun earlier, but I didn't want to cause any drama between you and your girlfriend."

At that moment, I didn't know if I was tripping or not. Was she jealous or did she feel some type of way seeing me with Tasha? The way she said *girlfriend* with her eyebrow up came out a little salty.

Let me find out she low-key checking for me, we'd never come out of this house.

"Naw, she isn't my girlfriend."

"I couldn't tell!" she snapped. I just smiled because, by that response, I knew she was a little in her feelings. I wanted to ease her mind, so I went on and explained who Tasha was.

"That was my baby moms. We haven't kicked it like that in some years. We have a three-year-old daughter together named Ta'Jae, but that's it. I don't know why she tried to pull that kissing stunt when you walked up. I checked her ass for that, though."

I could tell by the way she was looking at me that she was trying to see if I was being truthful. After she figured that I was, she invited me into her crib. I was down with hanging out with her. I was also happy as fuck. However, all that happiness went down the drain when some nigga I've never seen rolled up on us.

"What's good, JaNair?" He spoke with a little bit of bass in his voice. Who the fuck was this nigga? I didn't even hear him walk up behind me. He was on stealth mode or something.

"Jerome!" she squealed. "What are you doing here? I thought you were coming by later on tonight, baby."

*Baby?*

"I was," he said eyeing me. "But I was able to free up the rest of my day, so I decided to come spend some time with my lady."

*Lady?*

There was an awkward silence before he spoke again.

"If you had other plans," he said while looking at me, "by all means, handle your business. Don't let little ol' me stop you." He raised his hands up in a mock surrender.

I was hoping she chose to handle her business and let this nigga be on his way. I didn't know who this fuck boy was, and I didn't really give a damn. He was around the same height as me. His complexion a few shades darker. The nigga had a low-cut tapered fade with some sick-ass wave action. The only reason I noticed his dimples was because he smirked at me when we locked eyes. I guess he knew something was about to happen that I didn't.

"Jerome, stop being silly. *You* are my business. And before this gets any uglier than what it already is, Jerome, this is Semaj . . . Semaj, this is Jerome . . . my boyfriend."

*Word?* She had a nigga. I've never seen this cat before. Matter of fact, I haven't seen her with any nigga for a minute now. I guess she spent the night at his house more than he did over here. And I don't blame her, especially with the type of snake shit her cousin is on.

Back to the matter at hand, I wasn't a hater, so I gave dude a pound and told Jay that I'd talk to her later. I needed to hurry up, hop the fence, and get to the man cave. A smoking session was definitely needed to calm my nerves.

"Yo, nigga, what you doing back so fast? You and Jay was chopping it up for a minute. It even looked like you were about to go into her house."

I sat at the table and picked up the blunt Li'l Ray must've just put out. I lit that motherfucker and hit it hard as hell. As soon as the smoke hit my lungs, I started choking. I forgot you can't hit this hydro like that. After I controlled my coughing, I took another pull to let it settle my nerves, then passed the blunt to Li'l Ray.

"I was about to go in, man. But then her nigga showed up. Now pass that blunt back."

# Mya

A few weeks had passed, and I still hadn't run into Jerome. I know he's been here, though. I heard him and JaNair going at it a couple of times.

By the way, she was screaming his name and moaning. I can tell he has some good-ass dick.

Damn! I was so glad I didn't have on any panties right now. Them thangs would have been soaked with the way my pussy just juiced up thinking about fucking him.

I don't know what it was about my cousin's men. But for some reason, they seemed to be a perfect fit for me too. I need to start meeting these niggas first; then I won't have to sleep with them after Jay did.

My phone buzzing on my vanity brought me back from my thoughts. It was Ryan's ass again. I told that nigga that I was cool on having sex with him right now. I wasn't really feeling him that much anymore either. I hit the "ignore" button and continued to get ready.

I was in the mirror finishing up the last of my makeup when my best friend ShaNiece busted through my door.

"Hey, bitch. You ready yet?" she asked, plopping down on my bed.

"You know beauty takes time. Besides, Jay hasn't said anything about whether her friend could get us in tonight."

"Where are we going again?"

I just rolled my eyes. She gets on my nerves when she starts to ask twenty questions.

"We're supposed to be going to that new lounge Lotus Bomb. Supposedly, JaNair has a friend there that can get us in for free, plus a table in VIP."

As soon as the words left my mouth, my room door swung open again. I just kept getting myself ready as JaNair and her best friend LaNiece walked in.

"So my people said you're all set. Just give your name at the front and you're good to go."

I was actually surprised at the little bit of pull she had getting us into this spot. To be honest, I was low-key kind of jealous. How the hell did she pull that off? But then again, her hookup was my hookup. I should've mentioned wanting to go there weeks ago if she could get us in like that. I didn't want to seem ungrateful, so I thanked her and finished getting dressed.

"So, what y'all getting into tonight?" ShaNiece asked her twin sister LaNiece.

Looking at them sitting side by side had me wondering how people could ever tell them apart. They were identical in every way physically, but personality-wise, they were as different as night and day. I guess that's why LaLa and Jay clicked, and Niecey and I hung around each other.

We met the twins a few years ago through JaNair's ex-boyfriend and my current fuck buddy Ryan. He and the twins are first cousins. ShaNiece and I started kicking it really tough after she found out I was fucking Ryan behind Jay's back and never told a soul. Hell, she helped us hook up a few times. Of course, without her sister's knowledge. Now if it was LaNiece who had found out about me and Ryan, she would have definitely spilled the beans. She and Jay had become good friends the first day they met.

"We're going on a double date with Jerome and one of his boys," JaNair answered for her. Now see, that's the type of fucked-up shit I be talking about. She ain't never tried to hook me up with any of Jerome's friends. That's why I won't feel bad when I finally start fucking him.

"Damn, Jay. Why didn't you hook me and Mya up with blind dates? We need men too," Niecey whined.

I cut my eyes at this bitch. She already knows about operation *Take Down Jerome,* so I don't know why she even mentioned for me to get hooked up.

"I thought you were still fucking with Big Will, Niecey. He ain't about to kick my ass for giving his pussy away."

We all busted out laughing. Big Will was my girl's on-again, off-again boyfriend. And he did not play when it came to

Niecey giving up her goods, regardless of what their relationship status was at the time.

I went back to getting ready but couldn't help but to feel some type of way.

When Niecey asked JaNair why she didn't hook *"us"* up with friends, she didn't even acknowledge the question with a response.

Humph! Stuck-up bitch.

After LaLa and Jay finally left my room and ten more minutes had passed, I was ready to go.

# JaNair

"Did you see the look on Mya's face when you didn't say anything about hooking her up?" my best friend LaLa asked me as we sorted through the different outfits we had pulled out of my closet earlier.

"Yeah, but fuck her. She can hook herself up with someone else. She's never had no problem doing it before."

I know the way that I said that came out kind of nasty, but I didn't care. Mya was a sneaky-ass bitch. I just can't wait 'til her shit starts to blow up in her face.

LaLa must've sensed the hate I had laced in that last statement, so she asked me what was going on.

I went on and filled her in on what I'd found out about my dear ol' cousin. I was in the mall a week ago with Jerome, tearing it down as usual, when I ran into one of my old homegirls that we grew up with.

We were in Bath & Body Works, and I was stocking up on my Peaches and Cream smell-good when someone yelled my name.

*"Jay, is that you?" I turned around and damn near knocked another customer over with my shopping basket.*

*"Yeah, girl, it's you. Damn, bitch, you look good," Tamika said as she ran up to me and gave me a hug.*

*"How are you, Mika?" I asked looking her up and down. "I haven't seen you in years. How's your mom, brothers, and sisters?"*

After she ran down how everyone was doing, and I introduced her to Jerome, she asked me if Mya and I still kicked it.

"She actually lives with me now. My granny passed and left the house on Denker to me. I was there by myself for two years when she came knocking on my door crying and talking about she didn't have anywhere else to go. I was in the house by myself, so I didn't have a problem with letting her stay until she got back on her feet. That was four years ago."

"FOUR YEARS AGO!" she screamed in shock. I was kind of embarrassed because a few people stopped what they were doing and stared at us.

"Uh, yeah, girl. Four years ago. Why did you yell it out like that?"

She looked at me as if she was trying to tell me something with her eyes. After Jerome excused himself and went to Foot Locker, she finally spoke.

"The reason why I said it like that was because I ran into Mya a couple of years ago. I asked about you, but she said she hadn't spoken to you in a while. She said that you were dating some dude name Brian or Ryan and was so stuck up in his ass that you shut everyone out." Now it was my turn to be shocked. The expression on my face must have gone unnoticed by her, because she continued on with the story. "When she told me that, I kinda found it hard to believe because you were never love struck like that. Then, the way that she said it made it seem as if she was jealous or something. I just let that go and took it for what it was. I knew we'd run into each other eventually, and I'd get the truth. The thing I couldn't understand or figure out, though, was why she was holding hands and kissing on the nigga she was with."

"Who was she with?"

"Your ex . . . Jeremiah!"

What? Wait! Hold up now! I know she didn't just say Mya was booed up with my ex, Jeremiah. After reiterating that she was, Tamika told me that a few other people we used to roll with had seen them together on different occasions as well. The crazy thing about this whole conversation was, the information she had just given me about Mya and Jeremiah wasn't even the kicker. Mika went on to tell me that not only had Mya been chilling with Jeremiah, but she also was seen with Skyler and Robert as well. Two more of my exes. I didn't know what to think. On one hand, I could care less because I broke up with all them niggas for a reason. On the other hand, I couldn't help but to wonder when she started fucking with them. Robert was my first love and high school sweetheart, and we were together throughout most of my teen years.

Jeremiah is who I dated after Robert and later broke up with when I went away to college. Now, Skyler and I were never in a "relationship," but we hung out between breakups. This was all news to me. I was also mad as hell.

Tamika and I finally said our good-byes after catching up a little more and promising to keep in touch. I purchased my smell-good products, found Jerome, and left the mall loaded down with bags and pissed the fuck off. I couldn't wait to get home and cuss this bitch out. She was gonna have to pack all her shit too and get the fuck out of my house. When I pulled into my driveway, her car was there. But when I got in the house, she wasn't. I started to throw all her shit outside, but I decided against it. I hadn't even noticed Jerome had followed me into the house until he grabbed me from behind and asked me what was wrong. After I told him everything I had just found out about Mya, he was able to calm me down and help me to see things from a different perspective. I was so over the situation that I decided not to say anything to her about it.

I just went to my room, packed an overnight bag at my man's request, and headed to his house for the weekend.

After I was finished telling LaLa about what happened, she just sat on my bed with a stunned look on her face.

"I knew she was sneaky. Her and Niecey be doing some foul shit. I really can't say what it is, cuz I honestly don't know. But what I can say is that you need to watch her ass. Especially around Jerome."

"Girl, you don't think I know that already. That's why I rarely have him spend the night. I always go to his spot. And that's some bullshit too. I got to keep my man away from my own cousin."

"It is," LaLa said walking toward the bathroom to take a shower. "Enough about that, though, we got some dates to get ready for. So get your ass on up in here with me. Let's kill two birds with one stone and try to make it there on time.

"I'm right behind you, girlie. And once Jerome and his friend get a load of us in all our sexiness tonight, I wish a nigga would think about the next bitch."

# Mya

When we arrived at the Lotus Bomb, the line was already around the corner. Why? I don't even know.

This was a lounge bar, not a club. Other than the great food and tasty drinks Jay told us about, I didn't understand what else could have this place so packed.

We made our way to the front of the line, gave our names to the sexy-ass bouncer, and were immediately let in.

"I could get used to this. Did you see the way them bitches in line were hating when we walked in?" Niecey asked as we were led into the building.

Looking around and ignoring her, I was in complete awe when we stepped into this place. The only word that would describe both the inside and outside of this establishment was *gorgeous*.

The lounge was packed with a stylish clientele. I felt a little out of place with my green strapless freakum dress on. But with the way some of these men were already staring at me with lust in their eyes had me changing that tune real fast.

The interior had a green onyx fireplace as its masterpiece, along with a wood wine cabinet trimmed in 14k gold. There were plush white chairs that sat around tables draped with emerald-pleated tablecloths. Comfy, oversized couches lined the walls and sat underneath dimly lit lights for a more intimate feel. The large bar that was located in the middle of the lounge had nothing but the best liquor lining the shelves.

"I wasn't expecting it to look like this on the inside. This place is beautiful," I said to Niecey as I nudged her on the side.

"Yeah, so are the men," she responded while sipping on a drink I didn't even know she had.

"All right now, girl! Will's not going to kick my ass because you're in here trying to be a ho," I laughed.

She smacked her lips. "Girl, please! As of two weeks ago, I'm as single as a dollar bill. So I can talk to as many niggas as I want tonight."

I didn't even respond to her crazy ass. She knew damn well she and Big Will would be in each other's faces and all lovey-dovey tomorrow. Their asses are always breaking up just to make up. I didn't get it at all, but then again, it wasn't my problem to understand anyway.

We were taken to a sectioned-off area in the back of the lounge that was more decked out than the room we had just walked through.

*This must be the VIP section,* I thought to myself as we were led to our table.

Looking around, I could see and tell that there were all types of important people in here. Especially ones with deep pockets.

My eyes scanned the room again and came to a screeching halt when they landed on the chocolate Adonis standing at the minibar talking to one of the waitresses.

"I wonder who that is," I said to Niecey as I pointed my head into the direction of where he stood. Something about him was screaming at my body, face, and pussy. I don't know if it was the six foot three frame, smooth chocolate skin, pretty white teeth, athletically built body, slanted hazel-colored eyes, or the tapered haircut with the wave action on point.

"Oh, my damn!" I said as I grabbed my titties with one hand and Niecey's arm with the other. This beautiful creature just gave what to me was a million-dollar smile, which was accompanied by the sexiest set of dimples I've ever seen.

"I need to find out who this man is before I leave tonight or this earth. And, yes, if you're wondering, it's that serious!"

# Semaj

"Nigga, I don't even know why you dragged me down to this place. Look how long the line is. We are never gonna get in."

Man, I love my cousin to death, but he could get on my nerves like no one else. We were at this new hot spot in Hollywood called the Lotus Bomb. It opened a few months ago, but tonight was our first night trying to get in. The place was real snazzy too. It wasn't no ratchet hole-in-the-wall spot either.

The majority of the people here seemed to be the professional type that I needed to be around. I was used to this sort of crowd, so I fit right in.

I was rocking a pair of light washed Diesel jeans with my black Louis Vuitton V-neck shirt. My shoe game was on point as the new black Testoni shoes graced my feet. My dreads were twisted and pulled into a bun, and my chain, watch, and earrings shined just right. I was looking good and smelling even better. Li'l Ray, on the other hand, was hood nigga through and through.

Regardless of our different styles of dress, I had an agenda to stick to. The objective for tonight: Networking.

A chick I used to kick it with told me about this spot. She said if I wanted to jump-start my career in the music industry, this was the place I needed to be.

I had a degree in engineering and a love for producing, so the music industry is where I wanted to be. If I wanted to make a name for myself, I had to meet some of the right people. Hopefully, this would be the place.

We'd been standing in line for almost an hour and were still in the same spot. I was just about to give up and head out when I was stopped in my tracks by the one person who always seems to take my breath away.

"What's up, Ms. Jay? You look sexy as hell!"

She blushed. "Thanks, J2. You don't look so bad yourself."

I couldn't do anything but blush at that moment. Hearing her call me by the nickname she gave me a few weeks ago did something to a nigga. A couple of days after the brief run-in with her little boyfriend, she caught me outside and invited me over again. I was shocked at first but quickly got over it and went to chill with her. We talked about any and every-thing. From past relationships to favorite childhood games to favorite sexual positions. Not once did I come on to her or vice versa. It was like we were really starting a friendship.

Ever since our first kick-it day, as she calls it, we've chilled a few times more. Either I go over to her house, or she comes to mine. When we can't kick it, we usually text throughout the day, just checking on each other and whatnot. She showed me how she had me programmed in her phone under the name J2. I was cool with that, even though I think she only came up with that nickname because she still forgets my real name.

"What are you doing here?" she asked. "Hey, RayShaun!"

Li'l Ray nodded his head, then turned back to flirting with LaLa. They've also been chilling kind of heavy in the last few weeks.

"You know me. I'm trying to get up in here and politic with a few people. I was told that this was the place to be for what I'm trying to get into," I informed her.

"Why were you about to leave then?"

"Sexy face, do you see this line?" She blushed again. "We've been out here for an hour."

"When we talked on the phone today, why didn't you tell me you were coming? I could've got you in."

"How?" I asked, trying to remember if she ever mentioned this spot in one of our miniconversations.

"Because I know the owner. Come on."

She motioned for us to follow her, and we all fell in line. I wish I would've known that she had the hookup earlier. I just wasted an hour of networking time.

We headed to a door on the side of the lounge. When we got there, she took her phone out of her purse and texted someone. As she was scrolling through her phone contents,

I couldn't help but to admire her beauty. She had the softest caramel skin. Her lips were full, pouty, and pink. Her dark brown eyes were warm and even sexier with the little bit of eye shadow she had on. Those thick thighs, luscious hips, and fat ass were covered by a leopard pencil skirt. The black top that she had on rose high in the front and hung low in the back. You could see a little bit of her flat stomach and tattoo that I didn't even know she had there until right now. Man, she just screams sexiness, and my dick was getting hard just standing next to her.

All of a sudden, the side door swung open . . . and the last person I expected to see walked out.

"Hey, baby!" JaNair squealed as she gave him a hug. She then pulled LaLa away from whatever conversations she and Li'l Ray were having and introduced her to some Ginuwine-looking nigga.

"LaNiece, this is Jerome's friend Gerald . . . Gerald, this is my best friend, LaNiece."

They shook hands and exchanged pleasantries. He then whispered something into LaLa's ear that had her blushing and giggling like a schoolgirl. I looked over at Li'l Ray who had a fucked-up expression on his face. I just hope this nigga could keep his cool until after we leave this place.

The fuck boy Jerome looked at me and gave his usual smirk. He then grabbed Jay's hand and headed back into the lounge. I didn't want to disrespect this man's establishment or fuck up my networking chances. So before they were fully inside, I called JaNair's name. She turned around, smiled, and then asked Jerome if we could come in too.

This nigga's smirk was really starting to annoy me. But I chopped it up and let it go for now. If I had to play nice to jump-start my career, I had no problem doing so.

"Hey, Big Ben!" he called out to the gorilla-looking bouncer. "Take my girl's little friends to the VIP. Let Shelly know that they can order whatever they want and the bill is on the house."

I just laughed at this dude. I didn't want or need him to pay for a damn thing. But since he wants to make himself look good, I'm about to put a dent in this nigga's pocket.

We all started walking down the hall and entered what I took to be the part of the lounge where anyone can chill. We were then told to go through a sectioned-off part to the left, while Jay, LaLa, and their dates headed to a more secluded spot to the right.

Hopefully, I'll see her again before the night is over. If not, I'll just shoot her a text and thank her later.

As of right now, I had some socializing to do.

# JaNair

The sun shining brightly through the blinds is what woke me up out of the weird dream I was having.

*Why the hell was I dreaming about Semaj?* was all I could think about as my eyes focused on the digital clock on the nightstand next to me that read 10:45 in big red numbers.

"Wait! Why didn't my alarm go off? I'ma be late for school. Shit!" I moaned.

Finally noticing I wasn't in my own bed, I instantly sat up and pulled the cover over my naked body.

*What the fuck happened last night?* I thought to myself as I tried to remember.

"So, I treat you to a great night, shower you with gifts, fuck the shit out of you, and you calling this nigga's name out in my bed while you're dreaming?" Jerome asked me with a heated glare in his eyes.

I don't even remember what happened after we left Lotus Bomb last night. I do remember being in the secluded VIP area having a great time with Jerome, his friend, and . . . LaLa. Oh God, where the hell did I leave my best friend?

I reached for my phone on the nightstand but remembered I wasn't at home so it wouldn't be in its usual place. I jumped out of the bed and searched around the room for my purse. I finally found it slung over and partially opened on the bench that sat at the foot of the bed.

"You about to call that nigga?" Jerome spat in my face as he grabbed my wrist trying to get my phone.

"No, Jerome, I'm about to call LaLa to see if she's good. And let go of my arm. You're hurting me!" I screamed as he finally let me go.

"Your girl is good. She's in the guest room with my boy. We all came here this morning after getting something to eat at Jerry's Deli. You don't remember?"

I shook my head no and headed back for the bed. As if on cue, my head started to pound and spin at the same time.

"What all did I have to drink last night? My head is killing me right now."

"You had quite a few shots of Gaviota Tequila. Actually, you drank the whole bottle. Here!" he said as he handed me the two empty bottles.

I swear I loved this tequila. Not only was it smooth, but the bottle that it came in was so beautiful. The bottle was the shape of a woman's body, minus the head and legs. She had a Coca-Cola shape, with titties and ass. The strapless, heart-shaped minidress accentuated every curve on the bottle and/or body. I already had the bottle with the white dress on at home. I finally had the red and blue dress to add to my collection.

"Thanks, babe." I gathered my hair into a sloppy ponytail and pinned it up. "Why didn't you wake me up for class?"

"JaNair, it's Sunday. But besides all that, why the fuck were you dreaming about that bitch-ass nigga you had me get into the lounge last night? You fucking him too?" he asked as he stepped in my personal space.

"Whoa, Jerome. I need you to watch your tone and back up a few." He looked down at me and didn't budge, not one bit.

"Are . . . You . . . Fucking . . . That . . . Nigga?" he asked again through clenched teeth. The scowl he had on his face kind of scared me a little bit.

"Baby . . ."

*Knock, Knock, Knock!*

"Jay, you good in there, girl? C'mere for a minute!" LaLa said from the other side of the door.

"She'll be there in a minute!" Jerome snapped.

"Either she comes out now, or I'ma break this motherfucking door down, nigga. It's only for a second!" she yelled back.

Jerome looked from the door to me, then motioned with his head for me to open it. When I stepped into the hallway, LaLa grabbed my wrist and walked me into the room she must've spent the night in and closed the door.

"Did he hit you?" she asked as she looked at my face intently.

"Girl, please. Jerome knows better than that." I looked around the messy room. "He was all up in my face, though, talking about I was calling Semaj's name out in my sleep last night and shit."

"Wait! You did what?"

"He says I called out Semaj's—"

She cut me off laughing. "Jay, please don't tell me you called Jerome the next nigga's name while y'all were getting it on."

I rolled my eyes. This was the one thing I hated about my best friend. She didn't listen for shit. Nowhere in my response did I say *while we were having sex*. She was always so extra sometimes.

After explaining to her what happened again, I left her room and went back to Jerome's. I couldn't really remember what we did last night, but I was hoping to get a round two cracking of whatever it was.

When I got back to his room, Jerome was nowhere in sight. I checked the bathroom, still no Jerome.

I could tell that he was getting ready to hop in the shower, though. His favorite Ralph Lauren towel was laying on the edge of the bed like he always did.

I was just about to go to the front of his home to look for him when I heard my phone, which I don't remember being on his dresser, vibrate.

A small smile instantly came to my face when I saw who the text message I just received was from.

J2: Hey, J1, just checking on you and wanted to say thanks for last night. You seemed kind of upset when you were leaving, though. Are you OK? Hit me up later. Maybe we can have breakfast.

I responded back.

Me: Good morning to u 2, friend. And I'm good, just waking up. Thanx for askin'.

Not even ten seconds later, my phone was buzzing with a text alert again.

J2: YW . . . What you got going today?

Me: Idk yet. I'm at LaLa's house right now, and we are still kinda hung over . . .

Semaj had just sent back a response when Jerome came back into the room. He headed straight to the bathroom and started the shower. The thought of being pressed up against the tiled walls while Jerome pounded his dick into my pussy instantly had me wet.

I placed my phone back into my purse and took off the T-shirt I put on earlier. As soon as I opened the door, a big cloud of steam hit me. I could see the silhouette of Jerome's muscular frame through the foggy glass doors.

"Mind if I join you?" I asked as I stepped into the shower.

He didn't say anything or even acknowledge me. He just kept washing his body with the bar of Irish Spring.

"Babe, what's wrong? Are you mad that I left you to go talk to LaLa?" I purred into his ear as I wrapped my arms around his waist.

"Naw, it's all good," he finally said as he stepped out of the shower, leaving me to bathe by myself.

*What the fuck just happened?* I couldn't believe this nigga just left me hanging like that. Today was our six-month anniversary, and he promised me a day of wining, dining, and straight fucking. He had me fucked up if he thought he was gonna renege on that.

I shut the shower off and stormed into the bedroom. To say that I was surprised that he wasn't there would be an understatement. *I know this nigga better still be here,* I said to myself. But after searching the whole house and finally seeing his car gone, I got my answer.

My phone buzzing broke my train of thought. I walked over to my purse and picked it up. I had two new messages. One from Semaj, and one from Jerome. I scrolled to his message first.

My Bae: Went to take care of something. I'll be back in a few . . .

# Jerome

I hated to leave her stuck in the shower like that. I mean, I did promise her that we'd spend the day together since my schedule is going to be fucked up for the next couple of weeks. But a nigga needed a break. Don't get it twisted, though, I didn't need a break from the pussy, because she had that bomb. But her mouth and what came out of it at times was another thing. I get tired of hearing about school, LaLa, or her cousin she lives with.

I love JaNair with all my heart, even though it's only been a short time. She's what any and every nigga would want in a wife. Hard worker, educated, loyal, not a ho, family oriented, and she can cook her ass off. Let's not forget how her fly always matches my fly. Then her juicy-ass pussy and fiyah-ass head game is out of this world. She will be my wife one day. It's just not gonna be any time soon. Especially when she has yet to find out what I've been doing in my *free* time. Once that closet opens and the skeletons start to fall out, I just hope that Jay and I can work through it.

I'd just taken my exit off the 105 freeway to get to my boy G's place. I'm hoping this nigga is there. I know he's getting tired of me using him in my little schemes, but what other choice does he have? Best friends cover each other's asses regardless of what's right or wrong. They can call you on your bullshit all day, just as long as they have your back in the end. That's what I was taught.

I rode down the quiet residential street bumping YG's new shit, and just as I expected, his red Range Rover Sport was parked in front of his home. I must admit, I do envy Gerald at times. I mean, he's thirty-two, single, no kids, has a great job working for the local TV network ABC, and he owns his four-bedroom, two-and-a-half bathroom house.

I'd be living like a king right now if I were him. Bitches serving me naked and shit. But no, he's waiting for that "special one" to come into his life. JaNair tried to hook him up with her best friend LaLa a week or so ago. I knew right off the bat that he wasn't feeling her, even while having a good time together on our double date. LaLa wasn't Gerald's type of chick. She was great for fucking but not good enough to wife. I'm kind of glad that they didn't hit it off, though.

"What up, my dude?" I said to G as I grabbed his hand and pulled him into a half hug.

"Shit, nothing. About to dip out in a few and meet up with this chick I met a few weeks ago."

"Word! That's what's up. What she look like?"

"Man, this bitch is bad. Five foot seven, a buck fifty, light skin, long hair, and some pretty-ass green eyes," he said as he scrolled through his phone and lifted the screen to my face, showing me a picture of one of the sexiest females I've ever seen.

"Aye, she hot," I said as I eyed the picture one more time. "What's her creds?"

"She works at the Bank of America over there in Lakewood by the mall, and she's a part-time student at Cal State Long Beach."

"OK, OK. She has a little potential. Are you feeling her?"

He went into his kitchen and turned off the light, then motioned with his head for me to start heading to the door.

"Yeah, she cool so far. She just has a little baby daddy drama. Ol' boy ran up on us a couple days ago while we were having lunch at Red Lobster."

"Yeah? Did you throw a cheddar biscuit at him?" I asked, damn near tripping over the flower pot while I laughed walking down the stairs.

"OK, nigga," he laughed. "I actually didn't have to say anything. Day handled it."

"Day? She has to be a becky with a name like that."

"Nigga, what I look like fucking with a white girl? I mean, I have to fuck with them all day at work. But in my personal life, I only fucks with black girls. You know that shit. Her real name is Zadaya, but that's none of your business. Anyways, what's up? What can I do for you?"

Not even hesitating, I said, "Man, I need to use the Impala."

G just dropped his eyes to the ground and shook his head. I don't even know why he was tripping. He knows I have to be incognegro when I'm on my missions. With JaNair's ass always on the go, we tend to sometimes run into each other in the streets. My cocaine-white Chevy Camaro with the personalized plates "CHVYLVR" tends to stand out too.

"Rome, I hope this other chick is worth it," he said handing me the keys.

*Here we go,* I said to myself.

"Worth what?"

"JaNair, nigga! Dude, you have a loyal woman who loves your nasty-ass drawers. You wanna lose pussy that's yours and only yours for a bitch's pussy that every other nigga beating the bottom out of?" He shook his head. "I'd give my life for a girl like JaNair. I just hope you're ready for whatever happens if she ever finds out," he said, hopping in his truck and rolling down the window.

"Don't forget to close and lock my damn garage when you leave. Last time you left my shit wide open. I may live in a cool part of Inglewood, but it's not Beverly Hills."

I just nodded my head and went toward the car parked in the garage. By the time I reversed out, G was already gone. His warnings and words of wisdom are the only things I can do without. But, I guess he wouldn't be my boy if he didn't try to talk some sense into me.

The thing is, a nigga know he doing wrong. Especially with the person I'm doing the wrong with. But a nigga can't help it. It's like I can't stay away from that Forbidden Fruit. Something that accidentally happened one night started happening every week for the last two months.

So far, she's been okay with playing her role as the side chick, but there are those moments when she wants to talk about me being hers full time. I just laugh at her dumb ass. I don't know why she thinks that I'll leave my filet mignon for carne asada. That bitch is crazy. But that craziness isn't about to stop me from heading to her house right now and blowing her brains out.

My phone started buzzing on my hip. I didn't even answer it because I knew nine times out of ten it was Jay. I didn't want to hear that bitching and complaining right now about us spending the day together. I know I promised her, but damn, I'll just make it up to her later on tonight.

My phone started buzzing again for the third time in a row, and I knew this couldn't have been JaNair now. She normally only calls once. When I picked up the phone and saw Unique's name flash across the screen, I got an instant headache. I don't feel like hearing any of her bullshit either. I let the voice mail pick up. Once the little letter icon popped up, I checked my messages.

Message 1: *Jerome! I know you see me calling you. This is the third fucking time. Call me back!*

Message 2: *I don't understand why you can't Neeeeeevver answer your phone when I call. All I want to know is if you were still coming through.*

Message 3: (This bitch was crying now) *Jerome, please call me back. I'm sorry for the other messages. I love you, baby. I miss you and JJ does too. I hope you're coming to see us.*

Now do you see why I didn't answer my shit? I have a crazy-ass baby mama. If I would've known then what I know now, I would have strapped up twice when I fucked that bitch. JaNair doesn't even know about my son, and I intend to keep it that way. It's not like I had him on her. Some things are just on a need-to-know basis, and she didn't *need* to know that.

Instead of calling my BM back, I just shot her a quick text letting her know that I'd be through in a few hours. I had to make a couple of stops beforehand.

First things first, a nigga was hungry as hell. I decided to swing over to 3 Bears Burgers so that I could get me a Papa Bear combo and Red Bull. I need all the energy I can get for all the fucking I'm about to do today.

# Semaj

I just inhaled a big toke of Kush and held it in my mouth. I looked to my left and raised my eyebrows silently asking baby girl if she was ready. She looked at me nervously, then slowly nodded her head yes and moved in closer to me. I leaned over and placed my mouth onto her soft and juicy lips. When she slightly parted her mouth, I blew the contents of mine into hers.

"Now, act as if you are swallowing it and just hold it in your lungs."

She did as instructed, then looked back at me waiting for the rest of her lesson to be taught.

"When you're ready, slowly exhale the smoke right here."

Again, she did as she was instructed and had a light mist of Kush surrounding my face.

"So this is what you call a shotgun?" JaNair asked, lightly coughing.

"It sure is, and you did good for your first time. Most first-timers start choking as soon as this goodness hits their lungs. You took it like a champ."

She blushed, then giggled. "I wanna do another one."

I shook my head and smirked. We were on the couch in the man cave chilling, watching movies and conversing. We had a comfortable little setup going too. I sat in the middle of the couch kind of slouched down, while she sat in the corner with her legs stretched out and resting on my lap. Every now and then, I'd gently rub her feet.

For the last week, this has been the norm for me and JaNair. Either I was at her house, or she was over here after she got out of school. We even went to the park with my daughter one day and had a picnic. Of course, my little mama instantly fell in love with her and has been begging for us to go somewhere else ever since.

Although JaNair was putting up a good front, I could still see that something was bothering her. The fact that fuck boy Jerome hasn't popped up not once within the last week already told me what the deal was. I wanted to ask her about the nigga, but I didn't want to cause any drama between us. Whenever she was ready to talk, we would, and I would be here for her, ready to listen.

I gave her another shotgun. This time was a little bit heavier, and just like before, she took it like a champ. After taking a few tokes for myself, I was preparing to lean over and give her another charge, but she reached for the blunt and took a pull from it on her own instead.

"Damn, girl! No more baby steps, huh?"

"Semaj, this is not my first time smoking. I puffed a time or two before."

"You never told me that."

"I can't tell you *all* my secrets," she said as she playfully punched me in my shoulder.

There was an awkward silence as we sat there, lost in our own thoughts. After a couple of minutes, she removed her feet from my lap and got up.

"Y'all don't have no chips or cookies out here? I need something to snack on."

"Yeah, look in the cabinet above the fridge. That's normally where Ray keeps all the good stuff if he hasn't eaten it all."

When she stepped in front of the fridge, she had to step on her tiptoes a little to reach the cabinet. The little jean shorts she had on left nothing to the imagination. They were so short and fitted her frame so right, I couldn't help but stare. Seeing the bottom of her plump cheeks hanging out of the shorts when she bent over to look in the fridge had my dick slowly rising. The grey Minnie Mouse sweater she had on had slits going all down the back, exposing the fact that she didn't have a bra on. Just thinking about putting one of her perky-ass titties in my mouth had me hard as fuck now. When she was finished raiding the fridge, I had to quickly adjust myself before she came back. She would've definitely gotten a glimpse of the third member between my legs if I hadn't.

"Y'all got everything to snack on out here. I need to come over more often," she said as she started making her way back over to me.

She plopped down on the couch and placed her feet on my lap again. I knew when the back of her leg brushed over my crotch area, she was able to feel my semihard dick. I tried so hard to get him to go down before she got back, but nothing worked. Especially once that peach scent she always smelled like assaulted my nostrils. I almost lost it.

She gave me a little lopsided grin. "If I didn't know any better, Semaj, I'd think you were happy to see me."

Damn! Busted.

I chuckled for a second, then decided to hit her with some real nigga shit. "I'm always happy to see you, Jay, whether it's when you wave to me while you're on your way to your car or when you come over here and chill with your boy for a minute or two. Seeing your face always brightens my day."

She sat there frozen for a minute, a chip resting on her lip as she stared at me. I guess what I had just said finally started to register to her.

"Are you seri—" Before she could even finish her statement, I pressed my lips to hers and kissed her. I don't know why; I just did. Hell, let me stop lying. I *definitely* knew why I did it. I wanted JaNair like a fat kid wanted cake, and if she would keep it real with herself, she knew she wanted me too.

Over these past weeks of us talking and texting on the phone or chilling at each other's houses, we've gotten to know each other better. She even started calling me by my real name and not that J2 bullshit she came up with. She knew I was attracted to her, just like I knew she was attracted to me.

However, fucking with that bitch nigga Jerome had her mind conflicted.

I deepened our kiss, and she gladly followed. Her lips were so soft and plump. I took her bottom lip into my mouth and softly sucked on it. The sexiest moan escaped from the back of her throat and had my dick standing at full attention again. When she opened her mouth, I didn't hesitate to stick my tongue in to find hers. As soon as they touched, the sweet taste of pineapple juice and Kush greeted my taste buds.

Taking her tongue in between my lips, I sucked on that shit like it was a new flavor for Jolly Ranchers.

Her hands went to my head, and she lightly tugged on my dreads.

"Damn!" I mumbled against her lips as she grabbed another handful of my locks and pulled. For a moment I just sat there with my eyes closed, enjoying her touch as my forehead rested against hers. I needed a minute to calm down before I bent her little ass over this couch and fucked her ass to sleep.

I was just about to take her mouth again but was cut short when she jumped off the couch and started putting her red and black Jordans back on.

"What's wrong?"

"I . . . I . . . I gotta go," she stuttered. "That should've never happened."

"Wait, Jay, I'm sorry. I didn't mean—"

"No!" she cut me off. "It's not you. It's me."

"Well, you know you don't—" She cut me off again.

"I gotta go, Semaj. I . . . I'll talk to you later."

And with that, she disappeared out of the side door without glancing back once.

"Fuck!" I shouted in frustration. I hope I didn't just mess things up between us.

Wait! What the hell am I saying? I ain't mess up nothing. Even if she doesn't want to admit it right now, I know she enjoyed that moment just as much I did. Her body's reaction to my kiss and touch told that truth. I don't regret doing that shit at all.

I shook my head and smiled to myself as I sat back on the couch. If the opportunity ever presented itself again, I know, without a doubt, I'm going for it.

Fuck Jerome and whatever they have going.

Obviously, he ain't taking care of her like he should be. If he was, what we just did would've never happened. It's only going to be a matter of time before JaNair is mine, and I won't have anyone else to thank but Jerome.

Ol' boy was slipping. JaNair will be back, and I had no doubts about that. Especially when she realizes that what her nigga won't do, I surely will.

# Mya

"Damn it!"

My phone ringing for the tenth time in a row finally had me all the way up.

I sat on the side of my queen-sized bed and stretched my arms to the sky. For the last few days, I've been feeling kind of off. My lower back was hurting constantly, and I couldn't keep anything down. Niecey kept saying I was pregnant, but that was far from the truth. I went to Planned Parenthood like clockwork to get my depo shot. So me being with child was not the case.

With my phone ringing again, I finally picked it up and decided to answer it.

"What do you want, Ryan?"

"Bitch, watch your tone when you're talking to me."

I didn't give his ass a second thought when I hung up in his face. Disrespect was not gonna fly with me, regardless of who you were.

My phone rang again, but I ignored it. I had to use the bathroom bad and needed to head to the kitchen to try to find something I could eat and possibly hold down.

When I finished handling my business, I washed my hands, then headed straight to the fridge. JaNair's leftovers from different eateries were in there, as well as some fruit, sandwich meat, and a few things to make a light omelet. I gathered everything I needed and prayed like hell I would be able to keep these eggs, turkey, and spinach down.

Placing the skillet on the stove, I went back toward the fridge to grab the butter when the doorbell rang.

"Ugh, if this motherfucka showed up unannounced, we are gonna have a major problem," I mumbled to myself as I walked to the door.

I looked out the blinds and scanned the street for Ryan's car; then I silently thanked the heavens above when I didn't see it.

Whoever was at the door had just rung the bell again when I opened it.

"Helllllllll . . . Jesus Christ!" was all I managed to say as I stared into the face of one of the finest niggas I'd ever seen.

The waves in his hair almost had me seasick. His six foot three frame damn near blocked the whole door frame. The mysterious slanted hazel eyes complemented his smooth chocolate skin very well. As my eyes took in this bronze Adonis and all of his sexiness, I couldn't help but to feel that I knew this nigga from somewhere. I just couldn't place it.

When he flashed that million-dollar smile with the cutest pair of dimples, I finally remembered where I recognized him from. The Lotus Bomb.

This was the same dude I kept elbowing Niecey about all night long. I tried to get his attention whenever he was in my line of sight, but something or someone was always pulling him in another direction. I wasn't going to leave without one last desperate attempt to at least get sexy boy to call me. I asked the hating-ass waitress who served us for the night to slip him the napkin I'd written my number and address on before we left. She must've really been pleased with the three-dollar tip I left, because here he was in the flesh.

"How you doing today, Mya?" he said as he looked me over from head to toe.

"I'm doing OK. I've been a little under the weather lately, but I'm good now," I responded as I opened the door a little wider.

I had on a pair of lace cheeky panties and a matching bra. I wanted him to get a full view of everything I was working with since he didn't get to see it all that night.

He smiled as he appraised my body, then extended his hand for me to shake. "It's funny that we finally meet in person. I've heard so much about you that I feel like we already know each other."

*Heard so much about me? Who could . . .* Then it finally dawned on me.

"Jerome, right?" I said as I shook his hand, a devious smile plastered on my face. "I've heard so much about you too. You know, for a minute there, I thought my little cousin was making you up, talking about she had a man. But now that we've met, I see she was telling the truth."

He smirked, then licked his lips. Seeing his thick pink tongue dart out of his mouth like that had my clit thumping like crazy. *I wonder if his head game is on point.* Hell, who am I kidding? With the way he's looking at me right now, I could know the answer to that question in no time.

"Where are my manners, would you like to come in?" I asked as I gestured for him to enter our home. "I was just about to make me something to eat. I don't mind making enough for two."

He looked at me, then back down to his ringing phone. A slight frown crossed his face as the person who was calling picture-flashed across the screen. I couldn't get a good glimpse of who it was, but I could make out that the picture was a female. Being that he was at our home looking for JaNair, it definitely couldn't have been her. Whoever she was though really wanted his attention because she was blowing his shit up.

"Naw. I'm good. Thanks for the offer, though," he said as he backed away from the door. "Can you please tell JaNair I stopped by when she gets in."

I nodded my head and waved good-bye as he slid into the all-black Jaguar XFR and pulled off. I hurried up and ran to my room to get my phone. I scrolled down my call log until I got to the name of the person I was trying to call.

"Hello!" Niecey screamed into the phone because of her noisy background.

"Niecey, go into another room or something. I got something to tell you."

"Hold on, Mya, let me go to another room, because I can't hear you." I shook my head. Didn't I just say that?

"OK, I can hear you now. What's up?"

I went on and filled her in on everything I just found out about Mr. Jerome, including the way he couldn't stop looking at me. The lust he had in his eyes was pretty evident, and I'm pretty sure if that damn phone wasn't constantly going off, we would've been fucking right there on the living-room floor.

See, I told you before, I don't go after JaNair's men. For some reason, they always come to me. And this weekend won't be any different. If I'm guessing correctly, Jerome was the friend who got us into Lotus Bomb the last time we went. I don't know how he's connected to the lounge, but I'm pretty sure he'll be there . . . and so will I.

# JaNair

Jerome had finally hopped in his car and drove off. I've been standing on the side of my house for about ten or fifteen minutes waiting on him to leave.

I had just run from out of Semaj's man cave and was on my way home when I saw his car pull up. I knew part of the reason why Jerome has been igging me for the last week was because of how I called Semaj's name out while I was sleeping next to him. Let him tell it, though, he's just been real busy with work. Regardless of who was right or wrong, I wanted to avoid any further confrontation on the Semaj subject, so I ducked off into the little cubbyhole between our houses. They couldn't really see me, but I could see them just fine, especially with my living-room window on the side of the house being wide open.

Whoever was calling Jerome's phone really needed to get in touch with him, because it kept going off. I hope it didn't have anything to do with something at the lounge, because if it did, he would probably lose it. Lotus Bomb was his baby.

While peeping through the window like my name was Tom, I saw the whole little exchange thing he had with Mya. Although I couldn't hear a word that was being said, I can only imagine what was coming out of her mouth. She had the look in her eyes, though, the one she gave to a man right before she jumped his bones.

I shook my head and laughed at her and her ho-tactics. This bitch had another think coming if she thought I was going to let this one go just so she could go behind my back and date him. A few words with her ass was definitely going to be spoken as soon as I got into the house. All of that answering the door half-naked in lingerie was not gonna fly living with me. The shit was disrespectful and just downright trifling.

"Who we hiding from?" the baritone voice whispered into my ear, damn near scaring me half to death.

"Semaj, what the fuck! You scared the shit out of me." I didn't even hear him walk up.

"You should be more aware of your surroundings if you wanna play private eye," he said with a shrug of his shoulders.

He took the blunt from behind his ear, placed it in his mouth, and lit it up. When he took the first pull and blew the smoke out into my face, my eyes went directly to his lips. A tingly feeling crept down my spine as I remembered the way he attacked my lips earlier. It wasn't too sloppy or too conservative. It was just right. The way he sucked my tongue and bottom lip had me moaning and lightly pulling on his locks.

*Whew.* I just got goose bumps.

I looked up into his low-hooded eyes, just as he was taking another pull. If he ate pussy as good as he kissed, I'd probably be sprung as hell.

"If you want it, come get it," he said as he stared at me intently. He held out his hand and offered me the blunt, but I declined. I kind of had the feeling that what he said was meant as a double entendre, but I wasn't going to entertain either one.

"I'm done smoking for the day. I'm just about to head on in the house . . . and give Jerome a call. He just stopped by a few minutes ago, but I missed him."

He nodded his head slowly.

"All right, J2," I smiled. "I'll see you around."

I had just turned around to walk away when he grabbed my arm and spun me back around. He pulled me so close to him that my breasts were practically touching his chest. The impression of his dick could be felt against the top half of my stomach as it got bigger and bigger. I could feel the coolness of his breath on the top of my head, which had the tiny hairs on the back of my neck standing up. The aroma of Kush and whatever cologne he had on filled the air around me. My eyes closed and rolled to the back of my head as the intoxicating smell took over my senses.

*God, what is this man doing to me?* He had my body ready to explode just from being against his.

The few dreads that were hanging from underneath his fitted cap lightly tickled my shoulder as he leaned over and put his mouth next to my ear.

"JaNair, I want to taste you so bad right now, you just don't know. My dick is pressing against my jeans so hard that it hurts. That little kiss we shared a few moments ago isn't anywhere close to the type of kiss you'd get if you gave me the opportunity to show you." He rose up and looked me in my eyes before he continued. "The ball is in your court because I know you have certain . . . situations you need to deal with. But if he is who you really wanna be with, then I can't do anything but respect that. Just know that regardless of how I feel, I'm here for you and only a fence away if you ever need a listening ear."

He kissed me on my cheek, squeezed my chin, then turned around and walked off. Before he disappeared into the house, he called my name.

"Whenever you ready to let a real nigga show you how a queen should be treated, you also know where to find me. Both doors will always be open for you." And with that, he was finally gone.

All I could do as I sat there stuck on stupid was say, "Damn!"

# Jerome

"Are these the numbers for the night so far?" I asked while looking at the little sheet of paper that was just given to me.

"Yes, sir," he responded, all hype. "We're doing almost double of what we made opening night."

I nodded my head and smiled at my business partner Toby.

Tobias Wayne Wright was the smoothest and most down-to-earth cat I knew. We met our first year of business school and hit it off. The fact that he was the weed man was also another reason why we got along so well. Being one of the smartest kids in our class, Toby was well on his way to making a name for himself. However, one semester, he got caught up in some mess with this broad, and his weed operation was exposed. He ended up getting kicked out of the program at Anderson and cut off by his wealthy parents. We kept in touch over the years through social media and shit. I always told him that when I opened up a spot, I'd put him on. Not only was he great with numbers and real business savvy, he had connections with some of the most powerful people in the city. Toby only sold weed to high-end customers, some of which were a big help when we needed certain permits and licenses for the lounge.

I got up from behind my desk and started for the door, Toby right on my heels. We needed to make some rounds and show our faces to the huge crowd we had in the building.

"So how's that sexy little chick you've been seeing for a while now?"

"Ah, man, JaNair is good. She'll be here tonight with her homegirl," I answered back as I surveyed some of the people in VIP.

"Homegirl?" Toby asked as he turned to me. "It wouldn't be the same homegirl she tried to hook G up with, would it?"

I laughed because I already knew where this was going. "Yeah, it's the same one. Her name is LaNiece, but everyone calls her LaLa. She and JaNair are best friends."

"LaLa, huh?" He licked his lips and nodded his head. "Little mama hot, and if G ain't trying to fuck with her, hook your boy up."

After agreeing to put a bug in La's ear, I gave my mans a dap and headed toward the bar. Although we've been making crazy numbers at the door, the cash register at the bar has come up short at least twice in the last two weeks.

When I first noticed what was going on, I immediately had a staff meeting and raised all kinds of hell.

Niggas had another thang coming if they thought they were going to steal from me. The next day, I had my security guy come out and install small cameras above both registers and another one that gave me the ability to see if any of my bartenders were giving away alcohol for free.

I was so focused on watching my workers that I didn't feel my phone vibrate when JaNair called. Instead of calling a second time, she sent a text message saying that she was on her way. As soon as she walks through those doors, we're going straight to my office. It's been a minute since I dipped off in her pussy and before she starts to complain or question me about fucking other bitches, I was gonna break her ass off real good. Hopefully then she'd forget how long it's been, and the drama could be avoided.

I was still sitting at the bar, polishing off a shot of the drink my waitress just served me, when a familiar voice sounded in my ear.

"Bartender!" she shouted, waving the new chick Starlah over. "A59 Rémy Martin and apple juice for me, and a . . ."

"D'ussé," I said when she pointed to my empty glass. She looked me in the eyes, licked her lips, then turned back to Starlah.

"And another shot of D'ussé for this fine brother to my left."

We both silently stared at each other as our drink orders were being filled.

Her cinnamon color looked smooth as hell and had a little glow under the lounge's dim lighting. Her dark brown eyes gave off a little sparkle every time she smiled. When she licked her pouty lips again, that pretty pink tongue made my dick twitch. I stepped back a bit and took in her shapely body. She was thick in all the right places, minus not having as much ass as I liked, but her melon-sized titties made up for that.

My eyes rolled back up to her face. The sexy little smirk she now wore made my dick jump again.

"My . . . my . . . my . . . Mr. Jerome. If I didn't know any better, I'd assume you were checking me out just a few seconds ago."

I did not confirm or deny that allegation as I held her gaze. My silence must've given her the green light, though, because before I knew it, she stepped back into my personal space, rose up on her toes a little, and brushed her lips over my ear.

"If you were someone else, I'd probably take you to the bathroom and fuck the shit out of you," she said as she licked my earlobe, then kissed my neck. "But seeing as you belong to my cousin, I don't think that that would be such a good idea . . . Do you?"

Damn!

Decisions . . . decisions . . . decisions.

My dick wanted to take her up on the offer so bad, but something in the back of my mind kept telling me not to do it.

Remembering JaNair could be here at any moment, I backed up a bit and put some space between us. All I needed was for her to walk in and see her cousin all over me with my dick hard as hell. Damn! I needed to get away from her fast.

"Yo, Rome!" I heard over my shoulder. "We got a little situation outside that needs your immediate attention."

*"My nigga Toby,"* I thought as I left Mya standing at the bar and headed toward the front.

# JaNair

*"Girl, what's wrong? My man ain't shit. Girl, what's wrong? My man ain't shit. Girl, what's wrong? My man ain't shit.*

We were rolling down the 405 Freeway on our way to Lawndale bumping that Problem joint, "D2B." I had just texted Jerome to let him know that we were on our way.

"Damn, LaNiece! Slow your ass down. You know CHP stay pulling people over on this freeway," I tried to shout over the music.

"Huh? What you say? Go faster?" she shouted back as she pushed down harder on the gas and laughed.

"Damn it, LaLa! Stop fucking playing! If you wanna die, do that shit on your own time." I was freaking pissed now. She knows I hate that Vin Diesel, *Fast and Furious* shit. I've never been in an accident before, and I wasn't trying to be in one now. I should've gone with my first mind and drove my own car. But no, LaLa just had to show off her new whip.

"Stop crying, Jay. I was just playing," she said as she started to slow down. "Did you get a hold of Jerome?"

I shook my head no and continued staring out of the window. I was still pissed at her for playing with my life like that. She knew it too. That's why she turned the music back up, then picked up her phone and started texting.

"You have gots to be fucking kidding me!" I said turning the music back down.

"What?"

"As if driving over 90 mph wasn't a danger to my life, you switch to texting?"

She rolled her eyes. "What the fuck, JaNair? You wanted me to slow down, and I did. Now that I'm answering a few text messages, it's a problem? You're not the only one with a life around here!"

"And what the hell does that mean?"

She shook her head. "Nothing."

"Naw, sweetie! Don't go mute now. What the hell did you mean?" I said as I turned in my seat to face her.

"JaNair, you're my best friend, and I love you. But you act like you're the only one with a life. Like the world revolves around you and only you. Yeah, you got two of the finest niggas hounding your ass, but that doesn't mean shit. When was the last time you asked me about my love life or who I got hounding me?"

I didn't know where any of this was coming from. Hell, we were just joking and talking about her newest boo before she started driving all crazy and shit. To my knowledge, we talked about everything. Whether it's her life, my life, or some shit we did together.

"First off, LaNiece, I apologize if I ever made it seem as if your life doesn't matter to me. As you just said, you are my best friend, and I love you too, and I wanna know about any and everything that goes on in your world. With that being said, who are you texting over there that has you cheesing so hard?"

She smiled. "The nigga I was just telling you about while we were getting ready at your house."

"Oh yeah! You feeling him like that, huh? Is he hubby status?"

"Yeah, he is." She sighed. "There's a problem, though."

"And what's that?"

"He has a girlfriend already."

I didn't even respond to what she said. I just looked at her as she tried to text and keep her eyes on the road at the same time. I wanted to ask her so bad how can he be hubby status if he already has a girl? But with the way she just came at me, I didn't want her to start saying that I was hating now. Instead of harping on the fact that the nigga she was really feeling had a girl, I asked the one question that she shouldn't have a problem with me asking.

"So what's his name?"

She kept smiling and texting on her phone as if she didn't hear me. When I asked her again, she mumbled something under her breath.

"Wait, what did you say?" I asked after the second time of not understanding what she said.

"I said wouldn't you like—"

But before she could finish what she was saying, her answer was cut short . . . when we slammed into the back of a car that suddenly stopped in the middle of the freeway. The last thing I saw before total blackness took over was LaLa's head hit the steering wheel and a lot of blood gush out.

# Mya

So far, operation *Take Down Jerome* was live and in full effect. I wasn't going to abort this mission for nothing in the world. Not even family.

I knew that once he saw me in the black catsuit I found at H&M that I'd have his undivided attention. The thing fit my body like a glove. The push-up bra I got from Victoria's Secret had my perky C cups looking nice and ripe for the picking. The butt pad I had on gave me a little lift in the ass department and had me filling out the suit just right. My jet-black hair was in big spiral curls that framed my cute little round face. Thigh-high come fuck me boots set my whole outfit off. All eyes were on me as soon as I walked in, so I knew Jerome's eyes wouldn't be too far behind.

"Can we go sit back down now? My feet are starting to hurt!" Niecey whined from somewhere behind me. I was so caught up in eye fucking Jerome, I'd actually forgotten she was even there.

I don't even know why I brought her with me anyways. She's been acting real salty since I told her about my plan to fuck Jerome.

*"Are you really going to try to sleep with him?" she asked me as we walked through the mall looking for outfits to wear tonight.*

*"Hell, yeah! Have you seen that nigga?"*

*"Yeah, I've seen him. LaLa showed me a picture of her, Jay, him, and some other dude all out together. From what La says, JaNair really likes this dude."*

*"And?" I asked as we walked into Forever 21.*

*"And you don't feel bad? Including my cousin, you've slept with . . . like five of her dudes. You don't get tired of fucking her sloppy seconds?"*

*"If I didn't know you any better, ShaNiece, I would think that you were hating. You mad or something? What? Do you wanna fuck Jerome too? Hell, go right on ahead, honey. I mean, if you really wanna know, I wouldn't care if you were. That's still not gonna stop me from sampling a taste of his sexy ass. You fucking him first or him being my cousin's man, any way it goes . . . I don't care," I said with a shrug of my shoulders.*

*I looked up at Niecey who had suddenly become mute. The look she had on her face was a mixture between hate and disgust. I laughed inwardly to myself because this is one of the reasons why I don't have too many female friends.*

*Bitches kill me. It was okay for me to have sex with JaNair's man when he was your cousin and you were helping me sneak around with him. But now you want to question me about a nigga you not even related to?*

*We didn't stay in the mall too much longer after that conversation. After we stopped and got a couple of snacks from Wetzel's Pretzels, we headed out to our cars and went our separate ways.*

Still facing the direction that Jerome had just walked off in, I didn't even respond to her question. Hell, if your feet hurt, go sit your ass down. What do you need my permission for?

I caught another glimpse of Jerome across the lounge. He was smiling and talking to some chick who had just stepped in front of him. She was cute and from what I could see, had a nice little body, but I wasn't worried about her or any other bitch for that matter.

After watching the two disappear behind the double doors, I turned my attention toward a frowning Niecey. She didn't even notice that I was facing her until I cleared my throat. The daggers she was shooting at the double doors on the other side of the room had me thinking of the conversation we had at the mall.

"You didn't have to follow me over here, Niecey. You could've stayed at the table," I told her. When I looked over at our recently vacated seats, I noticed the dudes who were buying us drinks earlier had returned.

"Heckle and Jeckle are back." I tilted my head in their direction. "Go back over there and keep them company until I get back. Make sure you get me another apple juice and Rémy while you're at it too."

She twisted up her lips. "Bitch, please! What I look like going over there by myself to order your ass a drink?"

"Don't you need another glass of wine yourself?" I was on the verge of going off on her ass. She knew how we got down when we went out. All of a sudden she on some other shit.

"I do want another glass, but I don't need them niggas to get it! Unlike you, my dear *best* friend, I have a job, so I can buy my own drink."

Niecey had me all the way fucked up. Just because I wanted the next motherfucka to buy me a drink didn't mean that I couldn't buy one for myself. Hell, if I really wanted to, I could buy me, her, and them rounds for the whole night. I had some change in my clutch. Her sprung-ass cousin hit me off with a stack before we came out tonight. She didn't need to know that, though.

I had just sipped the last drop of drink I had in my cup when I felt something vibrating next to my arm. At first glance, I thought I'd mistakenly left my phone on top of the bar, but when a picture of JaNair popped up, with wifey flashing across the screen, I knew I hadn't.

"What the hell you smiling like that for?"

"Honey, my night just went from good to great." I showed her what I had just found. "Mr. Jerome left his phone."

"Soooo . . . what? You're going to call JaNair and pretend to be the other woman?"

"Hell, naw! I know it's only going to be a matter of time before he comes back over this way retracing his steps, looking for it. When he heads back to his office, I won't be too far behind. I'ma wait for a minute or two, then knock on the door and act as if I found his phone on the floor somewhere. Once I get in and close the door, I'ma work my magic and have him balls deep in this pussy before last call."

Niecey had this smug look on her face, and I didn't know why. It seemed like she low key had an attitude or something.

It was weird. If I didn't know any better, I'd think that she was . . . Naw, it can't be that. Niecey isn't Jerome's type at all. A man like him was attracted to women that looked like me or JaNair. That natural beauty. He didn't even acknowledge her ass earlier, and she was right behind me. I'm going to ask her ass about that shit later. Right now, I had other things to worry about, like putting my plan into action. Jerome's fine ass was on his way over here, and by the way he was looking around and checking his pockets, I knew he'd lost something.

# JaNair

"Baby, please!" I whined as he peppered light kisses down my smooth stomach.

He looked up at me with those sexy hooded eyes that I couldn't get enough of. The smirk on his face was a sure tell-tale sign that I was going to be begging for a lot more. Without even acknowledging my plea from earlier, he continued to blaze a trail of kisses down my body stopping at the gem buried between my thighs.

"Mmmm," he moaned softly as he nuzzled his nose between my slick folds. "You even smell like peaches down here. I wonder if you taste like them too."

I looked at him with eyes that mirrored his own and bit down on my bottom lip.

"There's only one way to find out" was all I said as I opened my legs a little wider, giving him full access to what he inquired about.

He gave me the sexiest lopsided grin before he took a deep breath and inhaled my scent for the third time. Lowering his head, he lightly brushed his mouth across my lips and kissed each one. Goose bumps tickled my whole body when the tip of his cool tongue found my throbbing clit.

"Shit!" I hissed after he lightly tugged on my pearl and pulled it into his mouth. A light coat of my juices sprayed his chin as if I were marking my territory.

The way he was eating my pussy was like something I've never experienced before. Within a matter of two minutes, I was on the verge of coming again. I tried to move away from his devouring session, but he locked his arms around my legs. When I tried to move his face from in between my thighs, he loosened his grip for a minute and swatted my hand away.

"Stop fighting me, JaNair. You're only making it worse for yourself when you do that," he said with my clit still in his mouth. I could feel his lips curling into a smile as he pressed his face back into his meal.

"Fuck, baby, what are you trying to do to me?" I hoarsely said between moans.

After ignoring me yet again, he gently pecked my clit and whispered that he'd see her later. As his face effortlessly glided its way back up my body, his fingers took turns diving into my wetness.

"You're so fucking hot," he whispered into my ear, giving me those goose bumps again. "My tongue fell in love with your taste. I can't wait for my dick to become infatuated with your feel."

He rubbed our cheeks against each other before placing feathered kisses all over my face. Once our lips connected, it seemed as if a magnetic pull drew us even closer to each other, deepening our kiss. Before I could even try to wrap my mind around what had just happened, he pushed himself into my slick opening.

"Ahhhhhhhhh!" I screamed out as he tried to bury himself deeper into me. My body froze and went stiff as a board. I tried to move my head but couldn't. When I tried to push him off of me, I couldn't. My arms felt as if they had thousand-pound weights tied to each one.

He looked at me with a shocked expression on his face. "Are you OK, JaNair?" he asked.

I tried to answer him, but I couldn't. Tears started rolling down my face.

"JaNair . . . baby . . . Are you all right? Tell me what's wrong," he asked again. This time I could hear the panic in his voice as he pulled out of me and turned on the bright-ass lights.

"JaNair!" he screamed, but I still couldn't respond. I felt my eyes roll to the back of my head as my body started to shake uncontrollably.

"She's seizing!" I heard a loud, high-pitched voice scream.

I opened my eyes when I heard it and was immediately blinded by the bright lights. When a few unfamiliar faces came into view, I tried to speak, but I couldn't. It felt as if my tongue was lodged into the back of my throat.

"Her blood pressure is 160/80 and steadily climbing!" the same voice shouted a few minutes later.

Fear instantly started to take over my body as so many people moved around me quickly. Questions I couldn't seem to ask them started to swarm around in my head like mad honeybees. Where the hell am I? Who are all these people? How did I end up here? And last but not least, what the hell happened to Semaj?

The slightly wrinkled Caucasian face of some woman appeared in my line of sight. The white coat she had on was as white as the walls around the room. She took a little flashlight out of her pocket and flashed it into both of my eyes. Next, she put what looked like headphones in her ears and some cold silver thing on my chest. When she was finished with that, she took the clipboard from the woman behind her and started flipping through the papers.

"Ms. Livingston, I know you can't move any limbs right now or talk, so what I need for you to do is move your eyes up and down if the answers to my questions are yes, then left to right if the answers are no. Do you understand?"

Up and down.

"Is your name JaNair Livingston?"

. . . Up and down.

"Are you twenty-five years old?"

. . . Up and down.

"Do you have any recollection of what happened to you tonight?"

. . . Left to right.

She touched the bottom of my foot with something, then asked, "Can you feel when I do this?"

. . . Up and down.

"How about this?" she asked as she moved whatever she had up my leg.

. . . Up and down.

She turned back to the woman behind her who smiled at me. After they discussed something I couldn't quite hear, the older woman said that she'd be right back and excused herself.

"She's going to check on your friend." I just stared at the brown-skinned woman who was now in my face. I had to close my eyes every ten seconds, because the crazy Mickey Mouse design on her top was making me dizzy. I wanted to ask her what friend she was talking about. As if reading my mind, she spoke.

"You know, Ms. Livingston, you are pretty lucky. The way your friend crashed into the back of that diesel truck . . ." She shook her head. "God is definitely good!"

*Crash . . . Diesel truck . . . Friend?* I lay there and thought about what she had just said to me for a few moments. Did Semaj and I just get into a car accident? Naw, that couldn't have happened, we were just in his bedroom. Then like a ton of bricks, it finally hit me.

I was in the car with LaLa!

# Mya

Uggggh! Jerome's constantly vibrating phone was working on my last nerve.

"Isn't that like the twentieth time JaNair has called his phone?" Niecey asked. "It might be important. You should probably answer it."

I sucked my teeth. "Niecey, you sound dumb as hell." Rolling my eyes, I continued. "Obviously, JaNair's insecure ass is on one. Jerome not answering his phone is making her think he's doing all kinds of things other than working, especially with me ignoring the last few calls she made."

"Maybe you should just give him his phone back, Mya." Her eyes shifted around the bar. "JaNair hasn't been the only one calling him either. Those other calls may be important to him."

For someone who didn't have any interest in Jerome, she sure was concerned about his phone. When he came over here earlier and asked if we'd seen his lost phone, I lied and told him no. He searched around for a bit, then finally turned on his heel and headed toward the kitchen area. As soon as he started walking down the hallway where the restrooms were, I was going to put my plan into action.

"That white boy know he fine as hell!" Niecey whispered in my ear as the tall, tanned, and boyishly handsome man I'd seen earlier with Jerome walked by.

The Clive Christian No. 1 cologne he had on invaded its way into my nostrils. A flutter of goose bumps trailed my arms as the intoxicating smell occupied my personal space. *Good God, he smells good,* I thought to myself as I tried to calm my throbbing pussy down.

"Don't tell me you want him too?" I heard Niecey say just before she gulped down the rest of her drink.

What the hell was her problem? My inner bitch was about to come out on her ass, and it was not going to be pretty.

She'd been sneak dissing and saying smart remarks all night, and I was tired of that shit. Right before I was about to let her ass have it, I saw Jerome head down the hallway and toward the offices.

I got up from my stool, smoothed out the invisible wrinkles in my outfit, and started walking in the direction of the hallway. I didn't even tell Niecey where I was headed because I didn't really feel like having to show my ass for whatever smart remark she was possibly going to say. I glanced over my shoulder to see if she was watching me, but was sorta surprised when I saw Jerome's sexy white friend talking to her.

*Bzzzz, Bzzzz.*

Jerome's phone vibrated in my hand again. This time, an unknown number popped up on the screen. I quickly declined the call after I let it ring for a few more seconds, then turned the phone over. I took my lifeless cell out of my purse and removed the battery. Since we had the same models, I replaced my battery with his, and his with mine. After switching those around, I didn't bother powering mine back on. We didn't need JaNair or anyone interrupting what was about to go down.

Walking down the dimly lit hallway, I passed both restrooms, then came upon two closed doors. I lightly knocked on the first and didn't receive an answer. I moved to the second door and did the same thing. I was just about to turn around and walk away when the heavy door swung open.

"Who is . . . Oh, hey, Mya . . . Wh . . . What can I do for you?" he asked with furrowed brows. His handsome face had a slight irritated look to it, but I didn't care. I was about to change all of that.

I pushed my way past him and walked into the office, making sure my ass rubbed against his midsection in the process.

"I didn't mean to bother you, Jerome, but I have a surprise for you."

He pinched the bridge of his nose and shook his head. "I really don't have time for this right now, Mya. I need to—"

"find this?" I said cutting him off and holding up his phone.

"Oh shit! Thank you, girl. I was about to die."

"And why was that?"

"I have a lot of shit in here that's not for everyone to see," he said as he tried to power it on. His eyes drifted over to me, then back to the device in his hand.

"You need to charge it right quick because it's dead. I tried to turn it on when I found it, but it wouldn't budge."

"Man, Mya, you don't know how happy I am you found it. How can I ever repay you?"

"I can think of a few things," I said as I walked around his big desk and placed my slim hand on his shoulder.

Jerome looked down at me and licked his lips. "I don't think that that would be such a good idea, Mya. Especially with JaNair being your cousin and all."

"Do you really thinks she cares about how you feel when she has that nigga Semaj all in our house and in her room?" I really didn't know what was up with JaNair and Semaj. They could really just be friends, but I needed to plant some sort of seed in his head to get him to let his guard down. And by the look he had in his eyes right now, I can tell I hit a sore spot.

I took things a little further and told Jerome how his girl and the nigga next door have been kicking it real heavy for the last few weeks. I also informed him of how JaNair had been at Semaj's house all day that time he came to the house looking for her. And if that wasn't enough to get his attention, I told him how JaNair had no intention of coming here tonight. That she was on a date with Semaj right now, and when he called to talk to her later, she was gonna make up some excuse about not feeling well.

"I knew that nigga was feeling my girl. But every time I asked her, she would say that they were just friends."

"Just friends, huh?" I asked doing air quotes. "Let me ask you this, Jerome. Do people who are *just friends* kiss?"

He shook his head. "They kissed?"

"Sure did. That same day you came over looking for her."

JaNair's ass thought that no one had seen her butt all on the side of the house with her tongue down Semaj's throat. After Jerome had left, I went to close the front window shades. When I looked out the window, I saw Semaj's tall, sexy ass hovering over JaNair before he pulled her into him. Yeah, you could tell that Semaj kissed her, but Jerome didn't need to know that.

I was just about to throw some more salt on my dear ol' cousin, but Jerome's lips crashing down on mine stopped that.

When he finally let me come up for some air, I was totally gone to la-la land.

"That . . . that . . . that kiss . . ."

"was everything," I said still dreaming.

"No, Mya." He shook his head. "That kiss should've never happened," he said as he backed away from me and sat down in his plush chair.

"Jerome, you know as well as I do that we're attracted to each other, so stop frontin'."

"But you're JaNair's cousin." The confused expression he had on his face almost made me laugh. Jerome and I were going to be fucking tonight, whether in this office or at one of those cheap little hotel rooms.

I slowly started to remove my catsuit from my body. When I got it down to my ankles, I sat on his desk, placed my heeled feet in his lap, and gestured for him to take the rest of the suit off. Jerome looked at me, then down at my ankles, then back up to my face again. He shook his head and closed his eyes. A slow breath escaped from his mouth as he rested his head on the back of his chair.

"This isn't right, Mya." This nigga needed to give it up. Especially with me knowing his dirty little secret. He was right when he said that his phone had stuff in there that a lot of people didn't need to see. One of them people being my cousin.

"This *is* right, Mr. Jerome, and this . . ." I pointed between the two of us "is going to happen," I said as I got up from the desk and straddled his lap. "What JaNair doesn't know won't hurt her. And I'm willing to keep our little secret if you are."

We sat and stared into each other's eyes for a moment, silently swearing to keep our little secret a secret. Once we both came to an understanding, he attacked my lips like his life depended on it.

# ShaNiece

"Hey! LaLa, right?" the sexy, tall, white dude who was with Jerome asked as he sat in the empty stool Mya just left.

"Um, no. It's Niecey, well, ShaNiece. LaLa, or LaNiece, is my sister."

"Twins?" he asked with a surprised expression.

"Yep. Twins. I'm five minutes older, and she's the bad one," I said, getting questions two and three out of the way. That's why I hated having someone who was identical to me. No one ever asked about me. It was always "we."

"That must really suck!" he said more as a statement rather than question.


I snapped my head in his direction. "What you say?"

He laughed. "I said, that must really suck. You know, being a twin and all. I bet you get tired of people asking you the same questions over and over."

Wow, he just said everything that I was just thinking.

I looked into his ocean-green eyes and couldn't help but to get lost. That sexy five o'clock shadow he had around his mouth was working for him overtime. His hair was shaved short on the sides and sat kind of long and wild at the top. He kind of reminded me of the dude who plays Thor, just with shorter and darker hair.

"You don't know how irritating it is to have to answer the same questions over and over again your whole life. No one ever wants to know who ShaNiece is. It's always twin this and twin that."

"Yeah, I know what you mean. I actually have a twin." He looked at me. "We're fraternal, though. He's seven minutes older, and *he's* the good one."

I just laughed and smiled at his silliness. With everything that has been going on in my life at the moment, I really needed that.

Starlah, the waitress who had been making our drinks since we got here, set a drink in front of him and refilled mine without me asking.

"Wait, I didn't order another one," I said to her as I pushed the drink back. I was already at my limit, drink and money-wise.

"You good, boo!" She nodded at Jerome's friend. "This here is on the house."

"Thank you," I said to her as she walked away. I turned to the sexy white hype. "You didn't have to do that."

"You're right. I didn't. But I did." Shrugging his shoulders, he took a sip of whatever brown liquor he was sipping.

"Who are you anyway? I mean, I know you're Jerome's friend, but you guys are that cool that you can give out free drinks?"

He laughed, showing off the prettiest set of white teeth I've ever seen. "My name is Tobias, but my friends call me Toby. Jerome and I have known each other for a very long time. We actually went to college together." He turned his full body toward me, brushing his knee against my thigh. "Now, as far as these free drinks go, when you own half of this place, you can practically do anything you like."

I looked at Toby with eyes wide open. The boyish grin he had on his face was making me feel all hot and bothered.

Before I could ask him another question, my phone started to go off with my mama's ringtone.

"Excuse me for one moment, I need to take this," I said to him as I hopped off the stool and stepped a few paces over.

"What's up, Ma?"

"Where the hell are you?" she screamed into the phone.

"I'm out with Mya, why?"

"LaLa and JaNair have been in a horrible accident."

"What!" I screamed a little louder than intended. I looked over at Toby, who was already getting out of his chair and walking over to me.

"We're at the hospital right now. I've been calling you and Mya's phone for the last forty-five minutes, and neither one of you bitches were answering. Get your ass up here right now, ShaNiece," my mom yelled into the phone as she started to cry.

"I'm on my way," was all I could get out before she hung up in my face.

"Is everything all right?" Toby asked once he got closer to me.

"I need to find my friend Mya. My sister and her cousin JaNair have been in a car accident."

"JaNair? Shit, I need to go tell Jerome," was all he said as he hurried off in the direction that I last saw Mya in.

While on his way, one of the waitresses flagged Toby down. From the way she was talking and waving her arms around, there must've been some sort of problem occurring that needed his attention since Jerome was nowhere to be found.

Not even waiting for him to take care of the situation, I headed straight down the dim hallway. As I got closer to one of the office doors, the sound of bodies smacking and moaning took over the air.

"Fuck me, baby!" I heard Mya purr.

The office door wasn't fully closed, so I could see the two of them going at it. Mya was bent over naked on his desk, with her ass tooted in the air. Jerome's muscular chest had sweat dripping all over it. His eyes were closed, and his mouth was sort of twisted. The fuck faces he was making instantly had my panties soaking. Every time he pounded his dick into Mya, the veins in his arms would flex, making my pussy thump more and more. My hands unknowingly went to my breasts, rubbing on my pebbled nipples.

Jerome fucked Mya in the position they were in for a few more minutes before he pulled out and told her to move. The sight of his eleven-inch sheathed dick, which was now in full display, had me drooling at the mouth.

"What's going on? Why aren't you telling them about the accident?" Toby asked me from behind, scaring the shit out of me. I tried to speak, but I couldn't. Embarrassment had me stuck on stupid. When he finally looked from me and followed my line of sight, his eyebrows rose, and he shook his head.

"Damn it!" he said before he busted through the door, startling Jerome and exciting Mya.

I quickly followed suit and stayed on his heels.

"Mya, Momma just called and said we need to get to the hospital ASAP!"

"Why?" she snapped as if she had an attitude.

"LaLa and JaNair were in a bad car accident."

I looked over at Jerome who looked as white as a ghost. All the color had drained from his face as soon as I broke the news. He hurriedly put his clothes back on and started to ask all kinds of questions. Once I answered all that I could, he grabbed his keys and ran out of the office. Toby was right behind him.

Not having anything else to say and needing to get to the hospital, I turned on my heels and was about to leave, but before I could get to the door, Mya stopped me.

"Uh, that couldn't have waited until we finished? I know you saw us in the middle of something," she smirked. "You were at the door for the longest before you barged in."

I couldn't believe the nerve of this bitch. Did she *really* just say that to me? Did she even *hear* what I said about LaLa and JaNair? Hell, does she even *care?* Right then and there told me all I needed to know about my so-called best friend. Whenever all her shit caught up with her, she was going to be in for a rude awakening. I shook my head at her trifling ass and turned around to leave. My damn sister was in the hospital, and I was not about to deal with Mya and her ho-ass shenanigans.

# Semaj

"Fuck!" was all I could say as I watched my dick disappear into the back of Tasha's throat.

I knew that what I was doing with her was dumb as shit, but right now, I didn't care. I needed to release this nut, and since JaNair still hasn't come to her senses, my baby mama would have to do.

Her head was bobbing up and down at a medium pace, just the way I liked it. Every now and then, she'd squeeze my balls with her hand, then juggle both of them in her mouth. She even went as far as lifting my sack up and licking the little area right underneath it. She knew I loved that shit. A chill ran down the back of my spine when she did that.

Hands down, Tasha was the best I ever had at giving head. She could do this trick with her tongue that I've never felt before. Even the way she suctioned her cheeks sometimes. It almost felt as if I was in some of the tightest pussy when indeed it was just her mouth.

Yeah, I know I told Jay that I didn't fuck with her like that, and on the real, I don't. It's been a couple of years since she had my dick anywhere near her pussy. I can't say the same for her mouth, though.

I had just lay my head back on the couch, getting ready to bust a fat load when the door to the man cave burst open.

"Sema—Oh hell, naw. Semaj, I know you don't have me in there watching your child while you're in here getting your dick slopped on," my aunt Shirley screamed. "You said that y'all needed to talk for a minute, not get some head. Put that damn thing back in your pants, and Tasha get your crazy ass up!"

"Auntie—"

"Don't auntie me, nigga! You know better than that," she said cutting me off. "What if it were Ta'Jae bursting through that door coming to look for your ass?"

"She would've knocked first," Tasha made the mistake of mumbling under her breath.

My auntie cut her eyes toward her. "Bitch, if you woman enough to be down on your knees sucking my nephew's dick in *my* house, you should be woman enough to say whatever it is you have to say out loud."

She looked from Tasha to me, then to Tasha again. It got so quiet in this bitch that you could hear a rat piss on cotton.

"Ms. Shirley, I'm so sorry. I didn't mean to disrespect your house at all," Tasha finally spoke.

"I don't believe that lie for one bit," she snapped, rolling her eyes at Tasha. She then turned her attention to me. "Nigga, what I tell you about going backward? Especially with someone loony like her?" She pointed at Tasha. "I tried to tell your simple ass the first time around to stop messing with this girl when you introduced me to her, but you didn't listen. Now you gotta deal with her and the precious baby of y'alls for the rest of your life. You made a mistake once fucking with her—don't do it again!"

Although I appreciated my auntie's realness sometimes, right now, I really didn't need it. Everything she just said to me was stuff I already knew. Tasha and I were never getting back together, and I've told her that a million times. Hell would be completely frozen over before I made her my girl again. We had one common denominator, and that was Ta'Jae. My baby girl was the only reason I dealt with Tasha as much as I did. Well, that and the occasional head sessions she would give.

We were still straightening up and getting lectured by Aunt Shirley when the door to the man cave swung open again. This time, Li'l Ray came flying through.

"Nigga, why haven't you been answering your phone? I've been calling you for the last five minutes!" he said out of breath. He took one look at me, Tasha, then to Aunt Shirley and figured out what had just happened. He shook his head as he continued. "Man, we need to get to the hospital like right now. LaLa's mom just called me and told me that she and JaNair were in an accident earlier."

"Wait, what?" I asked as I started to put on the rest of my clothes. *No wonder she hasn't been texting me back*, I thought to myself as I grabbed my keys and wallet, then headed for the door.

"Oh hell, naw, Semaj. You about to go running to the hospital bed of a bitch who don't even want you?" Tasha challenged as she stood in front of me with her hand on her hip.

"Humph!" I heard my aunt snort.

"Man, Tasha, don't start none of that dumb shit!" I thought about it, then turned back around to face her. "On second thought, what you getting mad about? I hope you don't think we're back together just because I let you swallow my dick whole for a minute or two!"

"Nigga, fuck you!" she screamed running up on me. "I hate you, Semaj . . . I fucking hate you! Where's my baby at so we can go? You don't have to worry about seeing her ass no more."

"Oh no, honey!" my aunt interjected. "You are *not* about to go and get that child and take her with you just because your feelings are hurt. That's what's wrong with you young parents now. You always wanna use your kids as pawns when you can't get your way. Semaj, you wrong for leading this girl on and still fucking with her like that, and, Tasha, you just dumb for thinking your lips is the best way to a man's heart."

Aunt Shirley headed for the door but stopped when she got in front of me. "You and Li'l Ray go on up there and check on y'all friend. Call me and let me know how she's doing when y'all get there, OK?" I nodded my head. "Tasha, you can gon' 'head and leave too. I'll watch the baby until Semaj gets back."

I looked over at Tasha and couldn't make out the look on her face. I didn't have time to try to decipher what was going on in her head, so I turned around and left.

As Li'l Ray was placing a call back to LaLa's mom to find out what hospital they were in, I said a silent prayer for her and JaNair.

"Man, did you find out where they are?" I asked Ray as we got into my car.

"Yeah, she said there at Cedar Sinai. She's gonna text me the room number any minute now."

"I didn't know you and La were kicking it like that. I mean, to the point that her mom is calling you in the case of an emergency and all," I said jokingly.

"Naw, you know we've been chilling off and on for a while. That's why I was kind of tripping when she was on a blind date with that nigga JaNair hooked her up with that night we ran into them at the Lotus Bomb. I thought we were good, but I guess not. She's been acting strange though for a minute now."

My eyebrows rose. "Strange . . . like what?"

"Strange like I used to be able to call her and get pussy whenever I wanted, but now whenever I call, she's either busy or not in the mood."

"Did you ask her what was up?"

He nodded his head. "Yeah, and she said it was nothing. I didn't really bother that subject again after that because I started fucking with that new chick I was telling you about."

After Li'l Ray finished telling me more about his newest bed buddy, I turned the music up and focused on the road. I kept wondering why he was running to the hospital to check on LaLa when he didn't seem too interested in her anymore. Then again, who am I to call the kettle black? Especially when Tasha was just gobbling up my dick a few minutes ago.

By the time we arrived at the hospital, we already knew where to go, thanks to the text Li'l Ray got. When we got off the elevator and over to the waiting area, there was nowhere to sit. The place was packed.

We spotted LaLa's mom in the corner sitting down with a few people huddled over her as she rocked back and forth.

"Hey!" Li'l Ray said as he bent down in front of her. "How is she?"

She looked up at him and began to cry. "I don't know, baby, I don't know. We've been sitting here for hours and can't nobody tell us anything. I even tried to see what was up with JaNair, but since I'm not family, they wouldn't tell me nothing."

"Where the hell is Mya?" Ray and I said at the same time.

"I called Niecey and Mya about an hour before I called you. They should've been here by now."

I shook my head. Anger had me balling up my fist real tight. I knew Mya was as trifling as they came, but to not be there for family in their time of need was beyond low.

I needed answers right now, though. I'd worry about Mya's ass later. I needed to see how JaNair was doing, and if I had to go through every room on this floor to find out, I would.

Before I had the chance to turn around, I heard an all-too-familiar voice boom from behind me.

*"What the fuck is he doing here?"*

# Jerome

"Samir, Samal, or whatever the fuck your name is, thanks for coming to see about *my* girl, but you're free to go."

I was burning up on the inside. Who the hell did this nigga think he was? Showing up to the hospital and shit, checking on JaNair like he was her man or something.

He slowly turned around and stood in my face.

"Why I'm here shouldn't even be *your* concern right now. However, JaNair's health should be." He leaned in closer to my ear so that only I could hear. "You might wanna take that opened condom wrapper from out of the cuff of your pants. If I can see it, I know everyone else can." He stepped back and smirked. "We wouldn't want *your* girl stressing over unnecessary bullshit now, would we?"

This dread-headed motherfucker was getting on my last nerve. I subtly looked down at my pant leg and saw the shine of the gold wrapper I'd opened earlier.

"Damn!" I silently cursed to myself. This bitch-ass nigga was right. And what made matters worse, it seemed as if everyone had zeroed in on what I was trying to cover up with my other leg.

"Family of JaNair Livingston!" a nasal voice announced.

I turned around and ran right smack into Mya's ass. I didn't even know she was so close behind me. The look on her face was sort of twisted, as if she was mad at something. Regret of what we were just doing earlier started to seep in.

"They just called JaNair's name. Shouldn't we be heading over there?" I asked as I tried to walk around her.

"So what we just did didn't mean shit to you, huh?"

What the hell? I looked at her, then around the little area that we were standing in. When I glanced toward the doctor who obviously had news about JaNair's condition, that snake-head motherfucka was all in her face. I noticed some woman who I hadn't seen earlier huddled in the circle too.

"Look, Mya, I need to go over there and see about JaNair. Don't start this bullshit in here!"

She walked into my face. "It's funny how you're so concerned about her now, but an hour ago, you were screaming how good my pussy felt!"

The moment those words left her mouth, it was as if the whole waiting room and hospital got quiet. Thank God everyone who we were around earlier happened to be over talking to the doctor.

Toby, who was sitting next to a crying Niecey, looked up at me and shook his head. Not trying to even go there with Mya, I forcefully pushed past her and walked over to where everyone was.

"What about LaNiece Taylor?" I heard someone ask.

"The last I heard, Ms. Taylor was still in surgery. I was not her attending physician. When I find out a little more information, I'll be sure to come out and inform you," was what she said as she turned to the nurse behind her, handed her a clipboard, and walked off.

"Did she say how JaNair was doing?" I asked no one in particular. They were all standing around the same doctor when they called her name, so I'm sure someone heard something.

"Where were you when the doctor was looking for any family or close relatives of JaNair? I'm pretty sure with her being *your* girl and all, you fit somewhere in that equation."

The smug look on this bitch-ass nigga's face had me balling up my fist. Semaj had another think coming if he thought that he could keep getting away with snide-ass remarks like that. I hope he wasn't letting the business attire I had on fool him.

I counted to ten in my head, then cracked my neck. After releasing a few deep breaths, I'd finally calmed down enough to ask my question again.

Instead of hearing bitch boy's smart-ass mouth, the woman I assumed to be LaLa and Niecey's mother answered the question for me.

"They said she's doing fine, baby. After they run a few more tests on her, we'll be able to go back there and see her," she said as she patted my arm and headed back to the waiting area.

I cut my eyes at a smirking Semaj, then excused myself to go to the restroom. I need to freshen up a bit and get rid of the condom wrapper that was now in my pocket.

While I was drying my hands, I heard my cell phone ding, indicating a text message had been sent. I pulled the phone out of the holster and scrolled through my log.

BM: Am I going to see you later on tonight after you close up?

Damn, I forgot I told my baby mother that I'd roll through tonight. I had to come up with a good lie for her ass, or else she'd be blowing my shit up all night.

Me: I'm gonna come by in the morning. Had to fire two waitresses tonight. Been behind the bar fucking all the drink orders up.

I was glad in that moment that I told her about the employees stealing from me a couple of weeks ago.

BM: LOL. I bet that's a sight to see. Too bad I was called into work tonight. I'll see you in the morning then.

Me: All right.

BM: I love you!

Me: Me too. Kiss my little man for me.

BM: OK.

When I finally returned to the waiting room, the doctor who had come out earlier with news about JaNair was just walking off. I looked to Mya for answers but was met with the coldest grill I've ever seen. Asking her what the doctor had just said was totally out of the question. I looked toward Semaj's punk ass and didn't even attempt to go in his direction.

"Aye, bro, where you been?" Toby said as he walked up beside me. "They're letting people go back to see her . . . Two at a time, though. I'll go back there with you if you want."

"Thanks, man, I really appreciate it," I said as we clasped hands.

"You know you done fucked up, right?"

I couldn't do anything but laugh at what he just said. Not only was that a poor imitation of the detective from *Menace II Society*, but the truth was funny as hell. I knew when Mya walked her ass up into my office that I should've just escorted her right back out. But those hips, lips, and perky-ass titties just kept calling a nigga.

On top of that, a few of the things she said while we were fucking on the desk kind of threw me for a loop.

*"JaNair's pussy ain't as good as this, huh? She can't fuck you like I can, Jerome! This is all your pussy from now on, baby. You won't need that bitch JaNair for shit!"*

At the time, all that shit she was moaning sounded real good while we were going at it, but now that I'm thinking with the head on my shoulders, the shit sounded kind of crazy. It's like she's obsessed with making me forget all about JaNair.

"Aye, the doctor just gave the green light to go back there to see your girl," Toby said, breaking me from my train of thought.

I looked over at Mya who was huddled in the corner with a woman I've never seen before. As soon as we made eye contact, both she and the woman she was talking to stared right back at me. A small smile spread across her face as she waved her fingers. The woman took one look from Mya, then to me, and started to smirk. She turned back around to Mya and said something to her, causing her gaze to fall from me.

I took that small opportunity and hurried in the direction of JaNair's room, dragging Toby right behind me.

"Dude, I feel sorry for your ass. That girl is going to make your life a living hell."

No truer words were ever spoken. Not only did I make the mistake of having sex with my girl's cousin, but I obviously made the mistake of fucking a psycho in the making.

# LaNiece

I sat in my hospital bed blankly staring at the TV which was on a rerun episode of *Cheaters*. I never understood how someone would want to go on national television to expose being cheated on. The thing is, they already knew what was going down before Joey and the crew even came to town. Women, as well as men, could always tell when their significant other is cheating. Whether they wanted to care or acknowledge it was a different story.

As the show went to another commercial, thoughts of my current situation started to invade my mind. Once my little secret came out, friendships, relationships, and lives would be changed.

A light knock on my door interrupted my thoughts.

"Come in!" I said as I pushed the tray of cold hospital food out of my way.

"Hey, baby. How you feeling today?"

"I'm good, Mom. My head still hurts every now and then, but besides that, I'm good."

"And my grandbaby?" she asked, sitting in the chair beside my bed.

I looked down at my little kangaroo pouch and smiled. God sure was watching over my little angel in that car accident. I placed my hand on top of my stomach. I couldn't believe that I was a little over twelve weeks pregnant.

"He or she is doing just fine, Mom. Did you bring what I asked for?" She dug into her big purse and handed me a brown paper bag that was covered in grease at the bottom.

"You know you shouldn't be eating that mess. All these monitors are gonna start going crazy when your blood pressure skyrockets. Plus you need to start eating a little healthier for my grandbaby."

I wasn't even trying to hear what she was talking about right now. The tantalizing smell of jalapenos and warm tortillas had all of my attention. I quickly unwrapped the big-ass carne asada burrito from Cliff's and dug in.

As I was stuffing a handful of french fries into my mouth, my mother decided to start up another conversation.

"So, LaLa, who's the daddy?"

I rolled my eyes. "Mom, can I please eat in peace? Don't you want me to feed your grandbaby?"

"I do. But I would also like to know what other bloodline is gonna be running through his or her veins as well."

I took another big bite of my burrito. "Why does it matter? Are you not going to claim my baby as your grandchild if it's by someone you don't like?"

"LaNiece, I'll slap the shit out of you if you say something stupid like that again," she scuffed. "I just want to know who your child's father is."

The truth of the matter was, I really didn't know who my baby's father was. There were two possibilities and a maybe. I'd never tell my mom that, but by the look on her face, I knew I needed to tell her something.

"Li'l Ray" was the first name that came out of my mouth.

A wide smile spread across my mother's face. "RayShaun, huh?" She nodded her head. "My grandbaby is gonna be cute as hell."

We both fell out laughing. That's the only reason why she wanted to know who the father was so badly. She always told me and Niecey that she couldn't be a fly-ass grandma with ugly-ass grandbabies.

While we sat there talking about baby clothes and names, my mind drifted off to Li'l Ray. I knew once it got out that I was pregnant, he would be questioning me.

For real for real, though, I was hoping and praying on the inside that Li'l Ray was indeed my baby's father. If it just so happened that he wasn't, all hell was going to break loose once the two possibilities were revealed.

"I knew it was your greedy ass that had the hallway smelling like that," JaNair said laughing as my sister rolled her into my room.

I was actually glad to see her moving around a bit. It was my fault that her pelvic bone was broken in three places. Had I not been texting like she said, the accident would've never happened.

"I saw JaNair's ass struggling out there with this wheelchair when I got off of the elevator, so I decided to help her out," Niecey informed us.

"And thank you so much for that, girl. It's already been a week, and I still don't have the hang of this."

"Well, you're looking good, honey," my mom interjected. "You and LaLa both. I'm so glad you guys made it out of that accident with nothing too major."

"Me too, Ms. Kat . . . me too!" JaNair turned her attention back toward me. "So what's happening with you, girlie? You ready to get out of here tomorrow?"

I nodded my head as I chewed the massive amount of food I had just shoved in my mouth. I don't know what it was about this burrito, but for some reason, it tasted ten times better than what it normally did. Maybe it was the extra jalapenos I requested.

"Sis?" Niecey said, looking at me side eyed. "You sure are taking that burrito down mighty fast." She paused for a second as I took another big bite. "Are those jalapenos you're eating?"

JaNair looked at my almost eaten burrito and cosigned. "Yeah, those are jalapenos. When did you start eating those? You can't stand spicy food."

I ignored their nosy asses and continued to eat, turning the volume up on the new episode of *Cheaters* that had just come on. I could feel them staring at me, but I didn't care. Telling them that I was pregnant was something I wanted to hold off on. Especially since I didn't know who the daddy really was. I knew that as soon as they found out that I was with child, the father's identity would come into question, and I wasn't ready for certain people to know.

# JaNair

A couple of weeks had passed, and I was finally being discharged. I was so tired of these hospital walls that I didn't know what to do. All I wanted was to lie in my own bed, eat my own food, and rest in the serenity of my own home.

I was mad as hell right now, though. Not only was I stranded at the hospital after I was discharged, I had to catch a fucking cab all the way home.

I glanced at the meter for the millionth time. I was already a little over fifty dollars. By the time we got to my house, I knew I'd be somewhere near eighty or ninety dollars.

I scrolled through my phone and looked at all the times I called Jerome, Mya, and even LaLa. But none of them answered my calls. All I kept getting was constant ringing or being sent straight to voice mail. I sent text messages and everything. Still, there was no response. I called Semaj, and he answered on the second ring to my delight. But when he told me that he was in the studio, I nixed the idea of asking him to come get me.

Letting my head fall back on the headrest, I closed my eyes and thought about everything that happened earlier.

*I looked at the clock on the nightstand beside my bed and frowned. 12 o'clock was quickly approaching, and there was no sign of Jerome anywhere. I told him a few days ago to have his ass here no later than 11:30. Here it was, fifteen minutes till, and he still hasn't shown up.*

*"Good morning, Ms. Livingston. I hear you're leaving us this morning," the nurse I've come to know as Tangie said.*

*"Yeah, I'm supposed to leave in about fifteen minutes, but my late-ass boyfriend hasn't shown up yet."*

*She laughed. "Girl, you know how men are when it comes to time. Let me help you get all of this stuff together, then put you in your wheelchair. He should be here by then."*

*After Tangie arranged all of my get well cards, balloons, flowers, and gifts on a roll-away cart, she helped me out of the bed and into the wheelchair the candy striper had just dropped off.*

*"I'm gonna push all this stuff to the front desk, then come back to get you, OK?" she announced as she was walking out of the room.*

*I looked at the time on the nightstand again. It was now ten minutes after 12:00, and Jerome's ass still wasn't here. I tried to reach for my ringing cell phone but didn't get to it in time before the caller hung up. I scrolled through the missed call log and saw that same unknown number that had been calling me for the last week was calling again.*

*I had just pressed the highlighted number to return the call when Tangie walked back into the room.*

*"Hey, girl! You all ready to go?"*

*I nodded my head yes and was chauffeured down to the waiting area in the lobby.*

*"Where the hell are you, Jerome? I told your ass to be here at 11:30 . . . It's now 2:35, and you're still not here!" I snapped as I left a third message on his voice mail. I was so pissed off that I didn't give a fuck that people were starting to stare at me all crazy.*

*"Hey, you've reached Mya. Leave a message if you want . . . Beep!"*

*"Uggh" I yelled out in frustration. This bitch's phone has been off for the last day or two. When she came up to the hospital a couple of days ago, it seemed as if she had an attitude. Especially when she saw all of the flowers, gifts, and cards Jerome had delivered to my room.*

*"Ms. Livingston, you're still here?" I heard come from behind me. When Tangie finally made her way in front of me, I lowered my head. Still sitting in the same spot she dropped me off at two hours ago was embarrassing.*

*She looked around the area as if she was searching for someone. When her eyes landed back on me, there was a look of empathy in them. "If you need a ride, I can give you a lift home. I don't mind at all. We just have to make a quick stop before we head your way."*

*With my head still down, I shook it no. "Thank you, Tangie, but I'm good. I finally talked to Jerome, and he should be here any minute."*

*I could feel her standing there staring at me before she squatted down before me.*

*"Are you sure he's coming, Ms. Liv—"*

*"JaNair," I said cutting her off and finally looking up. "You can call me JaNair."*

*She smiled. "In that case . . . JaNair, I wouldn't mind taking you home."*

*After declining her offer again and assuring her that Jerome was on his way, she finally decided to head out, but not before we exchanged numbers and agreed to hang out sometime.*

Being in the hospital for the last couple of weeks gave me the opportunity to get to know Tangie a little more. Out of all of the nurses that frequented my room to check on me, she was by far one of my favorites. She was around the same age as me, a single mother of one, and currently going to school in the day while working at the hospital overnight to pay the bills that financial aid or her baby's father didn't cover.

The cabdriver coming to a complete stop jolted my mind back into the present. When I looked out the window and noticed we were in front of my home, a smile stretched wide across my face. I've never seen a sight so beautiful. And the fact that Mya's car was nowhere in sight had my insides jumping for joy. I would finally get a few minutes of some peace and quiet.

"OK, ma'am. Your total is eighty-seven dollars and sixty-five cents. You can pay with cash or credit," the Hispanic driver said through the bulletproof partition.

"I have my debit card, but if you help me with my things, you can just slide my card for an even $100." Not even giving me the chance to ask a second time, he exited out of the driver's side and started to unload my things from the trunk.

It took me a minute to get out of the backseat and to my door to open it up for him. The crutches I had to use were new and uncomfortable to me. But it was either deal with these or roll around in the wheelchair for the next few weeks.

"Thank you so much!" I said to the driver as he brought my debit card and receipt back to me.

When I was finally settled in, I took a look around the house. I was surprised that everything was in its rightful place and still clean. It was as if no one had been here since I was gone.

*Mya must've found her a real good sucka this time,* I thought to myself as I slowly moved through the house. Being gone for two weeks and Mya living here by herself, the house should've been looking like a tornado ran through it.

I got to the dining-room table and started to sort through all of the papers and unopened letters that were thrown across it. There was junk mail, Pennysavers, sale ads, and a few bills. At first, I wasn't too worried about anything out of the ordinary, but when I came across a forty-eight-hour notice from Southern California Edison, I became a bit concerned.

I turned the flyer over in search of a date or something to see when this notice was sent out. Once I found it, my eyes damn near popped out of my head.

"A week ago," I said out loud as I made my way over to the light switch in the dining room. After flipping it back and forth a few times, still with no electricity to show, my blood started to boil.

No wonder the house was still up to par and looking neat. The bitch hadn't been here to mess anything up. It was just like her trifling ass to go and stay somewhere else until she came up with the money to pay the bill.

"Fucking dumb bitch!" I said to myself as I plopped down on the couch. The pain pills I'd taken earlier had started to kick in, and my eyes were starting to get low.

I sent out a few text messages, then started to doze off. I'd take care of this shit once I woke up. As for now, I needed to rest, and since it was already dark, I didn't have to worry about getting up and turning off any lights.

# Semaj

"All right, my nigga, J. I'm about to raise up out of here," Nip said as he gave me a pound-and-half hug. "When I get back next week, we can work out the kinks and everything so we can get this shit on the radio, all right?"

After another round of pounds, Nipsey Hustle and his crew started to file out of the studio.

"Yo, J! If this song blows up, homie, you're gonna be hard to get in touch with. I'ma have to schedule an appointment just to kick it with my fam," Li'l Ray said as he came from inside of the booth.

"Nigga, you tripping. You know if I'm on, you on. Aunt Shelia is not about to kick my ass for turning Hollywood on family."

We shared a few more jokes and laughs before I received the text message that I had been waiting on all day.

"Ah, man, JaNair just hit me to let me know she was at home. I'm about to be out. Did you need to ride with me, or was you gonna stay and chill for a minute." I looked at my watch. "The studio is paid up for another hour, so if you wanna fuck around with some shit, go right ahead and lay a few."

"Naw, I'm good. LaLa hit me earlier talking about we need to talk, so she's on her way to come scoop me. Tell Jay I said what's up, though, and let Moms know I might not be home tonight."

"I got you!" is what I threw over my shoulder as I walked out of the studio.

Traffic was fairly light tonight, so it didn't take me any time to make it back home. I parked my car in the driveway, went in the house, and chopped it up with my aunt and baby girl for a minute, then went next door to check on Jay.

*Knock . . . Knock . . . Knock!*

I stood there for a minute. When I didn't get an answer, I knocked again, but this time a little harder.

"It's open!" I heard someone yell from the other side of the door. At first, I was kind of skeptical about going in, but I said fuck it. It was pitch black and not a light on in sight. My eyes were still low from all the smoking I had done earlier, so I really couldn't see too much. I'd been inside JaNair's house enough to know the layout of the living room, so I'd be cool for a minute. Anywhere after that would be like an obstacle course.

"Jay, you in here?" I called out as I tried to adjust my eyes.

I heard a soft moan, then a loud thud.

"Ahhhhhhhh, shit!" she screamed out.

"What's wrong, Jay? You OK? Where you at?" I frantically asked as I tried to focus my eyes. The high I had a few seconds ago was rapidly coming down.

"I'm over here by the couch on the floor. I forgot I was on this motherfucka and rolled over thinking I was in my bed. Fuck! My shit is starting to hurt bad."

"OK, hold on! Let me help you up first. Then I'll go get some water so you can take your pain meds, OK?"

I still couldn't see her in this darkness, but I assumed she was nodding her head because she never gave a verbal response.

Putting my fist against the wall, I patted my hand around the smooth surface until I could feel a light switch. After flicking it on and off for the third time, JaNair finally told me that the lights were off and have been for the past week.

Removing my phone from out of my pocket, I went straight to the flashlight app I'd installed some months ago. I was so glad that I didn't erase it earlier when I was cleaning out my storage.

I made my way over to JaNair and helped her off of the floor. Once she was comfortably settled back on the couch, I made my way to the kitchen and got her a glass of tap water. I stopped at the fridge first to see if there was some bottled waters in there, but after almost choking on the smell of week-old food, I immediately closed the door. I made a mental note to stop by tomorrow to clean that stanking motherfucka out and throw away the old food.

Making my way back to the couch, I gave her the glass of
water as well as the pills she needed to take to help with the
pain.

"You haven't seen Mya, have you?" she asked as she swallowed another gulp of water.

I thought for a moment. "Naw, I haven't. The last time I saw
her was a week ago when she was coming out of the house
with an overnight bag and . . ." I trailed off. I didn't know if
she knew about Mya messing around with the dude she used
to fuck with.

"And what?"

"And a rollaway suitcase," I came up with. "Seemed like she
was going to be gone for a minute."

"Humph. Just like her ass. She knew the light bill needed to
be paid. And instead of paying that bitch, she leaves to go stay
with one of her little sponsors until she can come up with the
money."

I simply nodded my head as she went on and on about how
she hated having roommates and how she was going to kick
Mya out sooner than later. She then went on to tell me how
Jerome's bitch ass had left her stranded at the hospital after
promising he would be there to pick her up and bring her
home.

Now, I'm not gonna lie and say that I wasn't feeling some
type of way when she told me that. I wanted to ask her so
bad why she keeps staying with the nigga if all he does is
disappoint her. But, hey, that wasn't my seed to bring up.
She'd have to find out on her own what type of nigga she was
with. All I could do was sit back, be a listening ear, and be
me. Hopefully, one day, she'd recognize a real nigga when she
seen one.

In the middle of us talking, she dozed off and started to
snore lightly. I looked at my watch for the time. It was kind
of late, but with the installation of the electric meters, I
shouldn't run into any problems.

With the flashlight app on, I walked over to the pile of bills
on her dining-room table. After finding the SCE bill, I walked
back through the living room and out of the house. The
streetlights gave off a little more light, so I was able to see the
information that I needed much better.

I called the 800 number on the back of the envelope and listened to the automated system. After fifteen minutes of punching in account numbers, phone numbers, payment amounts, and credit card information, I finally received a confirmation number.

It wasn't even five minutes later before the lights popped back on.

"What? . . . How? . . ." I heard JaNair mumble as she shielded her eyes from the bright light. "Semaj, you didn't have to—"

"Shhh," I said cutting her off. "I didn't, but I did." I opened my hand out to her. "Now, come on so we can get you up off this hard-ass couch, into the shower, and then into your comfortable bed."

"Thank you so much, Semaj."

"No thanks needed, J1," I said, calling her by the name I'd given her.

When we got to the bathroom, I sat her on the sink and helped her get undressed. When it came time to remove her bra and panties, I figured that she'd ask me to turn around or leave for a minute. But to my surprise, she did neither.

I unhooked her bra from the back and slowly slid the straps down her arms. Her juicy cantaloupe-sized titties jiggled a little when I pulled the rest of the undergarment from beneath her breasts. After that, she lifted her ass up from the sink and slowly thrust her hips forward. In doing so, I was given full access to her panties and the perfect view to the imprint of her fat pussy. I licked my lips, then ran my hands down the sides of her soft body. When both hands were positioned above her panty line, I clamped my thumbs on both sides of the silky fabric and started to pull it down. The sweet scent of peaches wafted into my nose as I angled down to the ground and withdrew each leg one at a time.

Finally standing up, my eyes couldn't help but to roam every inch of her body. When my gaze landed on her face, the look of pure lust was evident in her eyes.

She opened her mouth and said something, but I had no idea of what she said. Her voice was so low I didn't catch it. I stepped into her space and in between her legs. I put my ear against her lips and asked her to repeat what she said.

"Semaj, please . . ." I lifted my head back to look into her face. Was she actually asking me to . . . ? That same look of lust she had a minute earlier was still in her eyes. When she bit down into her bottom lip, I had my answer and knew what time it was.

Without another word, I dropped down to my knees and went face-first into her pussy.

A moan escaped my lips as her juices coated my tongue. She tasted so good and sweet that my mind started to go into a frenzy. As if it couldn't get any better, I was damn near in love after her first climax hit. The stream of squirt she shot into my mouth was welcomed and very satisfying as I gulped it down.

"Fuck, Semaj!" she screamed as she grabbed a handful of my locks and pulled. Why she did that, I don't know. The last time she pulled my dreads like that, I attacked her lips something vicious.

I dug my face deeper into her goodness and latched on to her clit. As her whole body started to shake, I released the hold I had on her pearl and stuck my tongue into her opening. When her pussy muscle clamped on to my tongue and started to pulsate around it as she came, I was gone.

# Jerome

"Fuck, Mya! Suck that shit, girl." I moaned out as her pretty lips moved up and down my shaft. I knew I was wrong for what I was doing, but I couldn't help it. Whoever taught her how to deep throat some dick needed to get their ass whipped. The way she had my toes curling and butt cheeks tightening, I felt like a straight bitch.

I looked over at the picture I had on my desk of me and JaNair at the county fair and quickly picked it up and turned it over. I was on the verge of nutting, and seeing her face while her cousin was sucking on my dick would've halted any chance of that.

Focusing back on the task at hand, I grabbed a handful of Mya's hair, pushed her head down, and just held it there at the base. She didn't gag, she didn't cough, she didn't even try to push up for air. All I could feel was her throat constricting on my tip, and her mouth getting wetter and wetter.

"*Sssssss!*" I hissed when she did that rolling thing she does with her tongue and dug her nails into my thighs. My eyes rolled into the back of my head, and a chill ran down my spine, causing goose bumps to cover my arms.

"I'm about to come, Mya" was all that I was able to get out before I exploded a full load down her throat.

"Mmmm. You taste so good, Jerome," she said as she got up from under my desk. "I can drink you down every day."

I just nodded my head and smiled as I took a wet napkin and cleaned some of the spit she'd left in my lap. Clearing my throat, I stood up and looked her directly in the eyes.

"Mya . . . We can't do this anymore. The first time was a mistake, and this time . . . well, this time should've never happened."

She tilted her head to the side. "Why is that, baby?"

"First off, I'm not your baby. Second, you know I'm in a relationship with your cousin, yet you keep trying to throw the pussy at me every minute."

I knew that my holier-than-thou act was two seconds too late, but I was actually starting to feel bad about fucking JaNair's family behind her back. After the first time it happened, I tried my hardest to avoid Mya, but it was as if she had LoJack on a nigga or something. Everywhere I went, she seemed to pop up. Even at the hospital while I was visiting JaNair, the girl had no chill. She'd flash me while JaNair wasn't looking or she'd follow me into the bathroom trying to get a quickie while JaNair was asleep.

The only reason why I let her suck my dick right now was because I was horny as fuck. Her popping up at my office just to say hi is what started it all. I was doing good on dodging her advances, but when she took off her clothes and stood in the middle of my office butt naked, my dick almost busted through my pants. Hell, JaNair couldn't have sex right now, my baby mama was tripping because I wouldn't give her the amount of money she wanted, and the little side piece I was humping on, I cut her off a minute ago. A nigga was backed up for real.

"Jerome, stop playing. You and I both know we'll be fucking each other again, so you can miss me with all that *stop this* shit. You ain't no different from any of JaNair's other niggas that I've had. Once they get a taste of *this,*" she patted her pussy, "it's a done deal."

With what she just said, I knew I really fucked up by messing with this girl. She was as delusional as fuck. I knew I was partially to blame too for aiding in her delusion. That's why this was all going to end after today. I was just about to tell her about everything I had going through my mind when there was a knock on the door.

"Shit! Uh, just a minute," I yelled. I didn't know who was at the door. Being caught up with Mya's ass again was something that I could live without. It was already enough that Toby and Niecey walked in on us last time.

"You need to go in the bathroom, close the door, and be quiet."

"Why?" she said with a smirk. "Do you think JaNair hides Semaj when someone comes to the house?"

My nostrils flared, and my fist tightened just from her mentioning that nigga's name. That shit she told me about them kissing still pissed me off. That night at the hospital, I wanted to strangle the shit out of that nigga. He was real lucky Toby and security were there; otherwise, he would've been laid up next to JaNair.

When I asked her a couple of days later about their relationship and why he felt the need to come to the hospital, her response was that that were just friends and he was only worried about her. I searched her face for any hint of dishonesty. When I didn't see any, I couldn't do anything but believe what she was saying. Besides, I didn't have any real concrete evidence. Just Mya's hating ass planting that bug in my ear.

"Look, just get your ass in there and be quiet," I whispered harshly.

After standing there in defiance for a few more seconds, she turned on her heels and pranced her ass into the bathroom. But not before she turned around and blew me a kiss.

I shook my head and straightened up my desk a bit before I told whoever it was to enter.

When who was at the door walked in, my body instantly froze. I wanted to turn my head to see if the bathroom door was still closed, but I didn't want this person to follow my gaze and see that someone was in here too.

"Long time no see, huh, Jerome?"

I tried to swallow the lump in my throat but was having a hard time doing so. I was praying that this person would leave just as fast as she came.

"Cat got your tongue?" She walked around my desk. "That's funny, seeing how you always had shit to say when my ass was tooted up in the air on this very desk and your dick was drilling a hole deep in my pussy."

*Fuck! I hope Mya didn't hear that.*

"Wh . . . What can I do for you?" I asked, ignoring her previous statement.

She laughed as she looked around my office. When she saw the picture of me and JaNair turned over, she picked it up.

"I see you still get that guilty feeling when you in here fucking the next bitch. You know, turning over the picture won't make it hurt any less once she finds out."

I dragged my hand down my face and blew out a breath. My patience was really starting to wear thin now. This was one of the reasons why I wished I never started fucking with her. She was always on some bullshit.

"Look, LaLa, either state your business for coming here or get on. I got work to do," I said, gathering up a few pieces of paper from my desk.

She smirked. "Well, since you put it that way, let me get right to the point. I just wanted you to know that I'm a little over three months pregnant, and there's a possibility that you are the father."

As if anything at that moment couldn't get any worse . . . it did.

"You got this bitch pregnant, Jerome?" Mya screamed as she busted out of the bathroom.

LaLa looked from Mya then to me. She shook her head, then started to laugh so hard, tears were coming from her eyes.

"Wow. No wonder JaNair had to take a cab home from the hospital."

*Shit!* I cursed to myself. I was supposed to pick JaNair up after she was discharged at noon. I looked at the time and got mad as hell. It was already after four. I shot Mya a heated glare. Not only was my phone under my desk when I found it, but the ringer was turned all the way off. I didn't hear not one of the twenty calls JaNair placed to my phone.

"Look, y'all need to raise up out of here. I have to go see about Jay."

They both stopped midsentence in their argument and turned to look at me.

"Oh, so now you're worried about JaNair? You wasn't thinking about her ass ten minutes ago when your dick was down my throat," Mya screamed.

I didn't even respond to her simple ass. Mya really had another think coming if she thought I was going to leave

JaNair for her. LaLa, on the other hand, I'd have to deal with her on another day. I doubted the baby was mine. I made sure to strap up every time I dipped up in her pussy.

Shaking my head, I ushered both of them out of my office, locked up, and headed to JaNair.

# LaNiece

"Wow, Mya, is there any man of JaNair's that you won't sleep with?" I asked as I left her dumb ass standing in front of the door Jerome basically pushed us out of.

"Bitch, you're one to talk. Does JaNair know about your possible baby daddy being her man?"

I ignored this ho and kept on walking. I didn't need to explain shit to her—or anyone else, for that matter.

Yeah, I fucked up by having sex with my best friend's man, but the only person who would have the privilege of questioning me about that would be JaNair. Hell, I at least owe her that much for betraying our friendship the way I did.

"Look, Mya, I would appreciate it if you kept that little conversation you heard today between you, me, and Jerome."

"Why?" she asked as she folded her arms across her chest. "This may be more beneficial to me if she does find out. There's no way she would stay with Jerome after the news of her best friend carrying his unborn child comes to light. You've had the dick, so I know you remember how good it is, and I want it all for myself."

I rolled my eyes at this dumb bitch and walked to my car which was, ironically, parked next to hers. I don't see how I missed that. You would be able to tell her car from anywhere. Who gets a personalized license plate on a powder-blue 2003 Honda Accord that says "YNVMYA"? This pipe dream-having bitch, that's who.

"Mya, what makes you think that Jerome would come running to you once JaNair kicks his ass to the curb?"

She didn't even look away from her phone as she responded. "Because I know how to treat and keep a man."

I laughed at the crazy broad. If that was the case, why couldn't she find her own man? That was the question I should've asked her, but I wanted to know what her ho ass was talking about, so I asked the next logical question to her response.

"And how do you do that?"

She finally looked up from her phone. "By keeping his dick empty and his stomach full! You think if JaNair was fucking him right, he'd be breaking me off or letting me suck him up?"

She had a point there. But some niggas were supposed to be off-limits, especially when they belonged to family. Then again, who am I to talk? What was supposed to be a one-time accident turned into a few weeks of late-night accidents . . . and a possible baby.

"Where's Niecey?" she asked, breaking me from my train of thought.

"I don't know. The last time we talked, she was getting ready to go out on a date."

"With who?"

"Damn, bitch, call her and ask her."

"Well, I hope it ain't Big Will's trifling ass."

That comment sorta threw me for a loop. Why would she say something like that? There's no way she could possibly . . .

"You know, with all the secrets you got going for you, you should put a lock on this phone," she said as she held up my iPhone.

"How did you . . ."

"Jerome handed it to me when he kicked us out. He must've thought it was mine." She shrugged her shoulders and gave me my cell.

The dumb smirk she had on her face already told me that she knew my other little secret. I'm pretty sure her nosy ass went through all of the messages in my inbox. I don't know why I didn't erase any of this shit. This is the exact reason why niggas get caught up. Always saving shit they should've deleted after reading.

"LaLa, I see we have more in common than what I thought. I wonder what would happen if both JaNair and Niecey knew that their boyfriends could possibly be your baby daddy."

Damn, I was busted again. I shook my head in embarrassment. It was true. The third man who could possibly be the father of my child was my sister's on-again, off-again boyfriend, Big Will.

I hit him up a few days ago with the news, and he's been texting and calling me ever since, telling and asking me to get an abortion. The nigga was so worried about Niecey finding out that he even threatened to beat the baby out of me if I didn't.

I thought about it. I thought about it a lot. The two people who mean the most to me in this world were going to basically hate me once this shit got out. And now with Mya knowing this other secret I was trying to keep, I had to hurry up and decide on what I was going to do.

"Look, LaLa, I can see that you don't want this to get out yet, and I'm willing to keep your little secret . . . but only on one condition."

"What's that?"

She licked her lips. "You help me get Jerome all for myself."

Against my better judgment, I asked, "And how can I do that?"

"With one name . . . Semaj!"

# Mya

I left the parking lot of the Lotus Bomb happy as hell. Not only had operation *Take Down Jerome* been completed, but operation *Make Jerome My Man* was now in the works.

I shook my head. LaLa's ass has a lot of nerve talking about me and my extracurricular activities. Especially when she's been a busy little slut bucket herself.

I would be lying if I said I didn't feel some type of way about her possibly having Jerome's baby. Then again, I'm not his girl . . . yet, so I shouldn't be feeling shit.

The traffic on the 405 was surprisingly flowing, and that just made my night even better.

However, my phone buzzing again in my cup holder started to irritate me. I already knew it was this nigga named Cassan that I met a few days ago at the gas station. He was cute, and it looked like he had a little bit of money, so I gave him my number and told him to call me. The whole time I was in Jerome's office, he had been blowing me up. I made the mistake of texting that fool two hours ago and telling him that I would slide through. I guess he was getting a little impatient.

"Hello!" I yelled into the phone. I really didn't want to pick this bitch up, but I knew he'd continue to call until I did. Those damn talking-on-your-phone-while-driving tickets were a bitch, and if I got one, he would definitely be paying for it.

"Damn, baby, I've been calling you for the last thirty minutes."

*You mean hour!*

"I was busy. What's up, though?"

"Shit, I'm trying to see what's up with you."

See, this was the shit I hated about some niggas. All that beating around the bush stuff was so played out. He knew what he wanted, yet he sits on the phone trying to cupcake me first.

"Look, Cassan, I'm on the freeway right now headed toward the city. Text me the address when we get off the phone, and I'll be there within the next twenty minutes."

"That's what's up, Mia."

"You mean, Mya," I corrected. Did this fool really just call me by the wrong name? He most definitely was going to pay for that.

"My bad, Mya. I'm about to hit you with that text, though. See you in a minute."

I didn't even say bye before I hung up on his ass. Two minutes later, a text came through with the address.

*Damn, he practically lives right around the corner from me,* I thought as I listened to the directions coming from my GPS. *I wonder why we haven't met sooner,* I thought to myself as I drove toward the address he texted.

I was sorta glad that he was close to the house, though. I could stop by and freshen up a bit even if it will be in the dark. I hadn't been home since the day the lights got cut off. I know JaNair's ass was pissed when she got home, but, hey, what could I do?

When I didn't have the money to pay that light bill, I packed me a little overnight bag and went to stay at Ryan's. I knew I'd have to work my ass off to get the money from him if I asked, so why not stay somewhere where the lights are on in the process? After fucking and sucking him up for a week, he finally broke bread. I was planning on paying the bill today but got a little sidetracked when I popped up at Jerome's office. I'll pay that shit tomorrow.

Getting off of the freeway on my exit, I hit a few corners before I made it to our street. When I pulled up to the house, I instantly became pissed that there was a car in the driveway already, causing me to have to park my shit a few houses down.

I noticed that the porch light was on. JaNair must've gone on ahead and paid the electric bill when she got home and discovered that there were no lights. That was good looking on her part too, because now I can pocket that $250 Ryan had given me earlier.

I grabbed my bag and took my keys out of the ignition. I was just about to open my car door but closed it right back when a white car zoomed by.

"CHVYLVR" is what I read on the license plate, so I already knew who it was.

"On your way to do some damage control, aye, Jerome?" I said as I watched him block our driveway.

He left the parking lot of the lounge way before I did, so I'm kind of surprised that he's just now getting here. Hmm, I wonder where he went.

I watched as he hopped out of his car with the biggest bouquet of flowers that I've ever seen. I shook my head. This nigga.

He banged on the door for what seemed like ten minutes before it was finally opened. When I saw the way his body tensed up when Semaj's sexy ass answered the door, I laughed.

Jerome was fucking up big time and was making this so much easier for a wedge to be driven between him and JaNair. I might not even need LaLa's ass to help me with this operation after all, I thought as I started to pull off.

I knew I said I was going to go in, but I changed my mind about freshening up. I really didn't feel like hearing JaNair's mouth about the light bill, and I didn't want to interrupt whatever was about to go down between Semaj and Jerome. I decided to just head on over to Cassan's and do what I needed to do there.

I smirked as I passed by the house and saw their little standoff. Once I fuck Jerome a couple more times and show him how close Semaj and JaNair were becoming, this is gonna be like taking candy from a baby.

# JaNair

"Damn, Semaj!" I screamed out as I came for the third time. My legs clamped around his head while my hand pulled on his dreads.

"You keep pulling my hair like that and I won't ever stop," he said against my slick folds as his tongue traced my throbbing bud.

A smirk crossed my lips as I pulled on his hair again. Instantly, my eyes rolled to the back of my head when his cool tongue darted out of his mouth.

"Damn," was all I could say as I came for the fourth time. Semaj's head game was the truth. Never in my life have I come so many times just by dome alone.

When Semaj's grip around my waist became tighter, a frown decorated my face. Although those two weeks in the hospital gave me some time to heal up, I was still experiencing some sort of discomfort.

Coming yet again, I didn't know if I could take any more of his vicious assault on my clit. When I tried to scoot away from him, he locked his arms around my thighs and held me in place.

The pain from my injury was starting to get worse by the minute, and I couldn't take it any longer. I really needed to take some more of my pain pills.

Before I could even tell him we should pause for a second, there was a thunderous knock on my door.

"Semaj! Someone's . . . at . . . the . . . do . . . do . . . door," I managed to get out between breaths.

After repeating myself for a second time and hearing the door being banged on again, he slowly kissed my clit, then my lips a few more times before he rose up and stood between my legs.

"It's probably just Li'l Ray," he said as he nuzzled his nose into my neck. "I'll go get rid of him, then come back and finish what we started."

He pressed his bulging manhood against my center and stepped back.

Even through his jeans I could feel the heat radiating from that thang.

I nodded my head and slipped off of the sink, wincing from the pain that shot up to my hip when my feet hit the floor.

Unknowingly adding more pain to what I was already feeling, Semaj took it upon his self to smack me hard as hell on the ass as he was leaving.

The discomfort I was feeling as I pulled my pants back on had me moaning a bit. I tried to sit down on top of the toilet but had second thoughts when the pain started to intensify.

"Fuck!" I hissed as I placed my hands on both sides of the sink to steady myself.

I opened up the medicine cabinet and started to go through all of the junk that Mya had piled in it. I was hoping and praying that she had some sort of pain drug on deck.

I shook my head when a few boxes of Monistat 7 fell into the sink.

"Damn, she must stay with yeast infections," I said to myself as I continued my search.

I had just found a bottle of 800s when the sound of arguing echoed throughout my home.

"What the fuck are you doing answering my girl's door half-naked, nigga?" Jerome's voice boomed in my living room.

My body instantly froze. Hearing his voice had me feeling a little guilty. Not once did Jerome cross my mind as I let Semaj dine on me.

"That would be a question you need to ask your girl," I heard Semaj reply.

"Muthafucka, I'm asking you. Every time I come around, your ass is somewhere in the vicinity. JaNair!" he yelled.

"Nigga, keep your voice down," Semaj hissed. "You weren't worried about your girl when she needed a ride home or while the lights were turned off in this muthafucka."

"I don't have to explain shit to you, my nigga. And if you know what's best, you'd take your nappy-headed ass home and stay out of my girl's face."

I couldn't move as fast as I wanted to, but I was trying. It felt as if I were moving at a snail's pace.

Once I reached the living room, I saw Semaj walk up to Jerome, blocking his path into the house and whispering something into his ear. I don't know what he said, but whatever it was had Jerome rearing his fist back.

*God, I hope these niggas don't start fighting in my house* was all I could think about as I braced myself against the wall.

# Semaj

A smirk spread across my face when I opened up JaNair's door.

"Nigga, what the fuck you doing answering my girl's door with no clothes on?" Jerome screamed.

This fuck boy was always so extra with shit. I shook my head as I looked him up and down. The way his eyes narrowed and he balled his hands into a fist had me chuckle a bit.

"As you can see, my nigga, I have on some clothes," I said pointing to my opened button-down and Rock Revival jeans that were hanging off of my ass. "So you have nothing to worry about. Now when I answer this muthafucka with no clothes on . . ." I trailed off.

The look he had on his face had me dying on the inside. I can tell that this nigga was all bark and no bite. If this situation was the other way around, we would've been locking arms already.

"JaNair!" he yelled as he tried to step inside the house. I walked up and blocked his path.

"Nigga . . . You need to get out of my way! JaNair!" he yelled again.

I stood there with my arms crossed and legs apart. I wasn't moving shit. If he wanted to come in here, he'd have to move me out of the way. I didn't know what JaNair was doing, but she needed to hurry up and get her ass out here before I fucked her little boyfriend up.

I licked my lips. The sweet taste of JaNair's nectar still lingered on them. If she feels anywhere near as good as she tastes, I'd probably have to dead this nigga to make her mine.

"Semaj?" I heard her low voice call out from behind me.

When I turned around, she had one arm against the wall while her other arm looked as if it was cradling her side.

"You OK?" fuck boy and I asked at the same time. I cut my eyes at him, then turned my attention back to JaNair.

"Yeah, I'm good." She was lying. "I just need my pain pills."

While my back was turned, Jerome slipped his ass into the house.

"Where they at?" he asked as he rushed to her side, putting all of her weight on him.

"I'll get them," was all I said as I walked over to the table I'd placed them on earlier.

The look on Jerome's face was priceless. I went into the kitchen and grabbed a bottle of water out of the fridge. When I came back into the living room, this nigga was helping her onto the couch.

I laughed. It was funny watching his ass try to act as if he cared.

I gave JaNair her pills and water and sat on the couch across from her.

"Uh, my nigga, you can leave. Her man is here now."

I looked at JaNair. The expression on her face wasn't giving off the vibe that she felt the same way, so I didn't know what to do.

"Uh . . . I know you heard what I just said. You can go."

I shook my head and smirked. This dude was really trying to test my patience.

When I looked over at JaNair again, her eyes didn't connect with mine this time. She had them closed with her head back on the pillow.

*Wow!* I thought as I stared at her for a few more seconds. Not saying anything else, I nodded my head and stood up. I can admit that I was in my feelings about her not speaking up and letting this fuck boy dismiss me like he did, especially after the connection we just had.

"I'll get up with you later, Jay," I said as I kissed her on the cheek. That peach scent she always smells like invaded my nose and took over any rational thoughts I had. Closing my eyes and counting to ten was the only way I was able to fight off the urge to stick my tongue down her throat.

I finally pulled back. "Call me if you need anything, sexy face."

She looked up at me with a small smile on her face and nodded.

Jerome's bitch ass had the nerve to bump into me on the way out. I just laughed and kept on going.

Walking into my aunt's house, I slammed the door behind me and went straight to the kitchen table. The weed I had in my pocket was now lying in front of me, and I started to break it down. I needed to roll up something real fast to calm my nerves.

I was just about to fill my lungs up with that good Cali Kush when I heard my aunt's voice boom from behind me.

"Nigga, I know you done lost your damn mind! You know you don't smoke in my house."

"C'mon, Auntie, I just need to hit it a few times."

Her eyebrows scrunched. "What's wrong with you, Semaj? Ahhhh, hell, I hope you didn't get that little ratchet-ass girl pregnant again."

"Huh? Hell, no! Why would you say that?" I went to light the blunt again, but she smacked the lighter out of my hand.

"Because the last time you lost your mind and tried to smoke in my house, you found out she was pregnant with baby girl."

I nodded as the memory of that day flashed through my mind. I hated that I got Tasha pregnant, but I didn't regret having my daughter.

"So?"

"So what?" I asked coming back from my thoughts.

"Is she pregnant?"

"Hell, naw!" She cut her eyes at me. "I mean . . . no, Auntie. Me and Tasha don't fu . . . have sex anymore."

She laughed. "OK, Semaj, tell that to her mouth and your dick."

I shook my head and chuckled. My aunt was a God-fearing woman, but she always had some slick shit to say.

"If that's not what has you all riled up, then what is it?"

My aunt and I talked about a lot of things, so I didn't have any problem with filling her in. I went on and told her everything that has been going on with JaNair and me. From the times we were getting to know each other, to the time we kissed for the first time in the garage. I also told her about everything that happened earlier, including Jerome's bitch ass.

"So what you gonna do?" she asked as she started opening cans of string beans.

I wiped my hands down my face.

"What can I do, Auntie? She has a man who ain't shit, but I'm not gonna tell her that. She needs to figure that out on her own. I already told her how I felt, but she hasn't said anything about that either. I don't know what to do."

I stood up from the table and headed toward the patio. I really needed to smoke.

"If and when JaNair comes to me, I want it to be because she wants to, not because I or someone else made her."

My aunt wiped her hands on her apron and checked the smothered chicken that she had baking in the oven.

"Semaj, sometimes you have to just let people be. JaNair is a smart girl, and I'm pretty sure she'll do what she feels is right for her. Just keep being there for her as a friend, and whatever this is y'all have between y'all will fall into place when it's time."

I looked at my aunt through the sliding screen door that I was standing in front of. As the smoke from my blunt filled my lungs, I couldn't help but to give a little thanks to God for her. I don't know where I'd be if it wasn't for my aunt, Shirley. She was more of a mother to me than my own sorry-ass mother was.

"Did you hear me, J?"

I snapped back from my thoughts again. "Naw, Auntie, what did you say?"

"Boy, that girl has your ass all the way sprung, and all you did was taste her goodies. I hate to see what happens once you actually get them."

I couldn't do anything but laugh at her crazy ass.

"Dinner will be ready in a minute," she said as she took the chicken out of the oven. "Oh, and, Semaj, I hope JaNair does come to her senses soon. She'd be a fool to pass my baby up."

I smiled at her and then put the rest of my blunt out on the bottom of my shoe. Dinner smelled good, and I was hungry as hell.

After I polish off a few plates, I'll hit JaNair up to make sure she's good. If that bitch-ass nigga is gone, I might even ask her for another helping of dessert.

# Jerome

"So what's up with that, Jay?"

"What are you talking about, bae?"

"What am I talking about?" I stood up from her couch and paced the floor for a minute.

I needed to get the anger that was building up inside of me under control. The audacity of this nigga answering her door with barely any clothes on was still fucking with my mental. Then JaNair's ass wants to sit here and act like she doesn't know what I'm talking about.

Once I finally calmed down, I went and sat back down next to her.

"You fucking that nigga or something?" I didn't want it to come out as harsh as it did, but I couldn't help it. Just thinking about that nigga touching what was supposed to be mine had me getting mad all over again. I know I probably shouldn't be upset because of the things I've done with Mya and LaLa, but I couldn't help it. I love JaNair with everything in me, and I had plans of making her my wife one day.

"Jerome, please don't start this shit again," she said, trying to sit up. "I told you before that Semaj and I are just friends."

I looked into her eyes but couldn't tell if she was lying or not. She had the same blank expression she always has whenever I ask her about that snake-head nigga.

"Does he know that?" I had to ask.

She sighed. "It's funny how you want to question me about my relationship with Semaj when you have yet to tell me why *my* boyfriend was nowhere to be found when I needed to be picked up from the hospital."

Shit! I forgot all about not picking her up after she was discharged. With Mya's crazy ass coming to my office and sucking the life out of my dick, then LaLa dropping the news that I could possibly be her child's father, I lost track of time.

"I'm sorry about that, baby. Some shit came up at the lounge that needed my attention. I tried to get Toby to take care of it, but he wasn't answering his phone."

The frown she had on her face softened. "Is everything OK? I know how much you love that place."

"Yeah, baby, everything is fine now." I kissed her on her forehead. "We finally found out who was stealing from the register, and I had to file a police report. She got us for a little over $1,500."

"She?"

"Yeah, it was that new waitress Starlah we hired a few weeks ago. The funny thing is, we should've known it was her from the beginning. Not once had money come up missing before she started."

JaNair nodded her head, then attempted to stand up, but fell back down into the couch.

"You OK, babe? You need something?"

"Yeah. I took those pills without eating anything, so now my stomach hurts."

"Say no more."

I got up from my comfortable position next to her on the couch and went into the kitchen.

After searching the cabinets and the horribly smelling fridge, I couldn't come up with anything remotely edible to make. Not wanting to have to drive to get something, I took out my phone and went to the Grubhub app I downloaded a few days ago and ordered us some taco plates from the Mexican restaurant we sometimes ate at.

I had just finished processing our order when my phone started to ring with a number I've never seen before.

"Hello."

"Hey, baby."

*Baby?* "Who is this?"

"Oh, so now you don't know my voice, Jerome?" she laughed.

"Mya?"

 Silence.

"How the hell did you get my number?"

"From you, of course. I called myself from your phone before I turned your ringer off when I was in your office. How's my cousin doing, by the way? You know what? You don't have to answer that. I'll just call Semaj and ask him, seeing as you probably wouldn't know since you were getting some of my fiyah head when you should've been tending to her."

My nostrils began to flare as my anger started to rise. This bitch is crazy, I thought as her mechanical laugh rang in my ear.

"Look, Mya, what happened between us should've never happened." I looked over my shoulder to make sure JaNair was nowhere in hearing distance. "And it will never happen again, believe that. I'm with your cousin, and I plan to keep it that way. And as far as Semaj's bitch ass goes, I'm not worried about him. JaNair's too loyal to me to fall for any of his bullshit. Don't call my phone anymore or show up at my place of business again. If you do, I'm not going to be liable for what happens to your ass."

I disconnected the call before she could say anything else. When my phone started to go off again, I knew it was her calling back. I ignored her call and turned my phone completely off. She was not about to ruin my night or relationship with JaNair.

The doorbell ringing had me rushing out of the kitchen and into the living room. I tipped the young dude who handed me the food and drinks, then closed the door.

"What's that, bae?" JaNair asked waking up. She had dozed off that fast.

"Taco plates from that Mexican place up the street. I ordered fish tacos for you and carne asada for me. Extra cheese on the beans and a double order of rice."

She smiled as she sat up and took her plate.

We sat there and ate as we watched TV for the next hour. Who would've ever thought I'd enjoy a show about some chick named Mary Jane.

After the show went off and we finished eating, JaNair and I took a long, hot shower, then got into bed.

"Babe, I'm sorry about the not-picking-you-up thing. You forgive me?"

I could see her nodding her head. But I didn't like that nonverbal shit, so I turned her around to face me.

"You know I love you, right?"

She looked me in my face as if she was trying to search my eyes for something.

"Right?" I asked again.

She hesitated for a minute, then finally said yes and turned back around. I knew she wasn't going to say it back, because I could tell that she was still in her feelings. I didn't care, though. As long as she knew how I felt before we closed our eyes, I was cool with that.

I put my hands around her waist and pulled her body into mine. I know she felt my dick poking her in the back of her ass. I was horny as fuck. Especially after seeing and rubbing all over her naked body in the shower.

I wanted to feel her insides so bad, but seeing as she just got out of the hospital, I totally understood that she wasn't in the mood.

# Mya

"Ugh!" I screamed out in frustration as I threw my phone on the bed. "What the fuck!"

"Man, take your ass to sleep. It's like three o'clock in the morning," Ryan mumbled.

*I should've gone to Cassan's house*, I said to myself as I ignored his dumb ass and scrolled down to Jerome's name again. This was going to be the 100th time I've called his phone in the last week. He was straight igging the fuck out of me. At first, I thought Semaj might've sent his ass to the hospital the day that they were both at JaNair's house. But a phone call to Niecey and a text back from LaLa confirmed that nothing physical went down between the two.

I shook my head as I thought about how much I was starting to crave this man. The funny thing is, we've only fucked once. I pulled out all of my good pussy squeezing skills that day, so I didn't understand why he wasn't biting like the rest of them did once they got a taste of me. I knew for a fact that he loved my head. Why else would he let me top him off the day LaLa's bitch ass came through cock blocking?

LaLa . . .

Just thinking about that bitch had me on ten. Not only had she sampled that good dick before me, the bitch might possibly be pregnant by that nigga. If she played her cards right, and Jerome actually ended up being the father, she'd have unlimited access to his dick for the next eighteen years.

Fuck!

Why couldn't that be me?

A disturbing ache started to fill my loins. I needed to take some of this built-up aggression out on something. Since I couldn't have the dick that I wanted, I guess I had to go for the dick that I had.

"Ryan!" I whispered in his ear as I grabbed a hold of his deflated monster and started to stroke it nice and slow.

He didn't move a muscle at first, so I called his name again and squeezed on his semi-hard member a little more.

"Damn, Mya, what the fuck you want? You know I have to go to work in a few hours."

"You already know what I want," I said as I straddled his lap. "Your dick seems to know too, seeing as it's trying to poke a hole in my thigh right now."

He shot me that sexy grin of his and lifted his ass up a bit so that he could pull his pajama bottoms down. All of that bitching and complaining was so unnecessary, especially when he knew he wasn't going to pass up hitting this pussy.

I leaned down and pressed my lips to his ear. "I'm gonna fuck the shit out you right now, Jero . . . I mean Ryan."

I stuck my tongue out and played with his earlobe for a minute. I was hoping that my little slip-up had gone unnoticed.

When I sat back up and looked into his eyes, I knew all that hoping I was doing a few seconds ago was all done in vain. I didn't even have time to react before he threw me off of his lap, and my body went flying across the bed.


"I think you should go, Mya!" he said in the harshest tone.

"Wait . . . Ryan . . . I'm sorry!" I pleaded. "It was a mistake."

He gave a throaty laugh before he cut his eyes at me. "Mya, please save that bullshit for them other dumb niggas you fuck with." He got up from the bed. "You don't think I know you been humping on that nigga?"

I sat there with a blank expression on my face. How the fuck did he know?

"I can tell by that dumb-ass look on your face that you're wondering how I know, huh?"

I didn't say anything, so he continued.

"You really must think fat meat ain't greasy." He shook his head. "Do you ever think of what might happen to you when JaNair finds out all the shit you've been doing behind her back?"

I started to say something, but he raised his hand and cut me off.

"I already know what you were going to say: I'm just as dirty as you are, right? Especially since we started fucking while JaNair and I were together." He walked over to me. "I don't get it. What's your beef with JaNair? Y'all are family. It's like you take pride in taking her men. Why is that, Mya? Are you that jealous of your own cousin that you'll do any and everything just to make her look bad?"

Wait a second! A few minutes ago, he was acting so sleepy. Now this nigga wanted to be wide awake giving lectures and shit.

When he started handing me my things, I had to say something.

"So what? You're Dr. Phil now?" was the only response I could come up with.

Who the hell was he to be questioning me about my motives anyway? If memory serves me correct, he knocked on my door in the middle of the night. So why was it okay for him to do JaNair wrong, but not me?

To keep it real, he did have me thinking, though. What would JaNair do if she ever found out I've fucked damn near every one of her boyfriends, including Jerome?

I laughed. *Not a damn thing*, I said to myself.

JaNair wasn't about that life. At the most, she'd kick me out. I'd be okay with that, though, and that's only because I knew I had a few places that I could go. Niecey's door is always open for me, and even though I just called this nigga by someone else's name, he'd welcome me in to.

"Look, Ryan, I'm sorry about earlier, the whole calling you by someone else's name and shit." I was now standing between his legs fully dressed. I just remembered I'd asked him for a few dollars earlier, so I needed to play nice.

"Why don't you let me top you off before I leave, babe, just to show you how sorry I really am?"

When he didn't say anything in response, I took that as the green light to handle my business. I started to get down on my knees but was stopped when he pulled me up by my shoulders.

"I'm good, Mya. Just lock the bottom lock on your way out," he simply said.

*What the fuck! Did this nigga just dismiss me like that?*

His ass was really in his feelings right now. I laughed. If he didn't want me here anymore, that's cool. I'll leave, but not before he gave me the money I asked for.

I played as if I didn't hear what he said and tried to kiss him on his lips. He turned his head just before I was close enough, and I ended up kissing his cheek instead.

"OK, Ryan, I'ma go, but can I still get that money you said you'd give me?" *Shit! You thought I wasn't going to ask? I need those couple of dollars since they finally fired me from my job.*

I heard him smack his lips. "Bitch, you got me fucked up. You better go ask that nigga Jerome for that bread." He turned away from me and buried his face in his pillow. "Since there's nothing else we need to discuss, you can get the hell out of my house now. Don't forget to lock my door when you leave either."

I stood there shocked for a minute, but then quickly got over it.

I grabbed the rest of my things that were scattered around his room and finally headed to the door. Before I left, though, I threw a whole bag of flour all over his new suede couches. I even emptied the whole bowl of used grease I found on his stove.

Yeah, fat meat is greasy, and so are his couches too. I may have walked up out of here empty-handed, but I'm sure getting them muthafuckas cleaned will put a dent in his pockets.

# Jerome

"So, let me get this straight. While JaNair was laid up in the hospital, possibly damn near death, you were in your office fucking her cousin?"

I lowered my head in shame. Gerald always had a way of making me feel worse about a situation than what it was.

"Now that G said it like that, it does sound kind of fucked up, dude,"

Toby added as he took another swig of his beer.

I ran my hand down my face. "Man, it's not like I *wanted* that to happen. It just did." I looked over at my boys and noticed the smirks they both had on their faces.

"Nigga, tell that shit to someone who doesn't know your black ass."

Toby laughed. "For real, Rome, the way you two were staring at each other when y'all were at the bar, I thought you'd take her down right there."

"Aye, don't get me wrong, Mya is fine as hell, and I was low-key checking her out, but that was it."

"See, that's your problem right there. You already knew what time it was when she answered the door in lingerie and invited you in for a *bite* to eat. For a girl like Mya, checking her out only gave her the green light to think that it was okay for her to approach you on some fucking shit. You already know she doesn't care that you and her cousin are together."

"She had something for him to eat all right!" Toby laughed as he went to the fridge and grabbed another round of beers.

"Man, Toby, shut your corny white ass up."

"My ass may be white, but it's far from corny, dude. I bet I could pull JaNair."

The whole room went silent. Gerald and I looked at each other, then returned our focus back on Toby.

"Nigga, please!" we both shouted at the same time, which caused all of us to start laughing.

We were chilling in G's backyard, just shooting the shit and catching up with each other. I had a date later on with JaNair, so I just stopped by to get up with my boys.

Gerald had just got through telling us about the trip he had planned for him and his lady when my phone started to go off back to back.

"Yo, who is that calling you so much?" Toby asked as he responded to a text that just came through on his phone that had him smiling.

"Shit, I don't know. It's an unknown number, and you know I don't answer those."

My phone rang about five more times before whoever was calling stopped. Two minutes later, my phone started going off again, but this time with text messages.

Unknown: Jerome, I know you see me calling you. Pick up the phone!

Unknown: So you're still going to act like you don't see me calling you!

Unknown: I bet if I was JaNair you'd answer this mutha-fucka!

After reading the last text message, I had a pretty good idea of who it was that was now hitting me up. *Bitch is crazy* I thought as I deleted the texts. I don't know whose number Mya was calling me from this time. It didn't even matter really. That shit was going right on the blocked list just like the rest of them.

"Damn, man, who's got you over there frowning like that now? Unique tripping again?"

"Naw, I haven't heard from her in a few days. This is Mya's crazy ass calling and texting me from another number."

"Wait, before you even go in on her again, I'm still trying to understand how you and Unique never ran into each other at the hospital," Gerald said.

"That would be all in thanks to me," Toby quipped putting his arm around my shoulder. "The night the accident happened, she was there. It just so happened that I saw her first and ran a little interference before she saw him," Toby answered, pointing at me.

Gerald shook his head. "I don't see why you haven't told JaNair about your son anyway. You had him before you got with her. Plus, it's not like you and Unique are still together or anything."

I looked away. Unique and I weren't together, but we had slipped up a few times and had sex. Nothing recent, but it's been within the last few months.

"Nigga, don't tell me you still fucking with Unique too?" Gerald shook his head again. "I don't understand you, Rome. Why string both of these women along like that?"

"Man, it's not even as bad as you're saying. When I met JaNair, I wasn't really trying to be in no relationship because of the situation Unique and I had going on. But after being around her so much and getting to know her more, my feelings started to change. Plus, she's a good girl, and she's trying to add to our future, not just take away like most of these bitches. And to be real with you, Unique and I haven't messed around in a minute. She wants way more child support than I think she needs, so she ain't fucking with me like that anymore."

"Dude, you need to get your shit together on both ends. You wanna bitch about ole boy JaNair lives next door to being all in her face every chance he gets, yet you're making it easier and easier for him to take her away," Toby added.

I just waved his ass off. Toby's white ass was always trying to be on some self-righteous shit, when not so long ago, we were two of a kind.

Something he said though kind of had me feeling some type of way.

*"You're making it easier and easier!"* That's the same shit Semaj's ass whispered to me the day I found him at JaNair's house damn near naked. I wanted to knock that little smirk off of his face, but JaNair walked into the room.

I looked up at my boys, then down at my phone which was ringing once again, this time with Unique's name flashing across the screen.

*Maybe I am making it easy,* I thought to myself as I took another sip of my beer and sent her to voice mail. I need to change some shit before it's too late.

# ShaNiece

I stood in my bathroom staring at my reflection in the floor-length mirror. I couldn't help but to smile at the way my new moisturizer had my almond-colored skin glowing and feeling so smooth.

The earth tone makeup I had just applied to my face made my dark cocoa-brown eyes pop, while the Dynasty at Dusk Crèmesheen by MAC had my lips looking full and juicy.

The breath I'd been holding for the last two minutes finally decided to come out. I don't know why I was so nervous.

I looked at the tropical print cami and cuffed denim shorts I picked up from Forever 21 today. The way my shapely body filled out this outfit, I'm pretty sure my date would appreciate the thirty dollars I spent on it.

"Shit!" I said to myself when I saw what time it was. I had about thirty minutes before Toby would be here to pick me up for our date.

Since that night at the lounge, we've been talking on the phone and texting a lot. At first, I was tripping a little because I've never talked to a white boy in my life, let alone dated one. But there was something about Toby that had me ready to explore these uncharted territories.

*Bang! Bang! Bang!*

"Damn, Niecey, you've been in there for an hour already! Hurry the hell up, I gotta pee!"

I rolled my eyes and continued to get ready. LaLa had been a real pain in my ass since we found out that she was pregnant. If she wasn't eating up all of the food in the house, she was stretching my clothes out trying to stuff her fat ass in them. And don't let Mama be home. It's like ten times worse. She can't do shit for herself.

My mind drifted over to Li'l Ray for a moment. I felt kind of sorry for him. LaLa was really making him go through it from the late-night grocery store trip to the constant mood swings. One minute they're laughing and having fun, the next minute she's kicking him out and telling him that the baby isn't his. Mama told her that she needed to stop saying that shit to him because one day, he might just take her word for it and never come back.

"C'mon, Niecey! Damn! I'm about to pee on myself!" she screamed from the other side of the door.

After taking one last look at myself in the mirror, I opened the door and came face-to-face with a heavier version of myself.

"About damn time!" LaLa snapped as she ran past me and plopped down on the toilet.

"Do you really need that bowl of ice cream and pickles in there with you?"

She rolled her eyes as she scooped a big spoonful of the nasty mixture into her mouth.

"Mmmmm. You should try it, twin. I bet you'll like it," she said, offering me a scoop.

I shook my head and left her there to handle her business. As soon as I entered my bedroom, the Joe and Kelly Rowland ringtone I gave to Toby was going off. *"There's a difference between love and sex . . . But can I have both of them with you?"*

A big Kool-Aid smile crossed my face as I thought about the reason behind me giving him this ringtone.

*"Have you ever been in love before?"*

*"Once or twice. You?"*

I thought about my on-again, off-again relationship with Big Will. *"Yes."*

Toby laughed. *"You had to think about that question for a minute?"*

*"No, not really. Well, yes . . . a little."*

He laughed again. *"Which one is it, ShaNiece? No, not really, or yes?"*

*"It's yes, damn it! And why do you keep on laughing at me?"*

*"Because you're so cute."*

*I blushed.*

*"Hello!"*

*"Yeah, I'm still here," I said still blushing.*

*"I thought you hung up on me for laughing at you." I laughed. "Can I ask you something? I don't want you to get offended though when I ask you this."*

*"Naw, you good. Go ahead."*

*"OK. Well, do you know the difference between love and sex?"*

*I wasn't offended by his question. However, I was a little caught off guard. I thought he was about to ask me about my last boyfriend or something.*

*"Uh . . . yeah."*

*"Care to elaborate?"*

*I sat there and thought about his question for a minute, then answered. "Well, with sex, you can have that with anybody. Love, on the other hand, it takes a special somebody to have you feeling that way."*

*He got so quiet that I had to look at the screen on my phone just to make sure the call had not dropped.*

*"Hello!" It was my turn now.*

*"Yeah, I'm here."*

*"You OK?"*

*"Yeah, I'm good. I just never heard anyone answer that question with such simplicity. I like the way you put that."*

*We sat there quiet, lost in our own thoughts for a minute before I said thanks.*

*"You know what else I like?" he asked.*

*"What else do you like, Mr. Wright?"*

*He simply said, "You."*

My phone ringing in my hand again snapped me from my thoughts. When I looked down at the screen and saw Will's name flash across this time, I frowned.

"Ewwww. Who's got your face all screwed up like that?" LaLa asked from behind me.

I didn't even hear her walk up behind me, nor did I even respond to her ass. I looked out of my bedroom window and saw my sexy piece of white chocolate already waiting for me in his car.

I grabbed my purse and keys, slipped on my wedged sandals, and headed toward the front. As soon as I swung the door open, Toby was already standing there getting ready to knock.

"Damn," escaped his lips as he inspected my body from head to toe.

"Hey!"

"My bad. Hey, beautiful!" he said kissing me on my cheek. The touch of his lips to my skin had the hairs on the back of my neck standing straight up. A tingly feeling shot through my body which caused goose bumps to appear on my arms.

"I called your phone a few times, but you never answered. You ready to go?"

I nodded my head, and he smiled. Lacing his fingers with mine, he led me to his car, and we were on our way.

# LaNiece

I watched Niecey as she and her knockoff Justin Timberlake drove off. I wasn't hating or anything, but I really didn't know what it was that she was seeing in him. Yeah, he was nice looking, in a boy band type of way. You could tell he had a nice body underneath the fitted white V-neck shirt he had on. The Ralph Lauren tweed vest and matching fedora that he was rocking showed that he had a little bit of swag. But other than that, what else could it be?

I rubbed my big-ass belly as I walked back into the living room. That Cookies and Cream Ice Cream with a side of butter pickles was not agreeing with me or my baby right now. Another trip to the bathroom was definitely going to happen soon.

I was flipping through the channels on TV trying to find something to watch when I stumbled upon an episode of Maury Povich. As always, the question of some poor baby's paternity was in question.

*"Anika, how sure are you that Treyvon is the father of your child?" Maury asked.*

*The little ghetto bird started to smack her lips and roll her neck. "I'm 1,000 percent sure, Maury. Treyvon is the only (beep) I was sleeping with at the time that I got pregnant."*

*"Are you sure there's no other possible men who can be the father of your eighteen-month-old daughter Tarshay?"*

*"Uh-uh, uh-uh, Maury. There is no one else."*

*"OK, well, let's find out."*

*The crowd went wild as Maury stood up and walked over to the staff member who had the results. As soon as he sat back down and started to open up the envelope, it got so quiet that you could hear a rat piss on a cotton ball.*

*"In the case of eighteen-month-old Tarshay . . . Treyvon! . . . You are . . . not the father!"*

The look of sheer horror was etched on this girl's face after Maury read the results. She shouldn't have been mad at anyone else but her damn self. She knew before she even brought her ass up there that there was a possibility that Treyvon was not the baby's father.

I shook my head. "These bitches is dumb." I looked down at my protruding belly. "At least I know your daddy can be one of three," I said as I patted the spot where my baby just kicked.

I was flipping through the channels again when my text message notification ding started to go off.

Jay: Hey, girlie, how are you and my god baby doing?

I wonder how fast that title will change once she finds out I might be carrying her stepchild.

Me: We're doing fine. My stomach is just hurting a little.

Jay: Do you need to go to the doctor?

Me: No.

Jay: Ice cream and pickles?

Me: Yes. LOL!

I couldn't help but to smile at how well JaNair knew me. I know whenever the truth comes out about what Jerome and I did, our friendship will be over.

Jay: Let's do lunch or something this week. I have some juice.

Me: OK, just let me know . . .

I placed my phone back into my bra and got up from the couch. I wonder what type of juice her ass had to tell.

Oh shit! What if she found out about Jerome and Mya? Naw, she would have called and told me about that.

Hmmm. Ain't no use in trying to worry about it now, I'll find out whenever we do lunch.

The loud banging on the front door had my full attention now.

"Who is it?" I yelled as I walked closer to the front of the house.

"Where's Niecey?" Big Will's voice blared from the other side of the door.

I don't know why my body instantly froze at the sound of his tone. I grabbed my stomach and started to rub my hand back and forth. For some reason, my baby started going crazy as soon as Big Will's voice came vibrating through these walls.

"She's not here, Will. Come back later."

"Open the door, LaLa."

I thought about it for a moment. I didn't have anything to hide, and I doubted he'd do anything to me or my baby despite his numerous threats, so I opened the door. He walked in the house and looked around as if he was searching for something. Once he was done inspecting the place, he came back into the living room and stood in front of me.

I'd be lying if I said that Will wasn't fine. His six foot four corn-fed, linebacking ass always had these little chickenheads around the way falling all over him.

When Will and Niecey first got together, they were the couple that everybody in our high school envied. He was the huge football star destined for the NFL, and she was cocaptain of the cheerleading squad. During the Homecoming game our senior year, Will was tackled by five guys from the opposing team. While he was going down, his knee joint bent backward, tearing his ACL for the third time. His football career basically ended before it ever really started.

I guess he went through some sort of depression period, because after his dreams of making it to the NFL were basically flushed down the drain, he started to wild out. His and Niecey's relationship was really affected by his change, causing them to have this on-again, off-again shit they had.

Although the night that he and I shared was during one of their off periods, I know shit will most definitely hit the fan once it comes out.

"Niecey's not here, Will. She went on a date with her new friend."

"A date?"

I nodded my head.

"With some dude she's been talking to for a minute." I opened the door. Hopefully, he took the hint to get out. "I'll make sure to tell her you came by whenever she gets back."

"So I see you still going to have this baby?" he said as he walked up on me.

"It's a little too late for me to have an abortion now, don't you think? I already told you that there was a possibility that you weren't even the father. To be honest, I don't even think this baby is yours. The timeline just doesn't add up with how far along I am," I smirked. "You can stop tripping. Our little secret is still safe for now."

"What little secret?" My mom chimed in, causing us both to jump. I didn't even hear her walk up.

"Uh . . . Hey, Ms. Pam."

"Hey, Mama!" we spoke at the same time.

She looked from me to him, then back to me again.

"Where's Niecey?" she asked with raised eyebrows.

"She went out to dinner. She'll be back in an hour or two."

My mom turned her attention to Will. "What the hell you still doing here then?"

Will didn't say anything else. He walked out the door and left. Everybody knew that Ms. Pam didn't play. I closed the door behind him and turned around, only to have my mother standing directly in front of me. She was standing so close that my belly was touching hers.

I looked in her face and saw the questioning look she had in her eyes. That's why I wasn't too surprised with what came out of her mouth when she finally decided to speak.

"What little secret were you talking about? And you better not fix your face to tell that lie either."

"Damn!" was all I said as I hung my head low and told my mom everything.

# JaNair

"Tangie, girl, you are crazy. You better stop treating your baby daddy like that before he stops coming around."

"Honey, he ain't about to stop shit. All I have to do is text *come over* to that nigga, and he's dropping everything."

I shook my head. Tangie's ass always had me laughing. Ever since that first night at the hospital, I could tell that she was cool peoples. That's why when we kept in contact after I was discharged and a friendship started to form, I didn't have a problem with it. I could talk to her the way I could never talk to Mya or to LaLa as of lately.

"What's up with you and him, though? Are y'all together or just coparenting?" I asked as we looked through the clearance rack at Nordstrom's.

She shrugged her shoulders. "We're not together, but I'm pretty sure if we worked at it a little bit, we could be."

"Do you want to be with him?"

She shook her head. "No, not really. But I don't want our son to grow up like I did, you know, in a single-parent home."

"There's nothing wrong with that."

"Says the person who has both of her parents."

I did have both of my parents, but it wasn't like we were one big happy family. After my granny, which was my father's mother, died, he and my mom packed up and moved to Florida. They wanted me to sell the house and move to the Sunshine State with them, but I didn't want to have to transfer schools and go through everything that came along with that. The great thing about staying here, though, was the house was already paid for, so all I had to do was pay the property taxes at the beginning of the year.

"Hello, earth to JaNair, where did you go?" Tangie asked waving her hand in my face.

"My bad. You bringing up my parents had me thinking about them for a minute. Did you say something I missed?"

"Not really, I was just asking if your cousin came back home yet."

I rolled my eyes. "Yeah, she did. She pranced her ass in there a couple of days ago acting as if everything was good. I got all in her ass about the lights being cut off. She really had another think coming if she thought she still didn't have to pay that bill."

"You think she will pay it now that the lights are on?"

"She doesn't have any other choice. I told her to pay Semaj back the $250 or she could get the fuck out."

"Wait! What? Pay Semaj back?"

I couldn't hide the big-ass smile that was starting to appear on my face.

"Let me find out you and Semaj got something going on, JaNair." "Naw, it's nothing like that. Semaj and I are only friends. I just really appreciate what he did for me the day that I got discharged. When my own boyfriend was nowhere to be found, he was, and that touched my heart."

His thick and lethal tongue also touched my pussy, but that was none of her business. We shopped a little more, then finally decided to leave. Tangie had to go pick up some money from her baby daddy, and I had to go get ready for the date I had with Jerome.

"Really, babe? You're like an hour late."

"I know, I know, and I'm sorry. But I got caught up chopping it up with my boys." Jerome kissed me on my cheek, then gave me a warm hug.

"You know I hate getting ready and having to wait."

"I know, babe, and I'm sorry," he said, not even looking up from his cell that he'd been texting away on.

"If you put the phone away, maybe I'd believe that."

He didn't even respond as whatever he was looking at on his phone made him twist his face up. I walked up to him and tried to see what was on the screen, but he closed out of whatever he was in.

"So are we still going out or what?" I asked, irritation laced in every word.

He finally put his phone in his pocket, stood back, and stared at me for a while before he responded, that sexy little smirk he does gracing his handsome face.

"I don't know if we are going to make it anywhere, especially with you looking like that."

I glanced down at the white pleated crisscross cami dress that I had on. I thought I looked good. Paired with the Poseidon Vince Camuto Platform Booties I picked up at Nordstrom's earlier, I don't know what this nigga was talking about. I really didn't want to change, but if I had to in order to go out, then I would. I'll just save this outfit for my lunch date with Tangie and LaLa later on in the week.

"I can change into some—" I started to say, but was cut off by Jerome's lips crashing down on to mine.

A slight moan escaped my lips as our tongues danced to a song of their own.

"I don't want you to change into anything," he said between kisses. "I want you to take this shit off. I haven't had any of my pussy for some time now. I think you've healed enough, don't you?"

The tingly feeling that shot through my body had my clit thumping uncontrollably. I loved when Jerome demanded what he wanted. It turned me on like crazy. He was right. We hadn't had sex in almost two months now, and our time was way past due. I think part of the reason why I let Semaj sample a taste was because I needed a release.

I moaned again as Jerome's lips and tongue swirled around my neck. His hands that were just cupping my ass were now sliding the straps of my dress down my arms. When the thin pieces of fabric were finally removed, the dress fell down to the floor in a puddle.

Being braless and wearing nothing but a red lacy thong turned Jerome on even more. Before I even knew what was going on, I was lifted up into the air and slammed down onto his dick.

"Ahhhhh, shit, bae!" I screamed out as his third leg snaked its way to my cervix.

"Damn, I missed your pussy, baby. Don't ever keep her away that long."

"Jerome, wait, please. I need to adjust. You know, it's been awhile."

"I don't wanna hear that shit, JaNair. Stop acting like you're a virgin and take this dick." He lifted me up again and slammed me down on his member even harder.

My juices started to squirt everywhere, causing my tunnel to become easier for him to slide through.

"That's it, baby, quench his thirst. Rain all over your dick."

"This my dick?"

"He only belongs to you. Now show him how much you love him."

And I did just that. I placed my hands on Jerome's shoulders and wrapped my legs around his waist. As soon as I felt the coolness of the wall press up against my back, I started to go to work. I bounced up and down and even circled around, causing Jerome to moan and cuss at the same time.

"Let's take this to my room," I said, once I started to slow my pace. I didn't know where Mya's ass was, and I'd be damn if she walked in on us having sex.

Without another word and still connected to each other, we headed down the hallway and into my master bedroom. When Jerome got us to my bed, he gently laid me down and opened my legs as wide as they could go. As he started to lick at the glaze that coated my pussy lips, my body started to shake. I knew it would only be a matter of seconds before I shot my juices all over his face.

"Right there, baby, right there," I screamed when he took my clit into his mouth. I couldn't take it anymore and neither could my body, so I shot out another stream of come.

"Ugh, damn, JaNair! You shot that shit straight into my mouth. I almost choked."

I chuckled a little. "I'm sorry, bae, I couldn't help it. You made me do it."

"I know I did, just don't do it in my mouth next time, OK?" he said as he positioned himself at my entrance again.

This time when he plunged into my hotness, he made long, slow strokes, instead of the fast and short ones he pounded me with earlier.

"You love me, JaNair?" he whispered into my ear.

I nodded my head and bit my lip.

"Look at me," he said, his lips hovering above my own. Every time he pushed inside of me, his mouth would lightly brush over mine.

I opened my eyes and looked him in his face. When our eyes connected, it was as if a current shot through my body, but not strong enough to make the goose bumps rise.

"Tell me you love me, JaNair."

I moaned, "I love you."

He started to move faster. "You always gon' be mine?"

I breathlessly said, "Yes!"

He took both of my arms, placed them above my head, and peppered my face with kisses. The way that he started to rotate his hips and dive deeper into my pussy had my body ready to explode again.

"I'm about to come, baby, come with me," he said, beating my insides unmercifully. I knew once this was over I'd be swollen for days and a soak in the tub would be needed.

# Jerome

I woke up this morning to the feel of JaNair's velvet tongue moving up and down my shaft. The way she was licking me from base to tip had me softly moaning her name. Her soft, pouty lips circled the head of my dick and soon started to disappear before my eyes.

Grabbing a handful of her hair, I pushed her head down, trying to make her deep throat my shit. As soon as she started to gag, I released the hold I had on her head, then let her continue to do her thing.

"Damn, baby, that shit feels so good," I said, thrusting my hips up to meet her face. Toe-curling head is what she was giving me, and I didn't know how much more I could take.

She must've felt the way my body tensed up, alerting her that the end was almost near. When she switched from lying on her side to being on her knees in between my legs, I couldn't hold out anymore. The sight of her round ass being tooted up in the air is what took me over the edge.

"I'm about to come, baby," I warned in advance and got happy as hell when she didn't move.

However, all that happiness went out the window when she pulled her head back, causing the hot load of semen I just shot out to land all over my stomach.

"I hope you didn't think I'd let you come in mouth when it was such a problem for me to come in yours," she said laughing.

"Damn, Jay, that was fucked up."

She laughed again. "I only do that type of freaky stuff for my man."

"Oh, so I'm *not* your man now?" I asked with a raised eyebrow.

She shrugged her shoulders and poked out her bottom lip. "Maybe. Maybe not."

"I'll show your ass maybe," I said as I ran toward her little ass.

When I finally tackled her down onto the bed, I swiped my fingers through my wasted seed and smeared it all over her face.

"Damn it, Jerome! What the fuck?" she screamed, hopping out of the bed.

"What? I was just marking my territory and all, since you weren't sure if you were mine or not."

She threw one of her decorative pillows at me and stormed into the bathroom. The sound of the shower starting had me follow in right behind her. I tried to hop in and get a part two going since I let off that first round, but every time I tried to open the shower door, JaNair would slam it back shut.

After cleaning myself off, brushing my teeth, and still getting the silent treatment, I decided to make myself useful and make a little something to eat, so I headed into the kitchen.

I chuckled to myself because I thought that shit was funny, but I guess JaNair wasn't having that. Her ass wasn't screaming all that shit last night when she shot off all in my mouth. Hopefully, this little breakfast could be a peace offering amongst our sex wars though and that round two I was trying to get earlier could go down.

"I would've swallowed all of your babies if it were me sucking you off,"

I heard come from somewhere behind me.

Not even turning around to acknowledge her presence, I ignored her ass and continued on with breakfast. I could feel her burning a hole in my head, but I was not about to fall for that shit again, especially with Jay around here somewhere.

"Come on, Jerome, you know you liked it."

"You know he liked what?" JaNair's icy tone cut through the air as she walked into the kitchen.

I was stuck when I turned around and saw the look on her face. It felt as if we'd just got caught, but not really.

"I was talking about the way that D'ussé cognac tastes. Jerome was just saying that he was thinking about removing it from his bar."

JaNair looked at me, then back to Mya. Even I didn't believe the shit that just came out of her mouth, and the look on my face just told it all. Shit, I needed a distraction. When the smell of burnt toast rose into the air, I turned around so fast I almost got whiplash.

"Yeah, OK," was all she said as she came around the table and wrapped her arms around my waist.

"What you in here burning up, bae? It smelled good at first. Now I don't know if I want to eat."

"Shit, nothing really. The toast is just a tad bit darker than usual, but it ain't nothing a few scrapes with a butter knife can't handle." I kissed her forehead.

She went and sat at the little island next to an eye-rolling Mya. After I finished cooking, I made our plates which consisted of scrambled eggs, sausage, toast, and a few slices of fruit.

I set JaNair's plate in front of her and mine in front of myself.

"So, you didn't make enough for everybody?" Mya opened her big mouth to say.

"Why would he need to make enough food for you? He's not one of your little fuck flunkies."

A huge lump formed in my throat when I saw the smirk on Mya's face. If this bitch even attempted to open her mouth to say some shit, I'ma throw this whole plate of food down her throat.

She slowly rose from her seat and walked over to the fridge. After grabbing a cup of juice and a muffin, she headed toward the door.

"To answer your question, JaNair, he doesn't have to make any food for me. But it's rude as fuck to cook breakfast and not make sure that everybody has some."

Jay smacked her lips. "Just like you make sure there's enough food for me when you cook for your nigga of the day?"

All of the juice that I had in my mouth came flying out everywhere. I did not expect her to come back and say some shit like that.

Mya rolled her eyes and finally walked off, leaving JaNair and me to enjoy the rest of our breakfast. After filling our stomachs and having small talk, we cleaned up everything we messed up and headed back to her room.

"While you were in there burning my kitchen down, your phone went off a few times," she said walking into her closet.

I sat on the edge of her bed, pulled my cell out, and started to go through my logs. There were a few text messages from Toby and G and a couple of missed calls from Unique. Damn, I forgot I'm supposed to go pick up my son and spend some time with him today. I needed to hurry up and get out of here before Unique started to blow my shit up.

"Aye, baby, what do you have planned for your birthday? As of today, you have exactly six weeks and counting." "I know!" she said excitedly. "I think I might have a girl's weekend with LaLa and Tangie and just go to Vegas or something. If I don't do that, I was thinking about just having a small dinner party. I might even invite Niecey and Mya's ass."

I turned my nose up at that last statement, and I hope she didn't notice.

"Why not have both?"

"What do you mean?"

"Let me throw you a Vegas-style party at Lotus Bomb. We'll have whatever kind of food you want and plenty of alcohol."

"You'd do that for me?" she asked, jumping into my lap.

"I'd do anything for you, JaNair."

And I meant that. I kissed her lips softly and held her for a minute, then told her I had to go. We made plans to get together later on after she finished studying. With one last kiss, I grabbed my keys and headed for the door.

As soon as I stepped on the porch, the bright rays from the sun hit my face. I was blinded for a minute but quickly got over it as my eyes started to adjust to the light.

Before I made it to my car, which was parked in front of JaNair's house, the smell of someone smoking some of that good radiated around me.

I looked to my right, then over to my left and locked eyes with the last nigga I wanted to see.

"What's good?" he asked from across the fence. A smirk laced across his face. I lifted my head and kept it pushing to my car. I didn't have time for his shit today. Once I got in and plugged up my phone, I started the ignition and rolled down my window. I really didn't want to ask, but I just had to know. Whatever he was smoking had me wanting to hit that shit.

"Aye, what kind of Kush is that you're smoking?"

He took another pull. "This what you call that Cali's Finest. Peaches and Cream."

"That shit smell fiyah." I knew he was probably tripping out on me talking to him about weed. I may not smoke it anymore, but that doesn't mean I can't like the smell of some potent shit.

He smirked. "Yeah, it is fiyah. I stay smoking and eating on them good peaches."

See, that's why I couldn't fuck with this cocky-ass nigga. He was always on some dumb shit. What the fuck did eating peaches have to do with anything? I rolled up my window, turned the AC on, and left. I had way more shit to worry about other than his love for all things peaches.

# Semaj

*"I'm just tryna know you better . . ."*

I looked down at my phone and hit the "ignore" button for the second time. Her nigga hasn't been gone for five minutes yet and she already calling me. I know that sounded kind of salty, but I really didn't care.

"J, if you keep ignoring her, she'll stop calling you altogether," Li'l Ray said as he took the blunt from my hand.

"I know, and I'll call her back in a bit. I'm just tired of this back and forth with her ass. One minute we hanging and kicking it tough, the next minute she MIA."

He handed me the blunt again. "What do you expect when she got a nigga already? Is she supposed to spend all her time with you and only a little time with him? Look, man, I've known JaNair for a minute, and I can tell that she is feeling you some type of way. Hell, the fact that she now remembers your name should tell you that."

We both fell out laughing. Li'l Ray was right, though, things were different between us. Especially since that episode we had in her bathroom. Although it happened a few weeks ago, I could still smell her essence.

I looked down at my ringing phone and ignored the call again. Instead of JaNair calling this time, it was the same 713 number that's been calling me for the last week.

"Yo, who was that?"

"That out-of-state number I told you about. They call but never leave a message, so it must not be that important."

Ray nodded his head.

"What's up with you and LaLa? How are the parents-to-be doing these days?" I joked.

Li'l Ray started to rub the top of his head. Something he normally did when he was becoming real annoyed with something or someone.

"Man, I don't know what to say. Sometimes we good, then other times, I feel like choking the shit out of her ass." He took a long pull of the blunt. "This may sound harsh, but sometimes I hate that I might be this baby's daddy."

I looked at him with questioning eyes. "Might?"

"Yeah, man . . . might," he said as we headed back to the cave.

Ever since JaNair had started to become a little distant, I've been in the studio dropping all kinds of beats. In a way, I kind of have her to thank because if she didn't have me in my feelings like this, I don't know if these beats would've turned out the way they have.

"Aye, what did you mean by might?" I asked Li'l Ray as he stepped into the makeshift booth. I swear if I ever hit it big, I'ma upgrade the shit out of this muthafucka.

"I said might because the timing doesn't add up. Whenever I go to an appointment with her, she makes it a point to not discuss the due date. Then on top of that, Moms was talking about it's impossible for her to be pregnant by me."

"Wait, how would Aunt Shirley know? It wasn't like she was there at conception, was she?"

"Hell, no!" he laughed. "My dick wouldn't even get hard if Moms was in the room." He shook his head. "On the real, though, she said some crazy shit about her not having a dream about fish. She said if LaLa was really pregnant by me, she would've had that dream."

"That's that old Down South shit," I laughed but then got serious. "Do you think this is your baby?"

He shrugged his shoulders.

"OK, well, since you can't answer that, do you remember fucking her around the time she's claiming to have gotten pregnant?"

He nodded his head.

"OK, we're getting somewhere. Do you remember using protection?"

"Not all the time."

"Then there you have it. You remember having sex with her around the time of conception, but you didn't always strap up when y'all was fucking. I'm sorry to say, cuzzo, but there might be a possibility that the baby *is* yours."

"Yeah, I guess. Once you put it like that," he said stepping fully into the booth and closing the door. "Let's do that song from earlier. I got a few more verses to add."

I nodded my head and brought up the track he was talking about. Once I had everything set, I increased the volume in his headphones, then pointed to Ray.

*"Baby mama stay talking shit, so I stay smokin' kush.*
*Sometimes that don't work so a nigga gotta push.*
*Make money every day yeah true indeed*
*Real words to live by because money is all I need*
*I'ma get mine by all and any means*
*No bullshit shortcuts or small ass in betweens."*


I banged my head out as Ray kept flowing over the beat. The nigga was in rare form right now, I'll give him that.

I guess LaLa having him in his feelings was a good thing too. I had no doubt that out of the three songs we recorded today, this one right here was a certified banger. The rapid knocking on my door woke me up from my sleep.

After Li'l Ray and I finished that last song, I came in the house and lay down for a minute.

That was three hours ago. I reached for my phone to see what time it was. It was a little past seven, still kinda early, but a little too late to still be napping.

"Come in!" I mumbled as I scrolled through my call log. That same out-of-state number called me again as well as Tasha and JaNair.

"So are you done ignoring me now, J2?"

Speak of the devil. My head shot up quick when I heard her voice. I was expecting my aunt to be walking through the door telling me that dinner was ready.

"No one is ignoring you, JaNair. I've just been real busy." I turned over to face her. "I didn't think you'd notice, especially with the way you been dodging me for your little boyfriend."

She smiled. "Let me find out you feel some type of way about me."

I looked at her for a long moment, then sat up in my bed. I was starting to get tired of playing this game with her. Something had to give.

"Look, Jay, all bullshit aside, I'm a real nigga, and I don't know how to be no other way than straightforward and honest—" she cut me off.

"And I don't?"

"Not really! You can't even be honest with yourself half of the time."

"What do you mean by that, Semaj?" she asked, folding her arms under her soft and juicy titties. My dick twitched a little and started to rise up, so I pulled my comforter into my lap, then I ran my hand down my face.

"You know what, JaNair? I don't mean anything by it. If you can't figure the shit out for yourself, then I don't know what to tell you."

"What is there that I need to figure out, huh? That you like me? I know that already. What else? That I like you? You know that too." She came and sat on the bed next to me. "Semaj, I would be deaf, dumb, and blind if I couldn't see the attraction that we have for each other. It's like we're drawn together in some way. The thing is, I'm in a relationship with Jerome right now, and I owe it to him to at least try to make it work."

"That's what's up," I said as I started to get up, but her jumping on my lap had me falling back onto the bed.

We sat there and stared into each other's eyes for what seemed like twenty minutes before she grabbed a handful of my dreads and placed her soft lips on top of mine. As much as I enjoyed the feel of our tongues intertwined, I had to stop what was soon to happen.

"JaNair," I said placing my forehead against hers, "we need to stop."

Breathlessly she asked, "Why?"

"Didn't you just tell me you were trying to make things work with Jerome?"

She sat back and looked at me. The same look she had in her eyes the day I ate her pussy was there, and I almost lost it. I wanted to pull my dick out so bad and bury it deep inside of her body, but now wasn't the right time. Whenever JaNair and I did have sex, I needed her heart and soul to be here too. I wanted those as well.

"I'm sorry, Semaj, I shouldn't have done that," she said getting up from my lap. I know she saw and felt the way she had my dick standing straight at attention. I wasn't even going to hide it no more either.

"Are you really?"

"Am I really what?"

"Sorry?"

She opened her mouth, then snapped it right back shut. I could tell by the look she now had on her face that the answer to my question was swirling around in her head.

Her phone began to ring. She looked down at her screen and stared at the phone for a few seconds, then looked back up at me.

"I have to go," was all she said before she turned around and left, silently closing my door behind her.

I shook my head and laughed. This was the shit I was talking about. I don't know how much longer I'd be able to play second to a nigga she knows deep down she really isn't feeling anymore. Maybe this *thing* that I want JaNair and I to have is just what it is . . . a *thing,* I started to think. It might be time for me to fall all the way back and just let her do her like Aunt Shirley said.

I looked down at my dick which was still hard just thinking about her. JaNair needed to come to her senses real quick and real fast or I would have to move on. Walking around here with a hard-ass dick was not the business at all.

# LaNiece

It had been a week since I told my mother everything. To my surprise, she wasn't as upset as I thought she would be.

*"LaLa, you know that's foul as hell what you did, especially to your sister."*

*"I know, Ma. The thing is, I really do regret having sex with both Will and Jerome, but they're not going to see it that way. Not only will I lose my best friend, but I might lose my sister too."*

She rubbed my back. *"Baby, as far as JaNair goes, there is that possibility that she won't forgive you right now, but down the line, she will. With Niecey, she's going to be mad, maybe even beat your ass, but she'll get over it, and you'll go right back to being sisters again."*

After going over who I felt in my heart was my child's father, my mom suggested we have a little family dinner to air everything out. At first, I didn't agree with that shit. I wasn't planning on telling Niecey anything about Will possibly being the father until after the baby was born. But I figured it'll be less likely of a chance for her to come after me being pregnant than when I'm not.

I had just pulled into the overly crowded parking lot of California Fish Grill and had to drive around for about five minutes before I found somewhere to park.

JaNair, Tangie, and I were finally able to meet up for that lunch date we talked about some time ago.

At first, I was kind of in my feelings when JaNair told me that she was starting to hang out and become friends with the nurse from the hospital. But after chilling with Tangie a few times and getting to know her a little more, she was pretty cool.

When I walked into the small establishment, I immediately saw a frowning Tangie sitting at a booth near the window. I didn't know what any of that was about, but whatever she was looking down at had her face all screwed up.

"Hey, girl, where's JaNair?" I asked as I took off my coat and placed it on the back of the chair.

"She went to the restroom," Tangie responded, still looking down at what I now saw was JaNair's phone.

"What's the matter with you?"

She finally looked up, the frown she had a few seconds ago gone from her face. "Oh, nothing really. I just get kind of grumpy when I'm hungry."

I looked her in the eye for a minute and could tell she was lying. I wanted to ask her again, but JaNair finally returned from the bathroom.

"What's going on? What did I miss?" I looked at Tangie, and she looked at me.

"Your nosy ass ain't miss shit but me wobbling my greedy ass in here. Why haven't you ordered yet? You know we hungry."

"Speaking of we, how is my god baby?" JaNair asked as she started to rub my belly and talk to it in that baby Hebrew gibberish.

"*She* is fine. Although I should be the one you're concerned about since *I'm* the one in pain and gaining all of this weight."

It took her a minute to realize what I had just said. But once she did, her crazy ass started to yell and scream. It wasn't definite that I was pregnant with a girl, but with the way I've been craving dairy, I was hoping I was. The other patrons started to look at our little section after hearing all of the excitement and screaming.

I just shook my head and waited for her to calm down. JaNair's ass always got superexcited about the littlest shit.

"Congratulations, LaLa." Tangie finally said. "Did you and Li'l Ray want a girl?"

I opened my mouth but couldn't say anything. I don't know why I became speechless at that question, so I just nodded my head.

"I wish you would let me throw you a baby shower, LaLa. I don't understand why you want to wait until after the baby is here. You are such a party pooper."

*If only you knew the real reason why* was the thought that went through my head.

"Enough of this talking. What do you guys want to eat so I can go order our food?"

After we all decided on what we each wanted to chow down on, Tangie got up to stand in line.

JaNair and I sat there and chatted for the next ten minutes, talking about any and everything. She told me what had been going on in her and Jerome's relationship as well as what had been transpiring in her and Semaj's friendship.

Her phone started to buzz on the table again, but she just ignored it.

"Why aren't you answering the phone?" I asked, stuffing a fry into my mouth. Tangie had come back with our food, and we were already digging in.

"Because I don't want to talk to Semaj right now."

"Why not?" Tangie and I asked at the same time.

"Because the last time I was at his house, I embarrassed myself so bad." She covered her face with her hands, then went on and explained how she jumped on Semaj's lap and kissed him, only for him to stop her and remind her that she was trying to make things work with Jerome.

"Why would that embarrass you? If anything, you should be glad that he had enough respect for you and your feelings."

"What do you mean?"

Tangie went on to explain. "JaNair, anyone with eyes can see that Semaj has feelings for you, so finally being able to sleep with the woman he wants would be a no-brainer for him. The thing is, when he does sleep with you, he doesn't want you to wake up the next day regretting that shit, or even worse, going back to your boyfriend and leaving him high and dry."

I nodded my head in agreement with Tangie. What she just said was some real shit.

As the conversation went on, my phone started buzzing. I low-key rolled my eyes when I saw Mya's name pop up in my inbox.

Mya: Having fun at lunch with your best friend/baby's stepmom?

Me: What do you want, Mya . . .

Mya: Nothing really . . . I just wanted to see how the bffs were doing before your little secret comes out . . .

I didn't even feel like entertaining this bitch or her ho antics right now. I was just about to put my phone back into my purse when it buzzed again.

Mya: FYI, I don't need your help anymore with Operation Jerome. I'm handling that myself . . . However, I may need your assistance later on down the line. I'll keep in touch and so will you if you want your little secret to stay hidden . . . for right now!

Not even dignifying that nonsense with a response, I threw my phone back into my purse and finished off my grilled catfish, coleslaw, and fries.

I don't see how Niecey put up with her or any of her shit for all these years. This bitch was crazy and was always trying to come up off the next person. I couldn't wait for the day that Jay found out about her fucking Jerome. All hell was going to break loose and fists would definitely be flying.

I tried to ask Tangie and JaNair what they were about to get into, but by the looks on their faces, I could see that they were in the middle of a very deep discussion. Neither one of them acknowledged my question with an answer, so I took that as my cue to go since I was done eating anyway.

"All right, I'll see you guys later," I said as I walked around to each of them and gave them kisses on their cheeks. They both mumbled what seemed like good-bye and gave little waves, while still talking about whatever they were discussing.

I hopped in my car and was about to head home but decided that I didn't want to be there. With JaNair still eating with Tangie and Niecey somewhere with Jason Priestley, I really didn't have any or no one to kick it with.

Somehow, after ten minutes, I found myself parked and sitting in front of Li'l Ray's house. We had a falling out a couple of days ago and haven't talked since, so I was hoping he'd let me in.

"What's up, LaLa?" Semaj greeted as he opened up the door.

"Nothing much. Is Li'l Ray here?" He nodded his head and pointed to the back.

I couldn't help but to notice how fine Semaj really was once I looked up into his face. Being that I was fucking with Li'l Ray, I never really looked at him like that. But now with him standing here with his dreads pulled up into a high bun, the grey jogger pants with weed plants all over them hanging low off his waist, and the black wife beater displaying the outline of his toned stomach and the definition in his muscled arms, I stood there gawking at his ass.

"You OK, LaLa?" he asked, a small smirk settling on his face. JaNair's butt would be dumb as hell if she lets his fine ass pass her by for Jerome.

"I'm good. But, Semaj, let me ask you something." He leaned his back against the now-closed door and crossed his arms over his chest. "You really feeling my girl, huh?"

It seemed like he had to think for a minute, but then he finally answered. "I'm feeling her more than I should, especially with her having a man. Hopefully, she comes to her senses before I leave, though. If not, I guess we'll always just be friends."

"Before you leave?" I was confused. Where could he possibly be going? Li'l Ray never mentioned him moving away or leaving, so this was all news to me.

He smiled. "Yeah, I'm going to Texas for a few months to work on this new up-and-coming artist that was just signed to Rap-A-Lot Records. A few people that he's connected to heard some of the joints I did for Nipsey Hussle, Bad Lucc, and Glasses Malone, so they want me to come out and produce his whole album."

"*That's* what's up. Congratulations, man," I excitedly said as I gave him a hug. Li'l Ray told me a few times about Semaj and how good he was at producing music. I guess the right people finally took notice.

I stepped out of our embrace and was just about to turn around and walk down the hall, but something dawned on me.

"Does JaNair know you're leaving?"

He shook his head. "Not yet. I've been trying to call her since I got the news, but she won't answer my calls."

I knew I shouldn't be telling him this, but since I was going to be responsible for breaking up her current relationship, I might as well try to help her with the next.

"Semaj, don't give up on her, OK?" He looked at me with those sexy-lidded eyes, and I could tell he wanted me to further explain. "Look, JaNair would probably kill me if she knew I was telling you this, but I don't care." I blew out a breath. "She likes you, Semaj . . . a lot. And I know this much because I know my best friend. The only thing is, she's so blinded by this fake facade Jerome is putting on that she can't see a real nigga when she has one staring her right in the face. I can't tell you what's about to go down, but just know that within the next month or so, that little relationship she and Jerome have is going to be a distant memory, and she's going to need someone in her corner since I know it won't be me."

"Why won't it be you? You're her best friend, right?"

I wanted to tell him so badly why, but I couldn't do that without it getting back to Li'l Ray the second I did. I know that I was being a bit selfish, but honestly, out of all three of these niggas, Li'l Ray is the only one who's really been there for me.

"All that will come out in due time; just don't give up on her."

He nodded his head, then walked into the kitchen.

When I finally made it to Li'l Ray's room, he was lying across his bed snoring loud as hell. I smiled at his noisy ass, took off my shoes and jacket, then climbed into the bed with him. That grilled catfish, fries, and coleslaw had both me and my baby full and ready for a nap.

As if he sensed me in his sleep, Li'l Ray pulled me into his arms and laid his hand on my big belly. I fell right into a soothing slumber as soon as I closed my eyes.

# JaNair

"Why are you asking me all of these questions, Tangie?"

"Listen, JaNair, I don't like to beat around the bush or sugarcoat shit. Especially when it comes to someone I consider a friend."

I looked at Tangie and didn't know what to think. This line of questioning she was doing took me totally by surprise.

A little bit before LaLa left she pulled my ear to the side and started to ask me a lot of personal questions. A few of them were about my relationship with Jerome.

"I can most definitely agree with you about not beating around the bush or sugarcoating things, Tangie, because that's what I try not to do. I'm just having a hard time with why you're asking me these questions all of a sudden."

She chuckled, more so to herself than to me.

"This is some crazy shit! I don't know how we never figured any of this out."

"What are you talking about?" She was really starting to get on my nerves with these riddles and shit.

"JaNair, what's your boyfriend's name?"

"Why?"

"Can you just answer the question, please?" Her voice softened as she stared at me intently.

I sighed. "His name is Jerome. And now that you know that little bit of information, why is this information so important to you?"

She grabbed her phone out of her pocket, unlocked it, and started to scroll through it.

I could tell she was going through the phone's photo gallery, but she was swiping so fast, I couldn't really see anything.

"Is this him?"

When she lifted her phone screen to my face, my mouth almost hit the floor. There on the screen in my face was a picture of her and Jerome all hugged up. I could tell it wasn't a recent picture because Tangie's hair was cut into one of those cute Halle Berry pixie cuts, whereas her hair right now was a little bit above her shoulders in a fly-ass bob style. It looked like they were in some dimly lit club with a lot of shiny silver stuff in the background.

"Wait! How . . . How do you know Jerome?"

She scrolled past a few more pictures, then held her phone up to my face again.

"Because he's my son's father."

On the screen this time was a picture of Jerome and one of the cutest little boys I've ever seen. From the top of his head to the bottom of his chin, his face mirrored every part of Jerome's. That nigga couldn't deny him if he wanted to.

Sensing that she needed to further explain, Tangie went on and told me how she and Jerome met some years ago while she was dancing at some strip club. They hit it off that night and became inseparable. She said that after they had been dating for a few years, she ended up getting pregnant and having their son, JJ.

My hands started to shake uncontrollably, and my head started to pound. I was mad as hell. Although it was quite clear that he had his son before we got together, he still lied. When Jerome and I first started talking, I distinctly remember asking him if he had kids.

*"I want a little girl one day,"* was his response, so I just took it as if he didn't have any.

"JaNair, are you OK?" I heard Tangie ask, a bit of concern in her tone.

I turned my attention toward her. All I could think about was the look on her and Jerome's faces in that picture. They looked so happy. And if they were so happy then, I wondered how their relationship was now. Were they at each other's throat like most baby mamas and daddies, or were they still messing around?

I know I was being a little insecure at the moment, but if you could see the way Tangie looked, you'd probably feel the same way. I mean, I know I'm not an ugly girl and all, but there was always someone out there that made you second-guess yourself, if only for a minute. And although Tangie and I were becoming friends, she was that girl for me. Her cashew-colored skin was smooth and flawless, not a blemish in sight. Those greenish grey eyes would have the strongest man falling to his knees. The way all of her facial features blended together was crazy. It was like her eyes, nose, mouth, and ears were the perfect size and shape. In a way, she kind of reminded you of Alicia Keys . . . body, booty, and all.

I knew I shouldn't have been mad at her, but I couldn't help it. I started to wonder if she knew who I was from the very beginning. Jerome came to the hospital that night and left way after visiting hours. They had to have run into each other at some point in time. Did she only become my friend so that she could try to ruin our relationship?

All of the things that I told her about Semaj and I started to replay in my head at that moment. She even knew about the three times we kissed.

My anger started to boil over at this point. This bitch was really trying to play me. I snatched my arm from her grasp and was about to go in on her ass, but she held her hand up and cut me off.

"Before you even start, JaNair, let me just tell you a few more things. I didn't know that your boyfriend and my child's father were one and the same. You've always referred to him as your man, boyfriend, or boo. And I've always called him what he is, the father of my child. Second, the only reason why I asked you what his name was today was because while you were in the restroom, your phone was going off like crazy. After like the twentieth time, I finally turned your phone over so I could at least tell you who was blowing you up when you got back. Imagine my surprise when I turned it over and my son's father's face was flashing across the screen. Don't get me wrong, Jerome and I are not together, and I knew he'd end up with someone else. I was just a little caught off guard that that someone is actually you."

I understood everything she was saying, and by the look in her eyes, I could tell she was being sincere, but I still needed answers about a few things, and I'd be damn if I didn't ask them.

"I hear everything you're saying, Tangie, but I'm still trying to understand some things too, like the night I got into that accident. Jerome was there that night, and I find it kind of weird that you two didn't run into each other."

"Honestly, JaNair, we didn't run into each other. I didn't see him at all. I did text him though and asked him where he was and if he was all right. One of the times that I left your room, I ran into Toby which I thought was kind of weird, but I didn't think anything of it. When I asked him what he was doing there, he said something about one of their waitresses falling and he was just there to make sure she wasn't going to sue. After that, I went to make my other rounds. When I came back to your room, there was nobody there, and you were sound asleep."

My senses were telling me that she was telling the truth, but some shit just wasn't adding up.

The anger that was building toward her was slowly starting to dissipate. I didn't have a problem with Tangie at this point, but I still wanted to get out of here as soon as possible. I needed to find Jerome's ass and hear what he had to say about this.

"OK, Tangie, I believe you, and I'm sorry for coming at you the way I did. Thanks for lunch and everything, but I'm about to head out."

"Look, JaNair, my intentions for telling you that was not out of malicious intent. Jerome and I have been over for minute, and I've told you that a few times."

She was telling the truth there, so I nodded my head. But if I recall correctly, she cut him off because he started tripping about paying more child support. Who's to say that wouldn't change if he started to give her the amount of money she wanted.

She continued. "I know we haven't been friends that long, but I really do value our friendship and what we're trying to build. Now, as far as Jerome and I being around each other in regards to our child, there's nothing I can do about that. But as far as trying to get back with him or sleep with him again, you have nothing to worry about on my end."

"Thanks, Tangie," I said standing up. "I really do appreciate everything you said and coming at me on some grown-woman shit. I do have one question, though." She looked at me, waiting for me to continue. "I bet you made a lot of money with that big-ass booty you got, huh?"

She laughed. "You can say that. A lot of the girls couldn't make their asses clap like I could, so, yeah, I made enough. That was one of the reasons why I was given the stage name 'Unique.' To them men, this ass was unlike anything else."

We shared another laugh, then stood up. "OK, girlie, I'll talk to you later. Call me when you get home, all right?" I said as we hugged for a brief moment, then parted ways.

I jumped in my car and was headed right to Jerome's house. That nigga had some major explaining to do, and I prayed to God that he wouldn't lie to me again.

# ShaNiece

Joe was really doing something to me as I looked out at all the lights that illuminated the sky in the City of Angels. The view was so breathtaking.

Toby and I were at his loft in downtown L.A. When he told me that he lived down here, I was kind of skeptical to come. Yeah, there was the Staples Center and that big monstrosity known as L.A. Live, but there was also a lot, and I mean *a lot*, of crazy homeless people down here.

I remember when Mya and I came down this way to go to the fabric district one time. Somehow, we ended up getting lost with all of the one-way streets and ended up on Sixth and San Julian. When I say that both sides of the street were covered with tents, carts, cardboard huts, and dirty sleeping bags, I mean it.

The street had litter everywhere, and if you looked hard enough, you could see the rats rummaging through all of that trash.

While Mya and I were at a red light, this big black dude walked up to the car and asked if we had any change. After we both shook our heads no, we thought he'd turn around and walk away. Instead of doing that, he walked to the back door on the driver's side and opened that muthafucka up.

I didn't realize that both of our purses were back there until he stuck his stanking ass halfway into the car and tried to grab them. Mya's dumb ass finally registered in her mind what he was trying to do and took off, not even caring about running the red light. The shit happened so fast, all I remember seeing is the homeless dude falling out of the car with my new Michael Kors Peacoat still clenched in his dirty fist.

"What are you over there thinking about?" I heard Toby ask as he walked into the room.

When I turned around and saw what was standing before me, my voice got caught in my throat, and my eyes opened as wide as saucers.

I knew Toby would have a nice body by the way he filled out his clothes, but to see it up close and personal, I was freaking speechless.

He licked his lips and gave me that crooked signature smile of his. Cocky bastard. He continued to dry off with one towel while another was wrapped around his waist.

Embarrassed by how hard I was staring and practically salivating at the mouth, I turned my head. If I was anywhere near as light as my mama, I knew he'd of seen how red my cheeks were.

"What's up, ShaNiece? You good?" His voice vibrated through my body.

"Yes . . . I mean no . . . I mean yes!"

*What the fuck! Why was I stammering like that?*

"Look at me, ShaNiece."

It took me a minute, but I finally turned around. My eyes started at his feet which were quite nice for a man, then went up to the slight bulge that was slowly starting to form underneath that lucky towel. When my eyes took in that tight six-pack and sexy V-cut, I licked my lips. All of the tattoos that were covering his chest and both arms is what caught my attention next.

"Your tattoos are beautiful," I said once I finally spoke.

"Thanks! I think I wanna get my whole back done next."

I bit my bottom lip. "What did you have in mind?"

He shrugged his shoulders, then walked over to his dresser. "I haven't figured that out yet. Whatever it is, it'll go with all the other art I have on my body."

I nodded and watched as he pulled a pair of boxer briefs out of the drawer. Expecting him to go into the bathroom to slip those on, I gasped loudly when he let his towel that was around his waist drop to the floor, giving me the perfect view of his tanned white ass.

"I can feel you staring at my dunk, ShaNiece."

I started to laugh. "Boy, if you got a dunk, then I must have a super-duper dunk."

"Turn around and let me see so I can tell you if you're right."

"Boy, please! Now hurry up and get dressed so we can go. Didn't you say our reservations are at eight?"

He nodded his head again, then went on to finish getting dressed. While he was in the bathroom grooming, I started going through the iPod he had docked on the huge speaker.

I was kind of surprised that his library consisted of mainly R&B. There were a few white groups like Nickelback, Maroon 5, Fall Out Boy, and Crude. But besides all of that, he practically had everything I would have on mine.

"You ready?" I heard from behind me.

When I turned around this time, my pussy walls started contracting on their own.

*Damn,* was all I said to myself. If a man can look even better with his clothes on, I don't know how I'ma survive fucking with him.

Instead of engaging in another sprout of friendly banter, he walked over to me, grabbed my hand, and led me out of the loft.

We walked down the hallway for what seemed like ten seconds and stopped in front of a door I didn't notice when I walked past it earlier.

He typed in a code on the keypad, and the door cracked opened a little.

"Toby, where are we—"

He shushed me by pressing his big finger against my lips, then walked us all the way in.

The fear that was starting to build up instantly turned into awe as I looked at the beautiful setup before me.

"Perfect timing, sir. Your dinner is just about ready," some Alfred-looking dude said.

Toby led me over to a small table that was in the middle of the room. The red silk tablecloth looked beautiful as it flowed down to the floor. The stainless silverware shined bright as the flickering candlelight caused it to sparkle. There was a chilled bottle of some expensive wine in an ice-filled bucket accompanied by two long stem flute glasses. The beautiful floral centerpiece that sat in the middle of the table had the whole room smelling like fresh-cut roses. "Toby, this is . . . oh my God."

He did his little signature smile and pulled out my chair. After I sat down, he walked over to the white baby grand piano that was sitting beautifully in the corner.

"Did I ever mention to you that I play a few instruments?"

I shook my head.

"Well, my mom thought it was a good idea for me to learn how to play this little thing here, the violin, the saxophone, and the guitar."

At that moment, he pressed his fingers against the piano's keys and started to play a melody that sounded somewhat familiar. "Do you mind if I play a little something for you?"

Silently, I nodded my head.

I was shocked when I realized that the song he was playing was one of my favorites, by Jon B. Toby. He was a natural and could play the piano quite well. When he opened his mouth and started to sing the words of the song to me, I almost lost it.

*"All that you need is a little bit of tenderness, stability in your life. Pull a star out of the sky and place it on your hand . . ."*

I sat there with misty eyes as he continued to serenade me. No one has ever done anything for me this romantic.

The lyrics to the song really had me thinking too. My ex-boyfriend Will would never do anything like this for me. The closest he's ever come to being romantic was buying me a slow jam's CD from the DVD dude and taking me to dinner at Black Angus when they had the two for thirty-five-dollar deal. I don't know why I kept this on-again, off-again thing with him going. The love I used to have for Will went out the door a couple of years ago and never came back.

I looked over at Toby and could only imagine what going to bed with him would be like. I've never dated a white man, but so far, it was going great.

Once he was done playing around with those keys and entertaining me, he came back to the table and joined me for dinner. We enjoyed the rest of the night with good food, more great music, and a multitude of drinks before we both decided to call it a night, and Toby dropped me off at home.

# JaNair

I didn't even turn off my car when I pulled into Jerome's driveway. For some reason, I had the feeling that some straight bullshit was about to pop off.

I walked up to the door and rang the bell a couple of times. While I was waiting for him to answer, everything that Tangie and I talked about earlier started to replay in my mind.

Who doesn't tell the person they're in a relationship with about their kids? We've been together for some time now, and he's had plenty of time and opportunities to tell me about his son. Unless . . . Naw, Tangie said they haven't had sex in a minute, and she wasn't interested in him like that anymore. Then again, their "minute" could possibly be a month ago.

Yeah, I needed answers, and since I already got one side of the story from Tangie, it was now Jerome's turn to give me his.

I looked down at my watch. It was still early, so this nigga should be here. I walked to the edge of the porch and saw that his car was parked where it normally is behind the security gate. When there was still no answer after the second time I rang the bell, I started to bang on the door.

I was just about to head back to my car to get my phone when I heard the door crack open.

"Nigga, it's about goddamn ti—" was all I managed to get out before I was stopped in my tracks by the last person I expected to see answer the door.

We stared at each other for what seemed like forever. Him trying to figure out who I was, and I just amazed at how his parents made something so adorable.

My heart instantly melted when he started to smile back at me.

"Hey, li'l man, is your dad here?"

He nodded his head shyly.

"Can you go get him for me?"

He was on his way to turn around, but Jerome's loud voice met the door before he could.

"JJ, what I tell you about opening the door for strangers? You're supposed to come get Daddy when you hear someone knock or ring the doorbell," he chided.

After ruffling his head and sending him to his room, Jerome finally turned back to the door.

"I'm sorry about tha—JaNair? What . . . What are you doing here?" The shocked expression on his face almost made me laugh.

I stared at him for a minute. I was still trying to figure out why he'd keep something this important in his life from me. I was actually starting to feel hurt. Did he not trust me enough to take part in this chapter of his life?

"I just wanna know why, Jerome."

He wiped his hand down his handsome face.

"Can you come in and have a seat so we can talk about this for a minute?"

I shook my head. I could feel my eyes starting to get wet, but I kept telling myself not to cry.

"C'mon, JaNair. I was just getting dinner ready. I would love for you to join us."

"For what? How many other dinners have you had where you didn't think to invite your girlfriend to meet the son she never knew you had?"

"I'm sorry, baby. I shoulda . . . I mean, I wanted to tell you, I just didn't know how."

"You didn't know how? Well, how about when I asked . . . *Jerome, do you have any kids?* Why not answer with . . . *Yes, JaNair, I have a son* instead of answering with that bullshit about wanting a daughter in the future?" I said mocking him.

"I know, and I understand what you're saying, but in all fairness, I never said that I *didn't* have a child. I just never came straight out with it."

I had to laugh at that lame-ass response. It was just like a nigga to try to twist that shit around.

"On some real shit, what you did and or didn't say makes me wonder what else you haven't come straight out with, Jerome."

The look he had on his face after that statement was one of repulse and guilt. I thought for a second, *What else would he need to feel guilty about?* At that moment, a certain face flashed into my head, and like a dog in heat, I was on it.

"Are you still fucking Tangie?" I said a little louder than intended.

"What? No! Unique, I mean, Tangie and I haven't slept together in a long time," he stuttered. I didn't know if he was trying to convince me or himself with that lie. "Can you please come inside so we can talk about this some more, JaNair . . . please?"

I looked into his eyes and shook my head. This nigga couldn't possibly 196

be serious about me coming into his house still, especially with baby boy being here. His poor little ears didn't need to hear any of the slick shit I was about to say to his father.

"Jerome, you gots to be a dumb-ass muthafucka if you think I'ma step foot in that house to talk to you about some shit you should've been up front with in the beginning. Then when I ask you if you still fucking Tangie, you try to come up with some whack ass *long time ago* line." I stepped back from out of his face. This nigga had me hot as hell. When I looked down at my itching palm, I knew it was only going to be a matter of seconds before I slapped the shit out of his ass. I needed to leave, and I needed to leave now.

"Wait, JaNair, where are you going? We need to talk about this!" he said as he started to walk behind me. "Please, baby, just give me five minutes."

"Your five minutes passed them three hours we were on the phone the night I met you, so you can go fuck yourself with that. I don't wanna hear shit you gotta say other than 'What will be a good time for me to come and get the rest of my things from your house, JaNair?'"

"So it's like that? You ain't even gon' give me a chance to make this right?" he asked, sounding defeated.

"What can you possibly do to make this right, Jerome?"

We stood there staring at each other as I opened up my car door and got in.

"Exactly what I thought. Not a motherfucking thing," I said as I put my car in gear and drove off. When I got to the stop sign at the end of his street, the floodgates that I was trying so desperately to keep under control finally decided to burst open.

"You know, sooner or later, you're gonna have to answer his phone call and talk to him."

I blew out the smoke I'd been holding in my lungs for the last couple of seconds. "Says the nigga who can't even stand him."

He smirked. "But this ain't about me and fuck boy's beef. This is about you and how this can impact your future relationship."

I handed him back the blunt. "What do you mean?"

He placed the fiyah-filled, tightly wrapped swisher back into his mouth and took a pull. I couldn't help but to lick my lips as I watched him do what I've seen him do so many times before. For some reason, at that particular moment, I got so turned on at the sight of his juicy lips wrapped around the tip of the blunt like that. I guess memories of our little bathroom episode and the way he sucked on my clit started to flood my mind.

"Yo, JaNair, did you hear anything I just said?" Semaj snapped, breaking me from my freaky thoughts.

"Huh . . . I mean, what? I mean . . . what . . . What did you say?"

He chuckled. "If you're not going to pay attention to me or any of this free advice I'm giving you, maybe you should go home."

I playfully nudged him in his arm and snatched the blunt back. We were in Semaj's man cave/garage getting high, listening to his music and just shooting the shit like we've been doing for the last couple of weeks. After I left Jerome's house from confronting him, I came home and cried my eyes out. For two days I stayed locked up in my house not answering the door or phone for anybody. I was even ignoring Mya's ass when she dropped by. And, yes, I do mean dropped by seeing as she no longer lived with me. I changed the locks and everything on that ass. When the gas got cut off last week because of nonpayment, I couldn't do it anymore. That was the last straw for me. Besides, she hasn't stayed at the house in a minute, so it was like she was already gone.

Anyways, I guess Semaj wasn't feeling me closing off the world at all. So one day, he came to my house and banged on the door for damn near an hour straight while yelling my name. I got so tired of hearing the loud-ass noise and his big-ass mouth, that I finally opened the door. As soon as he saw the state that I was in and the mess that I'd made, he came into the house, cleaned it and me up, then rolled us a fat blunt of that loud. We've been smoking and chilling ever since.

# Semaj

"I was saying that you need to at least hear what he has to say. He may have a good reason as to why he didn't say anything about his son."

She rolled her eyes. "And what about Tangie?"

"What about Tangie? You said yourself that she told you they haven't had sex in a while, so maybe that part is true." I got up from the couch JaNair and I were sitting on and went to the fridge. "What's this really about, Jay?"

She shrugged her shoulders and got up. "It ain't about nothing. I just don't know if I can trust him anymore. If he could keep something so important like his son a secret, ain't no telling what else he's been up to and isn't telling me."

I took the fifth of Hennessy I had out of the freezer and grabbed a couple of cups. Dealing with JaNair and her ongoing bullshit with Jerome's ass had me drinking and smoking a little bit more than normal. Plus, I was kind of nervous about telling her I'd be leaving for Texas in a week.

"Look, Jay, as far as Tangie goes, I believe her. I mean, I met her a couple of times this past week, and she seems like a real genuine person. Even after finding out that Jerome was your boyfriend, she didn't trip like most baby mamas would. If they were still messing around, she would have told your ass that day, just to rub it in your face."

She nodded her head. "Yeah, I guess."

"And as far as Jerome goes, just give him a chance to explain. After you get all of the facts, then decide whether you wanna call it quits."

I really didn't want to give her that advice, but what type of nigga would I be if I didn't. I handed her a shot of the Henny, then poured me one. On second thought, I poured me a double. I needed to get buzzed a little bit faster if I was going to be giving her advice on getting back with fuck boy.

I thought back to two weeks ago. I knew something else must've happened between JaNair and Jerome the day I saw her run into the house crying with her head down. She doesn't even know that I saw her, but I did. I was buckling Ta'Jae into her car seat when JaNair pulled up into her driveway. She was so busy trying to hide her wet face that she never looked up and saw me staring at her.

After Tasha cussed me out for some unknown reason and left, I started blowing Jay's phone up. When she didn't answer the first night, I didn't trip because I figured she needed some space. But after the second night, I wasn't going for that shit, plus I was starting to become concerned.

Looking back on how she looked when she finally opened her door, I had to laugh a little. Baby girl was looking bad as hell. Her eyes were puffy and red, and her hair was all over the place. Her skin was real ashy, and her face was without any makeup. Even still, in the messed-up state she was in, JaNair was still the most beautiful girl I'd ever seen.

"What you over there laughing about?" I heard her say as she came and stood next to me.

I looked down at her. "You."

We stood and stared into each other's eyes for a minute until I cleared my throat and went to sit back down.

"So, what do you want to get into now? We can stay here and chill, listen to some music and get fucked up, or we can do whatever it is you wanna do." JaNair came and plopped down next to me on the sofa, snatching out of my hand the rolled up blunt I was about to put in my mouth.

"We can stay here, I guess. I'm tired of being at my house, and I don't feel like going anywhere. I am starting to get a little hungry, though."

I took the blunt back and lit it. "Me too. My aunt Shirley isn't here so I guess I can go in there and whip us up something real quick."

"Nigga, your ass can't cook," she laughed. "And I'm not talking about no bologna sandwiches, boiled hot dogs, or scrambled eggs either."

This girl really had life and bullshit fucked up. I could throw down in the kitchen. Although my aunt Shirley cooked 90 percent of the time around here, she still taught me a thing or two about cooking. She felt that I needed to know how to fend for myself just in case I got with a girl who couldn't burn like her or just couldn't cook at all.

"I can show you better than I can tell you," was all I said as I got up and headed into the house. I didn't even have to turn around to see if JaNair was behind me. Her scent gave her away.

I grabbed everything I needed from the fridge, freezer, and pantry, and ended up making us my famous bacon stuffed cheeseburgers with the works, homemade fries, and cherry Kool-Aid. After we both were filled to capacity, we went to my room and lay down on my bed. JaNair was the first to doze off, and I couldn't help but to lightly trace every gorgeous contour of her face with my finger. When I got to her lips, the urge to press mine against hers took over, and I did just that.

"What are you doing, Semaj?" she groggily asked with her eyes still closed.

"I couldn't help but to kiss you." She opened her eyes. At that moment, I knew I had to bring up the Texas subject. "I know you got the itis and everything right now, but I need to talk to you about something real quick, Jay."

She looked at me for a second, then sat up and propped herself on her arm. Her hair that was in a loose ponytail fell over her shoulder and covered half of her face. I took a few pieces and pushed them behind her ear.

The look in her eye was so intense and sexy, my dick started to twitch.

"Look, JaNair, I just wanted to let you—" was all I said before my bedroom door busted open.

"Daddy!" Ta'Jae yelled as she ran to my bed and jumped in the middle of Jay and me.

"Hey, Daddy's baby." I hugged her. "How did you get here?"

"Mommy." OK, I kind of figured that, but how in the hell did they get in the house? I distinctly remember locking the door, and I know my baby moms don't have a key.

Ta'Jae giggling had me look over in her direction. Damn that girl moved fast. She was just on my lap, now she was on JaNair's giving her kisses and hugs. It was crazy how attached those two have become since we've started hanging out.

Anytime Ta'Jae was here and Jay wasn't, she'd constantly ask where she was or ask if we could go next door to see her. Of course, Tasha had a problem with that, but I didn't give a fuck. She couldn't dictate who I chose to have my daughter around. As long as whoever it was wasn't mistreating our child, she shouldn't have shit to say.

"So what were you going to tell me?" JaNair asked as she and Ta'Jae played in each other's hair.

"Oh, I just wanted to let you know that—"

"What type of shit is this, Semaj?" I looked up at a twisted-faced Tasha and instantly got a headache. See, this was the shit I was just talking about. "Uh-huh, you got me fucked up for real. Bitches playing in my baby's hair and shit. C'mon, Ta'Jae, we about to go."

"But I wanna stay with Daddy, Mommy," she whined.

"No! Your daddy is out of his mind right now. How in the hell are you gonna be laid up with the next bitch and have my daughter in the same bed y'all probably just fucked in?"

"You got one more time to call me out of my name," JaNair smoothly said as she still had Ta'Jae on her lap. I knew I needed to get a hold of things before shit got way out of hand, so I hopped out of the bed and addressed my baby mama.

"Look, Tasha, first off, you're not going to come up in here and be rude to my company like that, so this name-calling shit is unnecessary. Second, I would never disrespect my daughter, myself, or whoever I'm with by putting them in an awkward situation. Lastly, I'm gonna tell you this, like I've told you so many times before. If I wanna have Ta'Jae around ten different women, that's none of your damn business. As long as my baby has a smile on her face and is enjoying herself, I'm cool with that. Now, if you don't have anything to tell me about *our* daughter, then you can go. I'll call you when I get ready to drop her off in a couple of days."

She looked at me, then over my shoulder at JaNair, back to me again, and rolled her eyes. I could tell she wanted to say something else, but thought against it and left.

For the next hour, we chilled and watched the Disney Channel until I finally couldn't take any more and dozed off. When I woke up a couple of hours later, both Ta'Jae and JaNair were lying next to me sound asleep.

I couldn't help but to smile at the way my two favorite ladies were cuddled up to each other. Just seeing the way JaNair held my daughter as if she was her own had me feeling her even more. I sure hope this trip down to Texas doesn't cause us to lose whatever it is that's happening between us, because I could get used to waking up to this every day.

# LaNiece

"Mama, do we really have to do this?" I whined as I walked around the kitchen. Who has a family dinner just to spill secrets anyway? This was the dumbest idea I've ever heard of. Maybe I should just leave and stay gone for a few hours. Naw, Ms. Pam would kick my ass up and down the street as soon as I got back.

"We . . ." she said pointing between the two of us, "aren't doing anything. This is all about *you*, LaNiece, and what you did. Don't nobody bring this on themselves but you, so, yes, this *is* about to happen.

"You know I don't like that sneaky shit, especially amongst family. So whether or not you like it, you're going to sit here like an adult, talk this shit out, and enjoy the home-cooked meal I've been slaving over all day."

"Well, can we at least leave the forks and knives in the kitchen, or better yet, can we use plastic and paper everything instead? I don't want Niecey to hurt me or my baby," I said rubbing my belly while popping one of the yeast rolls my mama just took out of the oven into my mouth.

"Girl, shut your scary ass up. Niecey isn't going to hurt you or my grandbaby. She's not crazy. You weren't scared when you opened up your legs to Will, so why be scared of what might happen now? Honestly, though, I don't think you have anything to really worry about. Niecey seems like she's really into that little white boy she's been seeing, so don't be so nervous."

I understood everything that my mom was saying, but still, you never know. Sister or no sister. Pregnant or not. When some people hear certain truths, they tend to snap, and Niecey was not to be excluded. They didn't have a show with that title for nothing.

I left my mom in the kitchen to finish getting everything ready. It was really no use for me to be in there, especially when all I was doing was sampling everything she had on the stove. I walked back into the living room, took a seat in my favorite recliner, and turned on the TV. As always, after flipping through damn near 500 channels, I still couldn't find anything to watch, so I decided to catch up on all of my shows I had recorded on DVR until the festivities started.

Those Memphis detectives on *The First 48* were just about to interrogate their prime suspect when the doorbell chimed.

"I got it!" I yelled out to my mom, although she wasn't showing any signs of getting it in the first place.

When I opened the door, my all-right mood instantly changed when I saw who was standing on the porch.

"What the fuck are you doing here, Mya?" I didn't even care about the annoyance dripping from each word.

"Well, hello to you, LaLa. I see you still trying to fit into those size nine clothes when you're obviously a what . . . 18/20 now?"

She smirked after her little jab, and I wanted to slap the hell out of her.

"Again, I ask . . . What the fuck are you doing here, Mya?"

She barged into the house without being invited in.

"Damn, Mama Pam has it smelling good as hell in here. Is she making roast?" She licked her lips. "Hell, whatever it is, I can't wait to eat it. I haven't had a home-cooked meal in a while."

"And I'm pretty sure it will be a little longer," I said standing by the door still holding it wide open. I guess she wasn't taking the hint that she wasn't welcomed because she went over to the couch and sat her ass down.

"Oh, you can close the door now. I'm not going anywhere. Niecey invited me over to eat with y'all tonight. She figured this would be the perfect time for her to introduce Justin Bieber Sr. to us since this is supposed to be a family dinner and all." She winked her eye. "Oh, and by the way, LaLa, will Li'l Ray or Big Will be joining us tonight? I mean, they are family too, right?"

See, this is why I hated this bitch. I couldn't wait until all the shit she's been doing caught up to her. I wouldn't be surprised if someone found her body thrown on the side of the road one day. I was just about to let off in her ass when Niecey burst through the door with a casually dressed Toby following behind her.

"Mama, we're here!" she yelled out closing the door and walking toward me. "Toby, this is my sister LaNiece, who you've probably seen before because she's best friends with JaNair. And this here," she said, rubbing my stomach, "is my nephew, Ray Jr."

"So you're having a boy?" Toby asked as he shook my hand.

"I'm not sure, but my sister seems to think I am. Every time we try to find out the sex, this little knucklehead closes its legs."

"Ray Jr., huh?" I heard Mya's ass question. "What if it's a girl? What are you going to name her then? Raynisha? Personally, I like the name Willow, but that's just me," she said trying to be funny.

"I like Willow, but Romella could be cute too, huh?" That shut her ass right up. I knew she couldn't stand the fact that I might be pregnant by Jerome. She'd never get him if I was.

"To be honest, sis, I hate both of those names, but if that's what you wanna name my niece, then I gotta live with it," Niecey said.

After we chatted for a few more minutes, my mom finally came out and told us that dinner was ready. Of course, Mya's bum ass was the first one to the table, but once we all sat down and Niecey formally introduced Toby to our mother, we dug in.

"Ms. Pam, I've never tasted a roast as tender and flavorful as yours. I hope the next time you make it, you give me a call or a plate."

"Ahh, thanks, baby. But you feel free to come by anytime I cook because everything I make is off the chain, so you'll love it all."

We all shared a laugh, then got quiet again. Everyone was lost in their own thoughts and enjoying the rest of their meal.

I was hoping and praying that my mom would forget about the big confession since technically, everyone was family, but as always, my hopes and prayers fell on deaf ears.

"OK, you guys. For dessert, I made a Pineapple Upside-Down Cake. While I clear this table and get dessert ready, LaLa, why don't you tell your sister what you needed to tell her."

I looked at my mom with pleading eyes as everyone else's looked at me. Even Mya's bitch ass was focused on me. She'd been texting away on her phone all night to only God knows who.

My mother cleared her throat and gave me that look she always gives when she wasn't playing. I also noticed how she discreetly raised her hand showing me that she had already collected all of the forks and knives from the table.

I gave her a small smile, then looked at my twin. I could tell the moment she knew some shit was about to go down because the happiness she just had on her face instantly mirrored the look of hurt I had on mine. It was one of the perks that came with being a twin, only this time, it didn't feel like a perk.

"What's wrong, LaLa? Is it the baby? You know you can tell me anything," she said as Toby rubbed her back.

I heard Mya smack her lips, but I paid her no mind. My mom finally returned with the cake and started to cut us each a piece.

"Niecey, I don't know how to tell you this, but—"

"Damn it, LaNiece, spit it out already!" Mother snapped.

I swallowed the lump in my throat. "Li'l Ray might not be my baby's father."

"OK . . . Who else could it be then?"

I went with the harmless name first. "Jerome."

A look of confusion came across her face. "JaNair's Jerome?"

I nodded my head yes. Toby, who was now on his second piece of cake, just shook his head. Mya started to text away on her phone again.

"Wow, LaLa! Does JaNair know?"

I shook my head no, then decided to put my big girl panties on and get this over with.

"Jerome isn't the only possibility. There's one more person." The room got so quiet I became nervous.

"Damn it, LaLa, stop beating around the bush and just spit it out already!"

# Mya

This shit was better than *The Jerry Springer Show*. I knew as soon as LaLa told Niecey who the other baby daddy could be, all hell was going to break loose.

"Yeah, LaLa, spit it out already," I taunted. She shot me a murderous look, but I didn't care. I just sat back in my seat and smiled.

I started to laugh when she whispered that name low as hell. I knew by the look on Niecey's face that she didn't catch it yet. So me being the messy person that I was, I spoke up again and asked her to repeat herself.

"Mya, shut your ass up. This is between LaNiece and ShaNiece unless you have some shit to add too?" Mama Pam hissed.

I started to say something back but thought about it. I liked to pick and choose my battles, and I knew I'd never win against Mama Pam, so I shut my mouth. Instead, I redirected my attention back to LaLa. Niecey had just asked her to restate the name she gave, and the spotlight was now on her.

"The other possible father is Big Will," LaLa finally blurted out.

My eyes instantly went to Niecey because I just knew shit was about to get real.

She blew out a breath, then sat back in her chair. She looked at Toby who was just sitting there all calm and collected like he didn't just hear what LaLa said.

"I'm so sorry, Niecey," LaLa cried. "I never meant for that to happen.

It was only one time, and if it's any consolation, it was during one of y'all's off-again periods."

Niecey threw her head back and started to laugh uncontrollably. Once she calmed down, she looked at Toby and asked, "Are you ready to go, baby, because I am?"

What! I silently screamed in my head. That was it? I was expecting so much more to happen.

Toby and Niecey got up from their chairs and went over to Mama Pam to say their good-byes. After hugs, kisses, and foil-wrapped plates were given, Niecey turned to face her twin.

"You know, LaLa, I'm not even tripping off of Will possibly being your child's father, because as you can see," she looked up at Toby lovingly, "I moved on to someone way better, someone who wouldn't even think about putting his dick in your corroded-ass pussy. So for that, you won't have any problem out of me."

I couldn't believe it. Niecey was taking this way better than I thought she would. I guess new dick will do that for you. Toby grabbed her hand and was leading their way to the door but suddenly stopped when Niecey jerked her hand from his hold.

She turned back to LaLa. "As far as us being sisters, I can forgive you one day, I'm sure. However, the fact that you are my sister and would do something like this to me will never be forgotten."

Niecey charged at LaLa so fast she never had time to react. When she drew back her arm and slapped the shit out of LaLa, Toby, Mama Pam, and I couldn't do anything but wince in pain and hold our cheeks.

"Just so you know, that's just a little taste of what's gonna happen to you once you drop that baby," she screamed as Toby pulled her off of a damn near unconscious LaLa.

I didn't want to laugh, but I couldn't stop it from coming. That's what LaLa's ass gets for fucking my—

"And what the fuck are you laughing at, Mya? I can't wait until JaNair finds out that you fucked Jerome too. You know as well as I do that she's gonna beat the brakes off of both y'all's ass when she does. Hell, she done already kick your ass outta her house and got you living from post to pillar. When will you ever learn? With friends like you and family like my sister, it's no wonder why bitches stay in and out of jail," Niecey screamed.

"Please know and understand that this friendship or whatever the fuck it is that we had is now null and void. Don't call me for shit, don't ask me for shit, and don't even speak to me for shit when you see me in the streets."

Mama Pam looked around the room and shook her head, disappointment etched across her face.

"Toby, can you please take Niecey with you for a few days. She and LaLa do not need to be in the same house right now." Toby nodded his head, grabbed Niecey's hand, and left. She then turned her attention toward me. "Mya, I think it's time for you to go as well. And I hope all that stuff that ShaNiece just said about you messing with your cousin's man isn't true. You young people are always burning the wrong bridges. What's gonna happen when that thing you have in between your legs stops working? What you gonna do when you really need someone to have your back and none of them so-called niggas you fuck with are nowhere to be found?" She shook her head and got up from the table. When she came back from the kitchen, she handed Niecey an ice pack for her cheek.

I wanted to ask for a to-go plate but thought against it. I made sure I had everything I came with and finally left. While pulling off, I thought about everything Mama Pam had just said to me. Maybe I do need to change some of my ways. Naw, who am I kidding? I'm not about to change shit, and Mama Pam's ass sure would be singing a different tune if Jerome gave her the dick one time.

When I got to Cassan's house, I unlocked the door with the key he had given to me and walked in. As always, the place was messy as ever. This nigga didn't believe in picking up shit. He'd come in from work, take off his clothes, and just throw them any and everywhere. I guess he felt that since I've been living here for the last few weeks, I'd clean up after him. His ass truly had another think coming if he believed that. My stay here was only temporary since JaNair's bitch ass changed the locks on me, so there was no use in me acting like wifey.

Just thinking about the way JaNair did me had me hot as hell. I could've been a real bitch and reported her for doing an unlawful eviction, but since I'd be taking her man from her soon, I felt payback would be served.

So far, the plan that I came up with for Jerome was going as planned. I ended up getting his new number from one of the new waitresses at Lotus Bomb. Of course, I had to hit her up in the parking lot since I was banned from coming back up in there. Surprisingly, whenever I do text Jerome, he hits me back, but that's only because I told him I could help him with getting JaNair back.

Yeah, I knew all about their little breakup. Unbeknownst to LaLa, she butt dialed my phone while they were in the restaurant that day. I didn't hear the whole conversation, but I did hear the part about Jerome and Tangie having a baby together and knowing JaNair, I knew the first place she was headed when she left was going to be to Jerome's house.

I made my way up to the restaurant undetected, thanks to Cassan's ride, and followed her for about forty-five minutes until we ended up in front of some house in the valley. The place was beautiful, and I could picture myself being Susie Homemaker and everything here.

I had parked about two houses down, so I couldn't make out what was being said, but when I saw JaNair storm off and Jerome chase after her, I knew something went down.

Shit was crazy how things were starting to happen on their own. That's why I told LaLa I didn't need her help with my plan. Besides, I knew sooner or later, her conscience was going to start fucking with her, and she'd end up telling JaNair everything before I wanted her to know. I had something for LaLa's ass, though.

Keys rattling in the door only told me one thing: Cassan was home. And as always when he walked in, everything went to the floor.

"What's up, Mya?" He looked around. "Why haven't you cleaned up around here?"

I rolled my eyes. "Because you don't pay me to."

"Because I don't pay you to? What do you think paying the rent, *so you can have a roof over your head*, the bills, *so you don't have to wash your ass in the dark,* and groceries, *so you won't starve to death,* means?" He laughed. "That's what's wrong with bitches like you. You think shit is just supposed to be handed to you and you can get anything that you want. But news flash, Mya, in the real world, it doesn't work like that. If that was the case, you'd still be at your cousin's house and not here."

See, this is why I hated living with him. Sometimes I wish Ryan's ass would get out of his feelings about me calling him the wrong name and fucking up his couches. I wouldn't have to go through this shit if I was over there.

"Yo, on some real shit, if you can't start helping around here, you gotta bounce."

Was he serious? I couldn't believe this nigga. He wants to treat me like this after what he did to me? I don't know where his mind was at, but it needed to get correct fast.

"Nigga, let's not forget that you owe me for what you did."

He blew out a breath. "Ah, hell, not this shit again. Mya, you need to get over it, because if anything, you gave that shit to *me*."

"Are you serious right now?" I laughed. "I stay at the clinic religiously, so I know damn well I didn't come here with any STDs. You, on the other hand, already knew you had it, then tried to put it on me."

"What the fuck are you talking about?"

"Cassan, after you fuck someone for the first time without protection, who says, *'If you gave me something, I won't be mad because I know you were messing with other niggas before me. But anything after this day will be a problem'*? It was like you were warning me already." I got up and went into the kitchen. "That's why I made an appointment at Planned Parenthood a few days later. And guess what I found out? Your nasty ass gave me chlamydia."

"Man, I didn't give you shit. If anything, you gave that mess to me. That's neither here nor there, though. We're both clean now, and that's all that matters."

See what I'm talking about? This nigga is always on some bullshit. If I had somewhere else to go right now, best believe I would sure be there, but since I don't, I just gotta sit here and wait it out until my plan falls into place.

After I grabbed everything out of the fridge that I needed to make a little something for him to eat, I made my way to the living room and cleaned up a little. I really didn't want to do it, but I needed him to be in a good mood before I asked him for a few dollars. And once I had his belly full and his dick empty, I knew that money would be as good as got.

# Jerome

I'd been going out of my mind for the last few weeks. JaNair was still ignoring my calls and any other form of communications I've tried. The flowers I've sent were turned away. The "I'm Sorry" cards I mailed were returned. She even went as far as to block both Gerald and Toby's numbers since I tried to call her from their phones a few times.

I was going crazy. Then to make matters worse, this crazy bitch Mya somehow got my phone number again and wouldn't stop texting me for shit.

The only reason why I hadn't changed my number again was because she claimed she could help me with getting JaNair back. Something on the inside was telling me that she was lying, but I was so desperate to get Jay back into my life that I'd do just about anything right now, including sleeping with the devil.

I pulled up to Toby's house and honked my horn. We had some business to handle at Lotus Bomb, and I offered to swing by and pick my boy up.

When he opened the door, I was surprised to see Niecey walk out behind him. He walked her to her car and opened the door for her. Before she got in, he grabbed a big handful of ass and pulled her close to his chest. I couldn't figure out what he was whispering into her ear, but whatever it was had Niecey blushing hard as hell. After kissing her a few more times and getting one last hug, he finally hopped into my car.

"Damn, nigga! Don't be slamming my door like that. I don't wanna have to sue your ass if you break my shit."

"Dude, I can buy you ten of these little Transformer cars, so shut the fuck up. Now, when you move up to the level with us big boys, *then* you can talk."

"Man, if I wanted a Range, Lex, or Benz, I could get one. But it would be a waste of my hard-earned money just to get a car and not drive it like your ass. I don't come from money like you, so I can't afford to have a showroom of luxury vehicles in my garage."

"Fuck you, man!"

I just laughed. I don't know why Toby hated to be reminded of his wealthy background. A nigga like me would be embracing the hell outta that shit.

Thankfully, there was no traffic on the freeway, so we made it to the lounge in thirty minutes.

After doing some inventory, unloading the alcohol shipment, taste testing the new menu our chef came up with and going through potential candidates for the waitress opening, we finally had a moment to sit back and catch up.

"Yo, have you talked to G lately? I haven't heard from him in a minute."

"Yeah, that nigga been spending all of his free time with that girl he was telling us about . . . Daya, Day Day or something like that. He finally made it official and wifed her up."

Toby nodded his head.

"What's up with you and Niecey? I see y'all been kicking it real tough lately."

He smiled. "Yeah . . . That girl is something else right there. At first, I thought she was gonna be a hit-it-and-quit-it situation, but after getting to know her and what she's all about, I can honestly say that I'm really feeling her."

"Damn, that pussy that good?" I laughed.

"I wouldn't know." He looked at me. "We haven't had sex yet."

"WHAT! I just knew you beat them panties up already." He shook his head. "Well, if it's true what they say about twins having the same everything, then I'm pretty sure she has some nice pussy because LaLa's was pretty good."

"See, that's your problem now, Rome, thinking with your dick and not your head. You think JaNair is tripping now? Just wait until she finds out that that baby LaLa's carrying might be yours too."

I spit my drink out of my mouth. "How . . . How do you know that?"

Toby went on to tell me about the family dinner he attended with Niecey a week ago and how LaLa revealed that she had three possible baby daddies.

"Your girl Mya was there, and Niecey put her ass on blast about fucking you behind JaNair's back too."

"Fuck!" I screamed out in frustration. This was all I needed.

"Yeah, man, fuck is right. Niecey's mom told her that LaLa's been at JaNair's house for the last week; said something about not feeling safe in the house after Niecey smacked fire from her ass."

I don't know why, but at that moment, I started to become hot as hell. I had to unbutton a few buttons on my shirt and call the bar for a glass of ice-cold water.

"Man, calm your ass down," Toby said laughing, but I didn't see shit funny. "I already know what you're probably thinking, and you shouldn't even be worried. It's obvious that if JaNair knew anything about the situation, LaLa would not be at her house right now. And she's probably not going to know anytime soon. LaLa needs her friend right now since she and her sister are at odds."

He was speaking some truth there, and to keep it all the way honest, LaLa would probably be in the hospital right now if Jay was aware. A lot of people didn't know this about her, but JaNair had a really bad temper when pushed.

Toby and I sat there and finished up the rest of the paperwork that we needed to do, then called it quits. Because neither one of us were going to be there that night, I made sure to call both assistant managers into work for the night before we left.

"So, are you still going to throw JaNair her birthday party next week? If not, you need to let me know as soon as possible. There's a couple of people interested in having their parties in the VIP section that night as well." He paused for a minute, then continued. "I was thinking we can just section off half of the room for Jay's party, then we can divide the other half in two parts, so they can have theirs. Just let them each have a twenty-five-guest limit, including themselves. That way, VIP won't be too crowded. Then we can have bottle service standard and make a few extra racks off of that."

Now do you see why I brought him on board? His white ass was always finding ways to make some extra money.

"I'm cool with that. Just as long as the surprises I have lined up for JaNair go on without a hitch, it's all good."

He side eyed me. "Surprises? What kind of surprises?"

"Let's just say that your boy is ready to get his life together and spend the rest of it with JaNair."

"Thanks for watching him on such short notice, Jerome. I really appreciate it."

"Unique . . . I mean Tangie, you don't have to thank me for watching my own son. It's my job too."

"Well, I didn't know if you had plans or anything tonight. And I didn't want to interrupt them if you did."

"Naw, you're good. But if you don't mind me asking, what are you about to get into?"

She kind of hesitated for a minute, then finally spoke, "Me and a few of my homegirls are going out for a little bit. One's having relationship problems, and the other is having family issues."

I nodded my head and followed her to the door to let her out. I had just locked the last lock and was getting ready to go catch up with some sports highlights when I started to really think about what she had just said: *A homegirl having relationship problems and one with family issues.*

Tangie was never one to make friends because a lot of chicks hated on her. They also thought she was really stuck-up based off of her looks when she was far from it. One of the reasons why I was attracted to Tangie when we first met was because of her sweet spirit. Yeah, she'd cut a bitch in a minute, but she also would give you the shirt off her back if she had to.

Going over what she just said in my head again, I hurried up and unlocked the doors and ran outside. I was just in time to see her getting ready to pull out of my driveway. I held up my hands and started to wave them around, hoping to grab her attention. When she finally noticed me, she stopped the car and rolled down her window.

"What's up, Jerome?"

I asked somewhat out of breath, "These homegirls you're talking about, they wouldn't happen to be JaNair and LaLa, would they?" She didn't respond, so I already knew my answer. "Look, Tangie, I know this is hella awkward because it wasn't too long ago that you and I were together, but I was hoping you could put in a good word for me with JaNair. She won't answer my phone calls or anything, and if you can't tell, I'm really torn up about it."

We both were silent for a few moments. I didn't know what she was thinking. I just hoped she'd look out for me this one time.

"I can tell that you're really feeling—"

I cut her off. "Love."

"OK, *love* JaNair, but you gotta give her some time, Jerome. I mean, you did lie—"

I cut her off again. "Didn't admit."

She rolled her eyes. "OK, you *didn't admit* that you had a child already. You need to understand, Jerome, that your whole relationship with JaNair is in question to her now. If you could easily *not admit* to having a son, what else are you not *admitting* to?"

I never looked at it from that point of view. I'd probably question our relationship as well if I found out she had a child she never admitted to either.

"Look, I gotta get going. But I'll make sure to bring you up to see where her head is at now when it comes to y'all's relationship, OK?"

"Thanks, U . . . I mean Tangie." I shook my head. I needed to get used to calling her by her real name. "I know this might be kind of weird because of our past, but I really do appreciate it."

"You're welcome, Jerome, and I'm not tripping about you and JaNair. I realize that what we had wasn't really what I thought it was. We never really got to know each other than sexually. A few months after we met, I ended up pregnant, which caused us to be together out of obligation. I had love confused with lust, and I know the difference now, so we good."

We talked for several more minutes before Tangie left. I rushed back into the house and turned on the heat. Those San Fernando Valley winds were no joke.

I checked in on JJ, then went in search for my cell phone. I wanted to send JaNair my nightly good night and I love you text. When I opened the door to my bedroom, I damn near shitted in my pants at the sight before me.

"What the fuck are you doing here?"

# Semaj

I was in my room packing the rest of the clothes I was taking with me for my stay in Texas. I'd be out there for the next three months or so, so I needed to have at least two suitcases full of clothes and one of shoes.

I couldn't believe that I was finally about to catch a break with this music-producing stuff. The A&R rep I spoke with said that the album I'd be working on should take no longer than a few months, but depending on how well shit started to move, I might be out there longer than that.

When I get out there, I was basically set up for my stay already. The label was providing a three-bedroom, two-bathroom, fully furnished condo, rental car to get around in, and a nice hefty signing bonus that was already sitting in my account. To say a nigga was on cloud nine would be an understatement. I was way higher than that, and I'm not speaking literally.

There was a light tap on my door, followed by my aunt poking her head into my room.

"Hey, J, you almost done in here?"

I stopped folding clothes. "Yeah, I just got a few more things I need to get into my suitcase, Auntie. Why? What's up?"

She came fully into the room and sat down on the edge of my king-sized bed. I could tell she was trying to keep from crying, but I knew that was about to be an epic failure.

"Semaj . . ." She put her head down, but not before I saw a tear roll down her cheek. "Semaj, you know you're my favorite nephew and I love you as if you were my own. I just want you to know that I am so proud of the man you've become and are becoming. From taking care of your responsibilities and being a great father for Ta'Jae to getting your degree and going on to do what you love with this music thing . . . I just want you to know that on behalf of your father, *God bless his soul,* and your triflin'-ass mama, *wherever she may be,* that it was my complete honor to be given the task to raise you. I hope and pray that you go on down there to Texas and knock 'em dead." She laughed. "I want a couple of them Oscars on my mantle above the fireplace."

"You mean Grammy's, Auntie?"

"Grammy, Oscar, a Steve Harvey Hoodie Award . . . Whatever it is, I just want one, gotdamn it."

I smiled and walked over to my aunt Shirley and gave her the biggest hug.

"Thank you so much for taking me in and being there for me when my own parents didn't want to," I said into her ear.

"You're welcome, baby, and make sure you go talk to that little girl next door before you leave." She pulled back from our embrace and looked me in the face. "I know she's still a little confused with things, but don't leave without telling her *good-bye* or *you'll see her soon.*" She raised her eyebrow up as if she was making sure I understood the difference between the two.

I nodded my head and went back to taking care of my to-do list. My aunt and I talked and joked around for a few more minutes before she gave me another hug and left to go fix lunch.

I looked down at my phone on the dresser and thought about calling JaNair, but figured a face-to-face would be better. Although we've seen each other and talked on the phone since the day me, her, and Ta'Jae fell asleep together, I still haven't told her about my trip. Honestly, I was hoping she would go with me. She'd be out of school for the semester, and this would be a great way to celebrate her birthday coming up.

I placed the last pair of shoes I wanted to take with me in the suitcase, then zipped it up. After moving all three of these heavy bags into the living room, I headed out of the door and across the fence to go see JaNair.

Ringing the doorbell for the third time without an answer, I was starting to become pissed. I knew she was here because her car was. Then again, I do remember her mentioning that she, Tangie, and LaLa were going to go shopping for her birthday outfit. Maybe she rode with one of them. I was just turning around to leave from her house when I noticed the blinds to the side window were open. I don't know why, but something was bugging me to go over and look inside.

My dick instantly got hard when I saw JaNair lying stomach down on the couch. The little dress she had on was raised up a little bit above her hips, causing you to get a real good view of that ass. She had on some purple silk panties that may have been a size too small because they weren't covering any of that extra booty meat she had.

"JaNair!" I yelled as I knocked on the window. Her ass must've been sleeping really good because she didn't move at all.

"JaNair!" I yelled again, this time knocking on the window a little harder. She started to stir a little bit, then finally shot up like a rocket when she realized someone was beating on the window.

"Semaj?" she asked, wiping the sleep from her eyes. Even with her hair all over the place and the dried-up drool on the side of her face, JaNair still was sexy as fuck to me.

"Open the door, Jay, we need to talk."

She stared at me for a minute, then motioned with her head for me to walk back over to the front entrance of her home. Once the wooden door was opened, that intoxicating smell of peaches wafted in the air.

After yawning and stretching, she spoke. "Hey, Semaj, what's up?"

I didn't even wait for her to invite me in. I just brushed past her, sat on the couch, and went right in on what we needed to talk about.

"Look, Jay, I came over here to tell you that I'm leaving for Texas tomorrow, and I'm gonna be gone for the next three months. I tried to tell you a few times before, but something else always came up."

She just stood there and stared at me. I couldn't tell how she was feeling because there was a blank expression on her face.

I continued anyway. "I got a call a couple of weeks ago from Rap-A-Lot Records, and they want me to come out there and produce that nigga Kirko Bangz's new album."

Still silence. I wanted her to say something—anything—to let me know she didn't want me to go, or that she'd miss me, but there was nothing.

I stood up, finally tired of this back-and-forth shit with her. If she didn't know what she wanted to do or how she felt, I'd just make that decision easier for her. "Well, since you don't have any questions or anything to say, I'll just be on my way. I just wanted to come by and say . . . I'll . . . good . . ." I put my head down and just shook it. "I just wanted to say see ya around."

I couldn't bring myself to say good-bye or see you later like my aunt told me. The thing was, I didn't know what I wanted to do when it came to JaNair.

I was halfway out of the door when I heard what sounded like sniffles. I froze my stride and just stood there. Was she crying?

When I heard the sound again, I turned around and found JaNair with her shoulders hunched over, head down, and hands covering her face.

"Jay, what's wrong? What's the matter?"

Again silence.

"Jay . . ."

"You know, I never answered your question that day I came to your room," I heard her say just above a whisper.

I stood there not knowing what to do or what to say. It was now my turn to be mute and give her the silent treatment. That, and I hadn't the slightest idea of what she was talking about.

She finally looked up at me with a tear-streaked face, and although her eyes were puffy and red, those cocoa-brown irises did it to me every time. I wanted to just grab her and hold her in my arms while wiping her tears away, but before I did that, I needed to hear what she had to say. She licked her pouty lips and tucked the bottom one into her mouth. God, she was trying to kill me right now. The simplest things

JaNair did turned me on like crazy. However, my patience was starting to wear thin, and I think she realized that, because a few seconds later, she started to speak again.

"I'm talking about the last time I was in your room, Semaj. You asked me if I was really sorry for kissing you, knowing that I was still in a relationship with Jerome."

I nodded my head. I remember what she was talking about now. She had my dick hard as hell that day too. I didn't know where this trip down memory lane was going, but she had my attention.

"OK! Sooo . . . some weeks later, you're ready to give me an answer?"

Ignoring my sarcastic response, she walked up to me, stood on her tippy toes, and pulled my head down to hers.

"Yes, I do have an answer." She looked me in the eyes. "I wasn't sorry then, and I'm damn sure not sorry now," she said as she placed her soft lips to mine.

# JaNair

*"Please don't reject me. Please don't reject me"* was all I kept saying as I slipped my tongue into Semaj's mouth. I don't know what came over me, but the need to feel his lips against mine took over. Maybe it was what he just said about leaving for Texas, or maybe it was the conversation LaLa, Tangie, and I had last night. It was so funny how one was all for Team Jerome, and the other was all about Team Semaj. Listening to their pros and cons on both men was kind of weird, especially with Tangie rooting for her baby daddy. However, at this moment, LaLa's favorite was winning. Whatever it was that we were doing felt so right.

I deepened the kiss, and he didn't resist. When he pulled my bottom lip in between his and started to suck on it the same way I remember him sucking on my clit, I totally lost my mind. Any thoughts of rejection that were floating through my head were easily pushed to the side.

I wrapped my arms around his neck, and he pulled me closer into his body. The sexiest moan escaped from his throat, and I could feel the wetness that soaked my panties starting to slide down my thigh.

"Are you sure you're ready to go there with me, Jay?" he asked between kisses. "Because once we get started, I'm not going to want to stop."

Not even entertaining the thought of stopping, I took his hand, laced it with mine, and walked him to my bedroom. As soon as I closed the door, he turned me around and gently pushed me up against the wall. I stared into his cocoa-colored eyes for a few seconds before I started to trace the outline of his facial features with my fingers. When I rested my open palm on the side of his face, he closed his eyes.

Semaj was indeed one of the most gorgeous men I've ever seen. His full lips were soft and inviting. His brown skin was smooth to the touch. The way he flexed that strong jawline whenever I touched him was sexy as fuck. My eyes traveled to his freshly twisted dreads which were pulled to the back of his head in a low ponytail. Not liking the fact that he had his locks tied down, I snatched the thin band off.

He opened his eyes and spoke in a low, husky voice. "What I tell you about pulling on my shit like that, JaNair?"

Looking into his hooded eyes, I didn't even answer. I just took another two handfuls of dreads and yanked those muthafuckas hard as hell.

I don't remember how or when it happened, but the white gown I had on was on the floor, my purple silk panties were ripped off, and my body was being turned upside down and hoisted into the air. We were now in the sixty-nine position but standing up. I could feel all the blood from my body rushing to my head. I started to tell Semaj to put me down, but when he blew on my pussy, then used his cool tongue to part my slick folds, I damn near fainted.

I could feel his legs start to move as he kept devouring my shit. Wherever he was taking me, he needed to hurry up and get there because I didn't know how much longer I could take being in this position and coming back-to-back. The first time I came, my head started to spin, so I knew that if I came again, I'd more than likely pass out.

When we got to what I guess was my bed, he stopped his deadly assault on my clit and laid me down. I watched as he undressed down to his boxer briefs and lay down in the bed next to me. He pressed his fingertip to my lip, and I opened my mouth and took it in. I sucked and twirled my tongue around his thick digit for a minute before he took it out and trailed a path down my body. Starting at my neck, he passed between my titties, circled my stomach, and stopped at the top of my pussy. He slid a finger inside of me and let my juices coat it real good before he took it out and put it in his mouth.

"Do you know that you taste and smell like peaches?" I shook my head. "Well, you do, and for the life of me, I can't get enough of it."

I didn't know what to say, so I just bit my bottom lip and nodded my head. I also made a mental note to visit Bath & Body Works to stock up on my Peach Bellini smell good since he liked the scent so much.

My phone which was on the nightstand started to go off. I knew by the ringtone who was calling, and for a small second, I started to feel bad about what I was doing. But then again, if memory serves me right, we weren't together right now anyway.

"Do you need to get that?" Semaj asked as he sat up on the bed.

I contemplated on that question for a minute, then shook my head. I reached out my hand for him to pass my phone to me. Just as he placed it into my palm, it started to go off again with the same ringtone. I quickly declined the call and turned my phone completely off.

"I don't think you're ready for this to happen, JaNair," Semaj said, blowing out a breath and wiping his hand down his face.

"I . . . I . . . I am ready." *What the hell?* Why was I stammering over my words?

He shook his head. "The way that you just said that lets me know that you're not."

"But I am, Semaj." *I think.*

"Then prove it and come with me."

Did he just ask me to—?

"Come with me to Texas and stay out there with me for the three months."

Wow! I was really speechless now. If he would've said a week or two, I would've been all for it. But *three* months? That would be a long-ass time for me to be away from my home and in a state that I didn't know anyone or anything about. Plus, I still had some unresolved issues with Jerome.

Yeah, I was really acting out of character with almost taking it there with Semaj, but that didn't mean that my feelings for Jerome weren't still there. And I would hate to lead Semaj on when I know I wouldn't be able to give him all of me right now.

I didn't want to say no, and I didn't want to say yes, so I did the next best thing, which was come up with excuses.

"I . . . I . . . I don't know, Semaj, what about school?"

"You can do some online courses, and there's always Texas A&M."

"What about a place to live? I don't want to invade your space."

"I'ma have more than enough room for both of us in the three-bedroom condo the label is providing for me."

*Shit.* He had an answer for everything. I was still on the fence on what I wanted to do, so I kept on going.

"Well, you know I'm on a budget since Mya doesn't live here anymore and I don't have any extra money to just be spending all willy-nilly. Plus I wouldn't feel right if you would have to pay for everything."

He stood up and started to put his clothes back on. "Why not, JaNair? I won't have a problem with taking care of you mentally, physically, or financially. And if you're really worried about money, I'm pretty sure I could pull a few strings with the label to put you somewhere. I mean, you already have a degree in business management, and you're going for your MBA, so it shouldn't be hard."

I smiled at him. He really had this all figured out. Yet and still, I wasn't sure whether I wanted to go. I was so caught up in the war that I had going on in my head that I never noticed that Semaj was now fully dressed. "You got the answer to everything, huh?" I teased.

"Only when it comes to something I want." He reached out his hand and pulled me up out of the bed. My naked body was still going through withdrawal of not having his tongue or touch on me. "So are you going to come with me and see how these country folks get down?" he asked as he pulled me into his embrace.

I know that this was probably the wrong answer and would probably be the worst choice I've ever made in my life, but right now, my mind was clouded with who and what I really wanted. Jerome was wrong for not telling me about his son, but was that little lie so unforgivable? God, I didn't know what I wanted to do. And the fact that I was so undecided helped me to make up my mind.

"Semaj, I would love to come out to Texas and kick it with you, but three months is too long for me. Maybe when you come back we can go out and celebrate all that new money you're going to be making once the world hears your music."

He let his arms fall from my waist and stepped back from out of my space. With me being naked, I felt as if he was staring through my soul with the way he was looking at me, so I grabbed the sheet from off of my bed and wrapped it around my body. We stood there and stared at each other for a moment before he turned around and headed for the door.

"Semaj, wait!" I screamed running behind him. He was walking so fast I didn't think I'd catch him before he reached the door. The sheet I was trying to hold up was so big around my body that I kept tripping with every step I took.

Before he left my house, he stopped and turned around to face me.

"We're good, JaNair, so don't trip about anything. I thought you wanted the same thing I did, and that's why I invited you to come out there with me, but obviously, I was wrong. I guess I'll see you when I get back. And if I don't get the chance to call you on your birthday, Happy Birthday! Good-bye."

And with that, he left my home and possibly left my life for good.

# Jerome

So much stuff has happened in the last week that I didn't know whether I was coming or going. First things first, JaNair finally started to accept my calls. We even went out to lunch and dinner a couple of times. I explained to her why I didn't tell her about JJ and apologized for not keep it real from the jump. I even answered any questions she had regarding Tangie's and my relationship. Although it was strictly coparenting now, I told her about the couple of times she and I did have sex in the beginning stages of our relationship. I thought that when I told her that, she'd jump up and walk out of the restaurant, but to my surprise, she stayed.

I did feel kind of bad when she asked me if I had sex with anyone else, and I said no. That would've been the perfect time to be honest, especially since we were starting over in a way. I knew that thing with LaLa wouldn't be a problem, only because I knew and felt in my heart that the baby wasn't going to be mine. Plus, LaLa was in the same boat as me. She didn't want to lose JaNair, so she'd be taking that secret about us to the grave. On the other hand, that bitch Mya was going to be a problem, and I needed to do something about her ass as soon as possible. I thought about calling in a favor and having her disappear, but I didn't want to spend the rest of my life in jail if it ever came to the light that I was behind it. I even thought about calling a couple of my ratchet female cousins who lived in South Central. I knew for a few dollars, they'd beat the hell out of her ass. But again, if the police ever caught up with them, I knew they'd dime me out for real.

Since I couldn't come up with any other alternatives on my own, I guess the one Mya presented to me would have to work for right now. When I walked into my room that night after Tangie dropped my son off, it was Mya's crazy ass that was in my bed. I'm not gonna lie, her lying there naked had my dick hard as fuck, but I couldn't take it there with her loony ass anymore. If she got into my house undetected, ain't no telling what else she could—and would—do. That conversation we had started to play in my head as I sat at my desk ignoring whatever my head of security for the club was saying.

*"What the fuck are you doing here?"*

*"Now, Jerome, you know you miss me just as much as I miss you. C'mon over here and let me take care of you real quick."* She licked her lips, then started to play with her titties.

*"Mya . . ."* I had a hard time concentrating. *My dick head was telling me to get on the bed and put him in her mouth while the head on my shoulders was telling me to get her the fuck out of my house. Thankfully, the right head prevailed.* "Look, Mya, you gotta go. I told you already that what we did was a mistake, and it will never happen again. I love and want to be with your cousin, so whatever this little infatuation is that you have with me, you need to get over it."

*She stopped pleasing herself and looked up at me.* "Whatever this is that we have between us will never stop, Jerome. Not unless you want JaNair to know all of your little secrets. And I'm pretty sure once she finds out you and her little nurse friend got something going on too, she's really not going to want your ass. But I will."

*I shook my head. This bitch was crazier and loonier than I thought.* "First off, JaNair already knows what's going on between Tangie and me. She's the mother of my son, even though that's none of your business. Second, I ain't got shit to worry about with LaLa, because you and I both know she'll never tell her what happened, even if her baby turns out to be mine."

*"So that only leaves me, right?"* she asked as she got up on her knees and started crawling toward me.

*"Yes, that only leaves you. But if you know what's best for you, you'll keep your mouth shut too."*

*She looked at me and smirked.* "Is that a threat, Jerome? If it is, there's no need for any of that. And to keep it real, I was hoping that we could come to a little agreement."

*Against my better judgment, I asked, "What type of agreement?"*

*She licked her lips again as she got up from my bed and pushed me against the wall. "I was thinking that I'd happily keep my mouth shut if you let me have some of this bomb-ass dick whenever I called for some."*

*As tempting as her offer was, I couldn't do it. Knowing Mya, she'd call every hour on the hour trying to get fucked, and I couldn't risk it. I told her my thoughts, and she backed up and sat back on the bed. She started to pick up the clothes she'd taken off and put them back on.*

*A sudden gush of relief flowed through my body. Was she actually going to just keep her mouth shut and leave JaNair and me alone? All the great thoughts swarming around in my head came crashing down when she said what I had to have her repeat. My ears must've been deceiving me right now. I know she didn't just say what I thought she said.*

*"What did you just say?"*

*"I said since you're not willing to fuck me for my silence, you will have to pay me instead."*

*Yep, that's what I thought she said.*

*"I don't have the money to pay you to keep your mouth shut. Are you crazy?"*

*She picked up her jacket and put it on, then grabbed her purse. Before she left my bedroom, she turned around.*

*"The fact that you would sit here and tell me that bold-faced lie just doubled the amount of what I want. Let me put you in on a little secret, my dear Jerome. The next time you have someone bent over your desk fucking the shit out of them, make sure you put up all of your business financial papers. You tend to learn just what kind of money people's business make when you don't." She turned around and started walking out. "I'll be in touch about that first payment" was all I heard as she closed my front door.*

"Mr. Hayes! Mr. Hayes! Are you all right?" I heard Roc ask, bringing me back from my thoughts.

"Ah, yeah. I'm good. I'm good." I shook my head and got back to boss mode. "So, you said that everything for the party is set up? Everything is delivered, and the decorator and her crew will be here a few hours before to set up, right?"

He nodded his head, then went over what bouncers and security guards were going to be working that night. After going over instructions for VIP and entrance fees, Roc finally got up and left.

I took my phone out of my pocket and sent JaNair a few text messages, letting her know that I was thinking about her and that I had a few surprises set up for her when I got to her house tonight. She responded and also asked me to pick up some food from her favorite Chinese spot before I got there.

There was a light knock on my door.

"Come in!" I yelled. I had the music from my computer's speakers playing kind of loud, so I hope whoever it was heard me.

"What's good, my dude?"

"Hey, G. What's up with you? When you get back in town?"

"Man, I got back a few hours ago. I just dropped Daya off at her mother's house down the street, so when I rolled past and saw your car, I decided to stop by. Where's Toby?"

"Shit, somewhere with Niecey. She got that white dude's nose wide open, and he hasn't even sampled the goods yet," I laughed.

"Well, he's getting older. Not everything has to be about sex. Daya and I didn't do it until two months after we started talking. Seems like you really get to know a person when there's no sex involved."

I just agreed and continued to look at the business bank statements in front of me. Both Toby and I were on the account, and I didn't know how I was going to be able to take sums of money from it without him noticing.

Yeah, I know. I should just come clean with JaNair and not pay Mya a dime, right? But I couldn't do that right now. Especially with what I planned on asking her tonight.

"So, I heard you and Toby went to his family jeweler yesterday. Is there any particular reason why?"

I wanted to slap that cheesy grin off of his face. But since he was my boy, I figured I'd let him in on my little secret.

"Yeah, I picked out a nice little ring. I think I'ma ask JaNair to marry me tomorrow night at her birthday party."

He looked at me for a moment. "Are you sure this is what you want to do, man? I mean, did you ever tell her what happened between you and her cousin?"

"Naw, I haven't. But I'm good on that end, though. She won't be saying anything anytime soon, I'm sure of that."

I debated on whether to tell him about the little blackmailing thing Mya hit me with, but thought against it. He and Toby gossiped just like females, and I couldn't chance him finding out yet.

"Man, you crazy if you think that girl isn't going to drop that bomb, especially if you said she's been stalking you like she has. What do you think is going to happen once JaNair knows?"

"G, you know my motto: It's not what you know, it's what you can prove. And since there is no proof of what went down between Mya and me, I'll just do what any man does in that situation . . . deny it until I die."

I know I was talking big shit, especially with me giving in to Mya's blackmailing plan. Honestly, I didn't know if she had proof or not, but knowing how she operates, I'm pretty sure she had something she'd be able to show JaNair, and I couldn't chance that.

I gathered up everything I needed for the night and finally left my office about twenty minutes after Gerald did. I had a few stops to make, before I went home to my baby. I really hope everything tomorrow night goes off without a hitch, and to make sure that happened, I'd be dropping off this first payment to Mya before I go shopping for the rest of JaNair's gifts.

# JaNair

The night of my twenty-sixth birthday party had finally arrived, but for some reason, I didn't feel like partying at all.

It's been a couple weeks since I last talked to Semaj, and I'd be lying if I said I didn't feel some type of way about that. I don't know if he's just been that busy out there in Texas or if he was just straight ignoring me.

When I ran into Li'l Ray a week ago and asked about Semaj, he told me that he was doing great and that he probably hasn't been able to answer any of my calls because he's been in the studio nonstop.

If I were anybody else, I probably would've believed that bold-faced lie, but since I'm not, I needed answers.

I picked up my cell phone and called Semaj again for the 1,000th time, and just like all the other 999 times before, my call went unanswered. I thought about leaving another voice mail, but that thought was immediately dismissed when the little automated lady announced that his mailbox was full.

I don't know what it was, but ever since that day before he left, it felt as if there was a change in our relationship. And I don't mean change in a bad way. It was as if we grew closer than we already were. Like our minds, bodies, hearts, and souls connected on a level that I've never felt before. Whatever it was, I had to get over it, especially since Jerome and I have been trying to work on our relationship.

I looked at myself in my bathroom mirror and couldn't deny how good I was looking.

A small smile crossed my face as I admired how the gold crystal-beaded Lorena Sarbu dress fit every curve of my body. The neckline slit and illusion waist detail gave the right amount of sassiness that I loved.

*Jerome really outdid himself,* I thought as I looked at myself again.

When I woke up this morning, there was a mountain of gifts piled up on my side of the bed. Boxes after boxes after boxes. I didn't know where to start. After opening up everything, I added eight dresses, ten pair of shoes, four beautiful purses, and a diamond necklace with matching earrings and bracelet to my wardrobe.

"You almost rea—Damn, JaNair. You look . . . beautiful," Jerome said walking into the bathroom.

"Thanks, babe," I replied, snapping my new bracelet around my wrist.

"Here, let me do that." Jerome took the matching necklace out of my hand and stood behind me. He placed it around the front of my neck and kissed my shoulder.

"Don't even try it, buddy. We're already thirty minutes late," I told him as I slipped from his embrace. I already knew what was on his mind, and I was not trying to go there. We hadn't had sex since we started back talking. I wanted to take things a little slower this time around.

*Ding dong.*

We both looked toward the hallway as the doorbell rang again.

"Who could that be?" Jerome asked, looking at his watch. "The limo driver said he was on his way from picking up Toby, Niecey, LaLa, and Li'l Ray only two minutes ago. I know he's not here that fast."

"Maybe it's Tangie. She said if she was able to get off of work early enough she'd come. I'll be right back. Let me go see who it is."

The bell rang one more time before I finally made it to the door.

"Hey, Ms. Shirley, how can I help you?" I asked a little surprised. I wasn't expecting her to be at the door.

"Hey, baby! Happy Birthday! You look beautiful."

"Thank you."

"You're welcome. And I'm sorry for interrupting you and all, but I just came by to drop off your gift."

I was taken aback. "Oh, Ms. Shirley, you didn't have to get me anything."

"Chile, I didn't!" she laughed. "My hardheaded nephew did. He had it sent to the house today and told me to bring it on over to you."

Now I was really shocked, let alone confused. Semaj hasn't answered any of my calls in weeks, yet he remembers my birthday and sends me a gift. I was literally speechless.

"Is everything OK, Jay?" I heard Jerome ask from behind me. "Yeah, everything is fine. It's just my next-door neighbor Ms. Shirley. She came to wish me a Happy Birthday."

"Oh, that's nice," he said going back into the room.

I turned my attention back to Ms. Shirley.

"I don't want to keep you any longer, sweetie, so here you go." She handed me a purple envelope that had my name written beautifully on the front.

"How is he?" I asked about Semaj. She looked past my shoulder, then back to me.

"You haven't talked to him?"

I don't know why her question had me wanting to break down and cry. For some reason, I just got all emotional about not being able to get ahold of Semaj for the last few weeks. I was so used to our daily talks and smoking and kicking it sessions that I was starting to really miss him being around.

I started to fan my face to stop the tears from coming. "No, I haven't. He won't answer or return any of my calls, and it's driving me crazy."

She looked at me for a moment before she smacked her lips and put her hand on her hip. "Can you blame him?"

*Wait! What?*

"Don't give me that look. You heard what I said." I was speechless yet again. "You young people are something else."

"I don't understand what you're saying."

She looked at me and shook her head. "Baby, I've seen you and my nephew around each other plenty of times, and it doesn't take a rocket scientist to see that you both have feelings for each other. You hurt not only his ego but his pride and heart as well that day you declined his offer. And before you even fix your mouth to say something, I know about everything that happened that day. Semaj talks to me about *everything*. He came back to the house that day so angry, I let him do something in my house that I never let him do. Smoke that weed shit y'all be puffing on. It was the only way I could get him to calm down and not turn down this great opportunity that was given to him."

"What do you mean, Ms. Shirley?" I kind of had an idea, but I wanted her to say the words.

"That boy was going to stay here and not go to Texas if that would've helped you see how much he's into you. After going back and forth with him for a couple of hours, I finally convinced him that it was probably time for him to let you go and see what God had in store for him. I didn't know it for sure, but now that I've seen that young man here getting ready to help you celebrate your birthday instead of my nephew, it's safe to say that you guys are back to being an item, right?"

I don't know why I hesitated at first, but I slowly nodded my head.

"So *now* do you see why I asked if you could blame Semaj for leaving and not having any contact with you right now?"

As gut punching as her words sounded, they were indeed the truth. I was wrong for leading Semaj on, knowing that I was still toying with the thought of giving Jerome another chance.

The loud sound of a low engine rumbling and laughter caught my attention. When I looked up, the limo with the rest of our party had finally made it. Jerome, who I didn't even notice was behind me, slipped my coat over my shoulders and handed me the gold clutch I'd already put all my things into, and the gold five-inch filigree leaves Giuseppe Zanotti heels I'd purchased for myself as an early birthday gift.

"Ms. Shirley, as you can see, our ride has arrived. If you're not doing anything tonight, you're welcome to come to my party," I said as we stepped out of my house and locked the doors.

She chuckled. "Maybe next time, honey. I have a date with my homemade peach cobbler and a few shows on HBO. You all have a great time, though. Be safe, OK?"

"We will. And thank you so much for the gift."

We waved good-bye once more and climbed into the limo. Li'l Ray looked down at the purple envelope that was still in my hand and smiled while nodding his head. LaLa, who was always so observant, saw what Ray did and was just about to say something, but Jerome beat her to it.

"So what did she get you?" he said, pointing to my gift.

I shrugged my shoulders. "I don't know. More than likely it's a few gift certificates to a spa or something of that nature. It doesn't feel like there's money in here, and it's light, so that can only mean some form or paper."

"Open it up and let's see what it is," LaLa exclaimed.

I heard Niecey smack her lips, then started to say something, but Toby squeezed her hand a little tighter and whispered something into her ear that made her blush. I was so glad that he did it too. I made Niecey and LaLa promise to not fuck up my party with their arguing back and forth. Real talk, I'm kind of surprised Niecey even said yes to riding in the limo with us. At first, it was only Li'l Ray and LaLa, but then Jerome wanted his boys to ride with us too. Gerald, of course, declined and said that he and his girlfriend would just meet us there. Toby, on the other hand, thought it would be better to be chauffeured around so he could get drunk. I don't know what it was with white people and loving to get drunk.

The fellas started going over the latest sports highlights while Niecey and LaLa sat in the own worlds trying their best to ignore each other. While everyone was doing their things, I slipped the envelope into my clutch and took my phone out. I scrolled down to Semaj's name and sent a text.

J2: Your aunt stopped by and gave me my gift. Haven't looked at it yet . . . but thank you!

I held my phone in my hand for the rest of our ride. By the time we arrived at the Lotus Bomb, I still hadn't received a response from Semaj. Instead of letting the hurt I was feeling at that moment show, I threw my phone back into my clutch, grabbed Jerome's hand, and strutted into my party like I owned the place.

# Mya

I walked into the Lotus Bomb and was in complete awe. Whoever decorated this place did an amazing job. If I'd never been to a Las Vegas casino before, I would've sworn we were really in one. There were blackjack and roulette tables spread throughout the place. A section of slot machines lined the back of the lounge. Red, gold, black, and green balloons completely covered the ceiling. Even the waitresses wore those feather outfits the show girls would wear. The table dealers were all dressed the same and looked the part. Jerome really outdid himself with this. And to think, the nigga was mad at the measly two grand I asked him for. Shit, he better be lucky I only asked him for that.

I grabbed a flute of champagne off of the tray the waitress who just walked in front of me had. I don't know why, but my insides started to boil as I looked at all of the pictures of JaNair that were plastered around the walls. I noticed that the playing cards they were using had JaNair's picture on the back as well.

"Well well well. Who do we have here?" came from behind me. I instantly froze, and a chill went down my body. I wasn't scared of who it was, just more so caught off guard. I wasn't expecting to run into him anytime soon, especially not at JaNair's birthday party.

"Baby, you're not going to introduce me to your friend," a female voice said as I turned around.

Looking at the way Ryan held her in his arms and kissed her on the forehead kind of had me in my feelings. He never showed that type of public display of affection with me.

I looked his little date up and down. She was cute in a Ciara sort of way. If there was a contest for a celebrity look-alike, she'd win hands down. If Ryan and I were still fucking around, and this was back in the day, I woulda had fun sampling her goodies. I laughed at that little joke in my head and extended my hand out to her.

"Hi, I'm Mya, and you are?"

"Genelle, but everyone calls me Nelly."

*But everyone calls me Nelly,* I mocked in my head. I was a little salty. Shit, even the way she talked was sexy. No wonder Ryan fell for her.

"So how do you and Ryan know each other?" she asked, looking between us.

Ryan answered. "Well, Mya here is cousins with my ex-girl-friend JaNair, who happens to be the birthday girl."

She looked at me for confirmation, so I nodded my head, but added, "He forgot to mention that we also started fucking while he and the birthday girl were together." I put my finger on my chin and looked up to the sky as if I was thinking. "If memory serves me right, we'd still be fucking if I wouldn't have called you by another nigga's name, correct?"

The steam that was blowing from his ears had me hot for a minute. I smiled, then waved good-bye to a very pissed off Ryan and a shocked-face Nelly. I'm pretty sure I just signed my death certificate fucking with Ryan like that, but I didn't give a rat's ass. Besides, I was on to bigger and better things anyway.

And speaking of bigger and better, a smile spread across my face as I watched Jerome walk into the door. He gave dap to a few of his security guards and kissed the cheeks of a few of his waitresses. He was just about to walk past me when I heard JaNair yell his name for him to come back. I watched with envy as they stood together as a couple and took pictures, then switched to a group once Niecey, Channing Tatum Sr., Li'l Ray, and LaLa joined in.

I had to give it to her, though, JaNair looked good. That gold dress went great with those—wait . . . Are those Giuseppe Zanottis? I took my phone out and went to the Giuseppe IG page, and sure enough, they were. Those were the same exact shoes I've been trying to get Cassan's tired ass to buy me, but he said no. With the two grand Jerome gave me, I could've bought them myself, but then I would have been left with only fifty dollars to my name. Her hair was up in a donut bun with some Chinese bangs covering her forehead.

*That should be me,* I said to myself as I watched them walk to VIP. I caught eye contact with Niecey, and she had the nerve to roll her eyes. I don't know what her beef was with me. It wasn't like I fucked Big Will and got pregnant. I'm surprised she and LaLa were playing nice too. The last time we were all together, I could tell it would be a minute before they were ever in the same place again.

I watched as Jerome introduced JaNair to a few people in VIP, then order a round of drinks. For some reason, JaNair kept taking her phone out of her purse and checking it. I guess she was waiting for a call or something. From whom was the question I wanted to know. I mean, her man and her friends were all around her. Everybody was laughing, dancing, and having a good time. Who could she possibly be waiting to get a call from?

On my way to the ladies' room, I ran into the little waitress bitch who helped me get Jerome's new number.

"Hey, Mya, what are you doing here?"

"Trying to have a good time and celebrate my cousin's birthday," I responded dryly.

"Your cousin? Who's your cousin?"

I looked at this girl, and for the first time, I realized why it was easy for me to get her to get Jerome's new number. She was dumb as hell. A black airhead.

"My cousin is JaNair."

"Oh, Mr. Hayes's girlfriend, or should I say, *fiancée*, if she says yes."

"Fiancée? They're not engaged."

"Not yet they're not. Once I take this birthday cake up there to VIP and they sing happy birthday, he's going to pop the question." She jumped up and down, squealing like she was the one getting proposed to.

My mind started to work overtime. Fiancée? What the hell. This could not be happening. This was *not* going to happen. I needed to come up with something quick and fast. I knew that the blackmailing thing was only going to go so far, but I was hoping that either he got tired of paying me and gave into fucking me instead or just told JaNair the truth and once she dumped him for good, he'd finally come running to me.

    I talked to ol' girl for a few more moments, trying to get as much information as I could. After coming up with nothing but what she had already told me, I went to the bathroom, handled my business, and thought of a plan.

# JaNair

I looked out into the crowd and scanned the many faces that were in attendance. Some I knew, some I've seen before, and some I wouldn't remember two days from now.

Once again, Jerome outdid himself with this whole birthday celebration. First, it was the mountain of gifts, and now the Las Vegas-style party I said I wanted awhile ago.

I turned around and looked at everyone sitting in my VIP section. With two other parties going on in the area, we still had enough room to have fifty more people come up here.

I looked at Li'l Ray and LaLa in the corner having a heated conversation about all the greasy food she'd been scarfing down since we got here. I laughed at how protective he was about her and the type of foods she was feeding their baby. Toby and Niecey were on the dance floor, and surprisingly, he was grooving and swaying his hips perfectly to the beat. Who would've thought a white boy could be so smooth? I could tell by the way he looked at her the whole time that they were dancing that he had some type of feelings for her. Niecey's face seemed to be glowing as well. She looked happy. Way happier than I ever seen her whenever Big Will was around.

My attention turned to Jerome who was talking to Gerald and his date. At first, I thought it was going to be kind of awkward, being that Gerald and LaLa hung out before, and they were both here with new people, but like Jerome explained, they weren't meant to be, and both of them understood that.

"Hey, Jay, I just wanted to come up here and wish you a Happy Birthday. This is my friend Genelle. Genelle, this is the birthday girl JaNair," Ryan said as he introduced me to the Ciara look-alike standing next to him.

"Thank you, Ryan, and it's nice to meet you, Genelle." She shook my hand but didn't say anything. The vibe that I was getting from her felt kind of weird, like she wanted to say something to me, but Ryan told her not to.

"Um, I hope you don't feel uncomfortable being here. Ryan and I haven't dated for a while, and we're simply just friends. His cousin and I are best friends, and since we still see each other sometimes because of her, I invited him."

She shook her head. "No, it's nothing to do with that. I know you are in a relationship with that fine-ass brother right there." She pointed at Jerome, who happened to look up at that moment and smile. "Whew, that man is gorgeous." Ryan cut his eyes at her and started to pull her away, but not before she left without a few more parting words. "If I were you, girl, I'd watch my man around all this trifling females . . . even family."

I scrunched my perfectly arched eyebrows as I watched her and Ryan walk out of the VIP arguing. That shit was hella weird, but I got over it.

I went and grabbed my purse and pulled my phone out. Semaj's ass still hadn't texted me back. Since we got here, I'd texted him again, thanking him again for the gift that he sent me. I was overexcited when I opened it up while I was in the bathroom and saw what it was.

"Happy Birthday, cousin," broke me from my thoughts. As much as I didn't care too much for Mya right now, I was glad to know that she came after I extended the invite and was doing OK.

"Thank you, Mya. You look nice tonight." I wasn't lying. She did. The two-piece red crop top and pencil skirt looked good on her. She had on some black pumps, and her hair was in a slick ponytail going to the back.

"Thank you, thank you. You look good yourself. Then again, you should since you're the birthday girl, right?" I nodded my head, not sure if I should take that as a compliment. "What are you drinking? Your next drink is on me."

"Oh no, you're good. Jerome paid for bottle service for the whole night, so I don't need anything else to drink. But check you out, offering to buy *me* a drink," I said joking around.

"Is that all you think I can buy you? Because if it is, you're sadly mistaken. I can buy you a bottle just like Jerome," she said with a smirk on her face.

I didn't know what that was all about, and I never got the chance to ask, because as soon as I opened my mouth, four waitresses walked into VIP holding a big-ass cake, with what looked like a 100 sparklers on it.

*"Happy Birthday to you, Happy Birthday to you, Happy Birthday dear JaNair (BFF, Bae, Baby Mama), Happy Birthday to you."*

I looked at Toby's crazy ass and shook my fist at him. I don't know when and or why he started calling me his baby mama, but if Jerome didn't get mad at it, neither did I.

I had just blown out all of the sparklers on my cake when Jerome took my hand and got down on one knee. My throat became dry as hell, and my heartbeat started to speed up. I looked around the small circle that seemed to unknowingly form around us.

LaLa, Niecey, Toby, and even Tangie who had just gotten there had smiles on their faces. The only person who wasn't wearing one was Mya. She didn't even try to disguise the smug look on her face when we locked eyes.

At that precise moment, the last few months begin to flash through my mind. In each thought that seemed to replay, the way Mya's ass would twist her face whenever Jerome and I were together started to stand out more and more. It was either that or she'd say something slick at the mouth that usually included Semaj's name somewhere in the mix.

I looked at her again, and it was obvious that she had some things she wanted to get off of her chest. So me being the caring cousin that I am, I just had to find out. Yeah, I was about to ask her in the middle of Jerome's proposal, and low key, I probably could've waited until he was finished. But at this point, I really didn't give a fuck.

"JaNair Simone Livingston, will—" was all Jerome got to say before I cut him off.

"Aye, Mya, what the fuck is your problem?" All eyes turned to her.

"What do you mean, JaNair? I'm standing here watching your man try to propose to you like everyone else." She looked around the crowd, then back at me. When her eyes traveled over to Jerome, he looked at her with a scowl on his face, then quickly turned his head. I took note of that little interaction, then turned my attention back to her. Something was definitely up with this bitch, and I was about to find out what.

I walked up to her with my hand on my hip and invaded all of her personal space.

"I wanna know what the fuck is your problem? I'm looking around at everybody's face, and I see nothing but smiles. However, when I look at yours, all I see is animosity. Are you angry about something, Mya?"

"She's jealous!" someone yelled while coughing at the same time.

I ice grilled the idiot for a moment, then waited for Mya to answer my question.

She looked at a belly-rubbing LaLa who was discreetly trying to shake her head no. She looked at Jerome again, and he still ignored any form of eye contact with her.

"So?" I asked, starting to get the feeling that something was about to pop off.

She smirked. "Yeah, Jay, I have a problem. But it doesn't have anything to do with being jealous of you," she smugly said as she started to walk around me. "You see, my problem happens to be the same one that you have."

I reared my head back and cocked it to the side. "And what problem would that be?"

"Jerome fucking your so-called best friend and possibly getting her pregnant."

The shit she had just said to me didn't really register with me until I saw Li'l Ray take his arm from around LaLa and mean mug the hell out of her. She tried to grab his face and say something, but he turned around and stormed out of the VIP section.

I looked over at Niecey and saw Toby firmly grab her arm trying to keep her from getting to a laughing Mya.

"Baby, please . . . Let me ex—" was all Jerome managed to get out before my open palm connected to the side of his face. I hit him so hard that his lip started to bleed. The shocked look that he had on his face told me that not only did he hear that shit, he felt it too.

"Bitch! Are you crazy?" he yelled as he stalked toward me. Before he could get any closer, Toby grabbed my arm and pushed me behind him.

"Rome, man, you know I will always have your back, and you're like a brother to me. But trying to attack a woman who only reacted to the shit you caused is not gonna fly while I'm here. Let me take you home so you can cool down, and if JaNair's up for talking to you in the morning, you can do it then. Cool?"

After looking around at all of the shocked faces, Jerome nodded his head and then turned his attention back to me. I wanted to say something real slick but didn't get the chance to due to LaLa's ear-piercing scream.

"Oh my God, I think my water just broke," she said as we all rushed to her side.

"Are you all right, LaLa? Do you need anything?" I asked kneeling in front of her. She nodded her head and started to scream again. That concern I was just giving her was all an act. I really didn't give a fuck how she was doing, to be honest. I just needed some way to get close to her without her suspecting anything.

After Mya dropped that little bomb about Jerome possibly being her baby daddy, she knew to keep some space between us. That's why I didn't get a chance to slap her right after I slapped Jerome.

"Are you sure you're OK, LaLa?" I asked looking her in the face.

When she nodded her head again and gave a quick smile, I nodded my head in return. Before I got up to give her some breathing room, however, I raised my arm up and sent my fist flying into her nose.

Blood instantly started to gush out. The *oohs* of some of the guests that were still in VIP started to echo throughout the confined space.

I didn't even look back to see the damage that I'd done to her face as I grabbed my clutch and jacket. The only thing that was on my mind was getting the hell out of there. My mental was so gone right now, I was liable to beat that damn baby outta her ass.

After making sure I had everything in my hand that I came with, I headed out of the club and to the limo.

Not even caring that the driver was obviously on a smoke break, I jumped in the back of the sedan and slammed the door.

"Uh . . . Where to, ma'am?" he said as he sat in the driver's seat.

"LAX."

He turned around and looked at me. "You don't want to wait for the rest of your—"

"No! LAX, please," I said as I closed the partition.

Once it finally registered to this fool that I didn't give a fuck that we were leaving the rest of my party behind, he put the key in the ignition and revved the engine up.

When the limo started to move, I opened up my clutch and took out my birthday gift from Semaj. A small smile began to form as the round-trip ticket to Texas stared me back in the face.

"I'm on my way, J2, and I'm really ready this time," I said to myself. Closing my eyes, I let the thoughts of tonight's event and seeing Semaj's smiling face lure me to sleep.

# LaNiece

"Aggggggggh!" I cried out in so much pain. Not only was my nose gushing out an insane amount of blood thanks to JaNair, but these contractions I was having every ten minutes had me ready to die.

"LaLa, I need you to stay with me. I know you're contracting right now, and it's hurting like hell, but I need you to hold your head back so we can get control of this nosebleed and calm you down so your blood pressure doesn't skyrocket," Tangie said as she kneeled down beside me.

"Can . . . someone . . . please . . . call . . . my . . . mama," I managed to get out between breaths.

"I think your sister already did."

I looked to my left and saw Niecey pacing the floor with the phone glued to her ear while Toby was in the corner having what seemed like a heated conversation with Jerome.

"Did . . . Li'l Ray . . . come back . . . yet?"

Tangie looked at me for a quick second, sheepishly smiled, then turned her attention toward the EMTs rushing into the lounge. I didn't know what that was about, but by that look on her face, I could tell that the answer was no. While Tangie briefed the paramedics on my condition and my mind drifted off to Li'l Ray, another contraction hit me a lot harder than the first and had me doubling over in more pain.

"Breathe, LaLa . . . breathe," I heard someone scream.

"How can I breathe?" I yelled back. "With your hand and this towel covering my face, it's kind of hard for me to do that shit."

I didn't mean to snap at the young girl like that, but when everything that caused this moment started to flash before my eyes, I got mad all over again. Mya was foul as hell for blurting that shit out like that. I couldn't wait until I dropped this baby.

I had something real special for her ass and couldn't nobody on God's green earth save her from it. Not only did she screw up JaNair's special moment, she probably cut any hope of my and Jay's friendship ever reconciling. I knew that bitch was up to something the minute I saw her ease her ho ass into the VIP section. I should've said something then, but didn't.

*"What the fuck is she doing up here?"*

*"Who you talkin' 'bout?" Li'l Ray asked as he took another sip of his drink.*

*"Mya's trifling and thirsty ass. She looks like she's up to something too."*

*Li'l Ray laughed. "How can you tell that? From what I see, she's up here just like we are, celebrating her cousin's birthday."*

*"Nigga, when was the last time you saw Jay and Mya together?" He thought about it for a second, then shrugged his shoulders. "See, that's what I'm talking about. I don't even think JaNair invited her to this party either, so why is she here?"*

*"You females kill me. Let that girl enjoy herself. Look, it's obvious Jay ain't tripping, or she wouldn't be talking to her right now."*

He nodded his head in their direction, and sure enough, the distant cousins were having some kind of awkward-looking conversation. I watched as both Mya and JaNair put on their fakest smile and exchanged pleasantries. Their interaction looked so forced and fake, I could only imagine what they were saying to each other.

*Yeah, that bitch is up to something,* I thought to myself as I watched Mya's gaze slide over to Jerome's every few seconds.

Twenty minutes, five songs, and two cranberry juices later, the waitresses of the lounge finally brought JaNair's lavish cake out. My stomach, which started to hurt after we ate all of the different foods, was now feeling a bit queasy. I was so ready for this night to end so that I could go home and lie down.

"Are you okay?" Li'l Ray asked as I grabbed my stomach and his shoulder at the same time. As a sharp pain shot through my belly, I gave a quick smile and head nod, just to avert any type of panic from him.

A few minutes later, another pain shot through my back which had my knees buckling a bit. When Li'l Ray looked at me again with concern laced across his face, I mustered up all the strength that I could and acted as if everything was still OK. I knew I should've said something then, but I wanted to see JaNair's face when she got her big surprise.

Jerome going down on one knee with a small black velvet box in his hand had everyone in the VIP gasping at the same time. The look on JaNair's face was indescribable, and I couldn't tell whether she was shocked or annoyed. When I followed her line of sight and saw the expression on Mya's face, I just knew some shit was about to pop off.

Even though we were mad and hadn't talked to each other in a minute, that twin telepathy thing Niecey and I sometimes had must've kicked in. Either that or she must've noticed what was about to happen because she and Toby came and stood next to me.

*When JaNair started to question Mya about the look on her face, I just knew she was about to tell Jay about her and Jerome fucking around. But when I heard her say "Jerome fucking your so-called best friend and possibly getting her pregnant," I could feel all the color drain from my face as the pressure that was building up at the bottom of my stomach suddenly released and went spilling all down my legs.*

*I reached out for Li'l Ray after Mya revealed my dirty little secret, but was met with a scowl and him shrugging his arm from my hold. Not even bothering to look back, he stormed out of the VIP area.*

"Ray . . . RayShaun!" *I cried out, only to be ignored.*

"LaNiece, we were able to stop the nosebleed, but now we need to get you to the hospital," the young paramedic said, breaking me from my thoughts.

"Hospital? But why?"

She looked around at everyone standing around me. "Um, we need to take you to the hospital because your water broke, and it seems like this baby wants to come out tonight."

"WHAT!" I yelled at the top of my lungs. "It's too early. I have two more months to go." I was becoming scared now. I didn't have anyone by my side, and I didn't want my baby to be premature.

"That's why we're on our way to the hospital now. We've already called your doctor and informed him about what's going on. He's already in the delivery ward waiting for your arrival."

I didn't know what to say or how to feel after that. Li'l Ray was nowhere to be found, and I even managed to lose sight of Niecey and Toby as the EMTs pushed me through the lounge and into the ambulance that was waiting for me outside.

The ride to the hospital was short. We got there within fifteen minutes. When we got to the room that I would be delivering in, the first familiar face I saw was my mother's. JaNair was supposed to be the second person I allowed to witness the birth, but we all know that wouldn't be happening anytime soon. I was so happy that I finally had someone there with me that I started to cry while the doctors and nurses stood around me telling me to push.

After being in labor for twelve hours straight, I finally gave birth to my beautiful, brown-eyed, curly-haired, and cara-mel-colored princess. Weighing four pounds, one ounce, and eighteen inches long, my little angel was the most adorable baby I'd ever seen. Due to having thrush, she stayed in the NICU for three days, but after it cleared up, she was by my side day and night.

"Ahhhh, LaLa, my grandbaby is beautiful," my mom said as I nursed my bundle of joy. "What are you going to name her?"

"I was thinking—" I started to say, but was interrupted when my room door was pushed open.

Shock instantly covered my face as Li'l Ray walked in smelling like a goddamn weed dispensary. Before I could even get into his ass, the door opened once again with Niecey, Toby, and a distraught Jerome walking in.

My baby must've sensed my mood change, because as soon as the door closed, she started to cry at the top of her lungs. With every eye now on me, I tried to calm her down any way I could. I bounced her, swayed her, patted her back, checked her diaper, and even tried to feed her again, but nothing seem to be working.

Finally, Niecey stepped forward with a tear-streaked face and said, "Let me hold her for a minute."

Seeing the tears fall from her eyes had a few tears start to fall from mine. I didn't know if this was her way of forgiving me for what happened, but I'd take whatever I could to have my sister's and my relationship back to the way it was. We looked at each other and nodded our heads at the same time, silently agreeing to put our differences aside for the time being. When Niecey walked closer to me and was in a comfortable standing position, I gently placed my baby in her arms. It was just that fast that my love baby started to quiet down and soon fell asleep.

"I guess my niece likes me a little better than her own mama, huh?" Niecey joked, which caused everyone to chuckle a bit, including Jerome.

"So what are you going to name her?" Toby asked as he stood behind Niecey and smiled down at the sight before him.

I was just about to answer his question when the room door swung open again.

"Oh, I'm sorry, you guys, but there are way too many people in the room right now. That's not healthy for the little beauty you got there in your arms," the nurse who was assigned to my room, said. "How about granny and the proud father stay for right now, then after fifteen minutes or so, the next round can come in."

I don't know why, but her mentioning the proud father had me dropping my head down in embarrassment.

Jerome, who had been sulking in the corner, cleared his throat and spoke up. "Unfortunately, it would be kind of hard for us to decipher who the child belongs to, seeing as we have two possible fathers in the room."

The nurse scrunched her eyebrows, then looked from me to Jerome, then to Li'l Ray. I don't know if she crossed out Toby because he was white or because he was standing close to Niecey, but she never glanced his way.

"Okay . . . I see. Well, if you want, I can go get two DNA kits so we can clear this whole thing up about the baby's paternity."

We all nodded our heads in agreement as there was a knock followed by a familiar voice pushing through the door.

"Excuse me, ma'am, but do you mind making that *three* DNA tests. I need one too since LaLa here slept with me and these two other niggas around the time of conception," Big Will said as he strolled into the room. Then to add more insults to injury, he added, "Oh, and by the way, can you please make sure it's the rapid one. I don't wanna be here any longer than I have to."

The shocked look on the nurse's face and everyone else's was priceless. The only thing I could think of as I sank deeper into the hospital bed while pulling the sheet over my head was, *Shit!*